**"You have to bel**
**fighting for. You h**
**to say it, too."**

"I'm worth it," Jen whispered softly. "We're worth it," she corrected. "Both of us. Me and you."

At her words Nick's gaze fell, silver-blue eyes fastening on her mouth until she felt compelled to wet her lips.

He stilled, the tension between them rising like a flash flood, all rush and noise and chaotic thoughts before he lowered his head as though he simply couldn't help himself and gave her a kiss no dam could contain.

A low groan escaped him, rough and seductive, bone-melting hot to her starved-for-attention ears. She shivered in response, slipping her arms beneath his lightweight suit jacket to the expanse of his back, the heat radiating off his body warming her as no blanket ever could.

He lifted his head to give her a sexy smile. "You know, a confident woman turns me on."

Dear Reader,

I don't know of a single person who hasn't had something negative said about them, something that harmed their self-image and put a rather large chink in their self-esteem. Whether it's a stammer, a weight issue or a problem with looks, most of us can sympathize due to something we've encountered over the years. I'm no exception, and neither is Jennifer Rose, the heroine in *His Son's Teacher.* Jen's gone through a nasty divorce from a cheating spouse, eaten her emotions since childhood and wants to overcome her issues with weight. And Nick Tulane is just the man to help her do it.

But Nick has his own set of problems. Estranged from his supersuccessful family, Nick is the black sheep. He has secrets that no one, especially not his family, knows. But when Jen breaches Nick's protective walls, they discover they have a lot more in common than they think.

I hope you enjoy Nick and Jennifer's story, and will check out the entire THE TULANES OF TENNESSEE series. I love to hear from my readers, too, so please write to me at P.O. Box 232, Minford, Ohio 45653, or e-mail me at kay@kaystockham.com. For more information on my books, monthly contests, newsletters and more, check out my Web site at www.kaystockham.com, and friend me on Myspace.com at www.myspace.com/kaystockham. I look forward to hearing from you!

God bless,

*Kay Stockham*

# HIS SON'S TEACHER
*Kay Stockham*

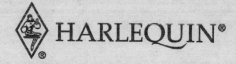

HARLEQUIN®

TORONTO • NEW YORK • LONDON
AMSTERDAM • PARIS • SYDNEY • HAMBURG
STOCKHOLM • ATHENS • TOKYO • MILAN • MADRID
PRAGUE • WARSAW • BUDAPEST • AUCKLAND

ISBN-13: 978-0-373-71502-2
ISBN-10:     0-373-71502-1

HIS SON'S TEACHER

This edition published by arrangement with Harlequin Books S.A.

® and TM are trademarks of the publisher. Trademarks indicated with
® are registered in the United States Patent and Trademark Office, the
Canadian Trade Marks Office and in other countries.

www.eHarlequin.com

**Printed in U.S.A.**

# ABOUT THE AUTHOR

Kay Stockham has always wanted to be a writer, ever since she copied the pictures out of a Charlie Brown book and rewrote the story because she didn't like the plot. Formerly a secretary/office manager for a large commercial real estate development company, she's now a full-time writer and stay-at-home mom who firmly believes being a mom/wife/homemaker is the hardest job of all. Happily married for over fifteen years and the somewhat frazzled mother of two, she's sold seven books to Harlequin Superromance. Her first release, *Montana Secrets*, hit the Waldenbooks bestseller list and was chosen as a Holt Medallion finalist for Best First Book. Kay has garnered praise from reviewers for her emotional, heart-wrenching stories and looks forward to a long career writing a genre she loves.

**Books by Kay Stockham**

**HARLEQUIN SUPERROMANCE**

*The Tulanes of Tennessee

Don't miss any of our special offers. Write to us at the following address for information on our newest releases.

Harlequin Reader Service
U.S.: 3010 Walden Ave., P.O. Box 1325, Buffalo, NY 14269
Canadian: P.O. Box 609, Fort Erie, Ont. L2A 5X3

This book is dedicated to all the people out there who've struggled with their weight. Some of us have won the battle, some of us have lost it and some of us are still fighting. It's never too late to be healthy—and learn to be happy with ourselves. Good luck!

As always, to my family for their love and support.

To Jane Hilal for always answering the phone when I call with yet another plotting problem. Jane, you rock! :)

To Mrs. Kim Evans, third-grade teacher, for answering so many questions on testing, elementary school procedures, etc. Any mistake is entirely my own. Thanks, Kim!

And last but not least, to the teachers out there preparing our children for the future. Where would we be without you? This is for you.

# CHAPTER ONE

"YOU FORGED MY SIGNATURE? You're only eight years old!"

Nick Tulane shifted his butt on a child's chair five sizes too small for his six-foot-three frame and stared down at the top of his son's head. Talk about déjà vu. How many times had he been the kid sitting there beside his dad, head bent low, waiting for the bad news to be delivered?

The other kids in Matt's class had left fifteen minutes earlier, filing out of the room with their backpacks and bags in tow, all of them chattering, yelling. Laughing. But Matt wasn't laughing. And that, more than anything, cemented the truth in Nick's mind. His son had actually—

"I didn't mean to—I just did. The teacher didn't say anything."

"So you thought you were going to get away with it?"

The knot in Nick's stomach tightened. Matt's voice trembled, but there was something more there. And whatever it was, whatever reason Matt had for doing such a thing, it was *big*. Why else would the counselor have called both of Nick's businesses in order to track him down and set up a mandatory meeting on the last day of school? "What was in the note? Did you play a prank on the teacher?"

*Following in your footsteps already, eh, Nick?*

In his head, his father's voice mocked him. Said scenes like this were the first of many paybacks he'd receive for all the problems he'd caused his parents when he was growing up. "What did the note say?"

A big, fat tear rolled down Matt's cheek and fell onto his hand. Matt wiped it on his cupcake- and juice-stained shorts. "Just…stuff."

"Yeah, I got that. But why didn't you give it to me?"

"Because I didn't want you to *know*."

"Know what? What did—" He reined in his anger and forced himself to soften his tone. "What did your teacher say when she didn't hear from me?" Nick was not his father's son. He flat out refused to yell and shout at Matt, when the kid was already terrified. What's done is done, as Nick's grandfather always used to say.

Nick was twelve the first time he'd altered his grade on a school paper, having wised up by then to the fact that it would buy him some time and delay punishment. But for Matt to be doing this stuff at *eight*…? Not good.

"It wasn't her. We had a substitute. A lot of 'em, 'cause Mrs. Reeder got sick and had to leave. Remember?"

Vaguely. Nick waited for his son to continue, his heart pumping so loud he could hear the blood roaring in his ears. Damn. He should've been paying more attention. But the boy had seemed to be handling school okay. Did he need to go through Matt's backpack every night? "How'd you do it?"

"I copied your name from one of your work papers. I said you were too busy to come in, but that you'd come in later."

"And the substitute bought that?" How naive were these teachers—she couldn't tell the difference in handwriting? Granted, his signature wasn't much more than a capital *T* and a scrawl, but still… Nick struggled to remain even-tempered. "You haven't told me *why*." He rubbed a hand over his mouth and chin, the rough stubble reminding him he'd forgotten to shave this morning because he'd been in such a hurry to get Matt to school and himself to work. "What's so bad that you didn't want me to know about it?"

Had his father felt this way? Was that why Alan Tulane had always ripped the air blue when Nick had been in trouble? Because here and now Nick felt like a total loser of a parent. How many men had an eight-year-old con man for a son?

"Just…*stuff*. You were supposed to sign my homework and test papers. I thought I'd do better. Honest, Dad. I didn't want you to worry or—"

"Or what?"

Matt sniffled loudly. "I didn't want you to be mad or, you know, disappointed."

Nick's anger deflated in an instant. Of all the things Matt could have said, he'd just hit his father where it hurt most. Disappointing a parent was something Nick identified with all too well. "You can come to me about anything. I thought you knew that."

A shrug was his answer. A loud and clear *no*.

"Well, you *should* know that," he said, nudging Matt with his elbow. "We stick together, right? Just us bachelors."

Matt gulped and wiped his wet cheeks with a sticky hand. "I tried *really hard*. I thought I'd do better. I'm sorry, Dad."

The words, Matt's tone, were painfully sincere. "You should be sorry. What you did was wrong. But let's take this one step at a time, okay? From what I gather, they don't know you forged my signature on those papers. All they know is that I didn't show up to talk to them, right? Since they don't know what you did, I think maybe we won't tell them."

*"Really?"*

"We'll handle that between us," he promised. "But—"

The classroom door swung open. "Mr. Tulane, thank you for coming."

Nick pushed himself to his feet and shook hands with the woman who must be the school counselor. Mr. Keener, the principal, came next. Nick remained standing while the two seated themselves, then reluctantly returned to his uncomfortable chair.

"I'm Mrs. Chambers, and I understand you already know Mr. Keener?"

Nick nodded. "Nice to see you again, Mr. Keener. I've been helping Uncle C. out at the Coyote, and we got a great shipment of steaks in last night. You'll have to stop by."

The balding man perked up at the mention of his favorite meal. "I'll do that," he said, patting his protruding stomach. The counselor glanced at her watch pointedly and Keener cleared his throat. "Well, uh, Nick, I'm sure you need to get back to work so how 'bout we get down to why we asked you here? Mrs. Chambers will go over the situation for us, since we're without a regular classroom teacher for Matt."

Nick glanced down at Matt. "Shouldn't we talk privately?"

The woman shifted in her seat, her gaze not quite meeting his. "There are times when we feel it best if the student is involved in the decision-making process, and this is one of those occasions. Mr. Tulane, we're sorry for calling you in on such short notice but when it came to our attention that the letter Mrs. Reeder had sent home some time ago wasn't followed up on and the postponed meeting hadn't been rescheduled, well... It *is* the last day of school. All I can do is apologize on the school's behalf for our mistake. I hope you'll support the suggestions we're about to make. Matt has had a bit of a rough year, but he'll continue on to the fourth grade in the fall."

Matt's head snapped up, his expression so relieved it brought a lump to Nick's throat. His son *couldn't* have flunked the school year without Nick knowing. Could he? Just how many papers and notes had Matt kept to himself?

"But in order for Matt to stay current," Mrs. Chambers added after a slight pause, "we'd like him to join us for summer school."

*"Summer school!"*

Nick hushed Matt with a look his son instantly obeyed. Yet another indication of the trouble that Matt already knew he was in.

"While your son's grades have always fluctuated, in Mrs. Reeder's absence Matt has truly struggled. Thus the note requesting a meeting with you, and the request for you to sign Matt's homework papers. It was a way to keep you informed of his progress."

"I see." He hadn't signed any papers, not a single one. Meaning Matt had? Nick fidgeted, his toes tingling from cut-off circulation.

"We're to blame, too, Mr. Tulane. We do hope you understand this is an unusual situation and not the norm for our school. We want all our children to grow and prosper here at Beauty Elementary, and as I said, we take partial blame for failing to reschedule the meeting."

Nick wanted to tell her to skip the B.S., but was afraid to open his mouth. He reminded himself that he had worked hard to *not* behave like his father, who would have jumped to his feet and exploded in a fury long before now.

"Again, I want to stress the importance of your support, Mr. Tulane. We realize it may be an inconvenience, but we strongly recommend it for Matt. Even though—" she paused here "—we have no way of actively enforcing his participation. Summer school is voluntary, and parental cooperation is key."

"Why am I getting the feeling this is about more than a few papers?"

Mr. Keener cleared his throat and stood. "Matt? Why don't you come with me? We'll go see how many of the teachers are left sorting out their rooms and get something to drink."

Matt obediently rose and headed for the door, glancing over his shoulder at his dad. The expression on his face was like a punch in the gut to Nick. "What's going on?" he demanded the moment the door closed. "Why does Matt need summer school?"

The counselor inhaled then sighed. "First off, we recommend summer school to *all* of our students as a way of retaining what they've been taught during the school year. For the students who've done poorly in class or for those who didn't perform well on the standardized tests, we find it's *crucial* to keeping up. Before I get into the details, the school asks that the parents not disclose test scores to the child because of emotional problems that can arise in relation to self-esteem. We don't want Matt comparing himself to his peers. Every child is different and we realize that."

"Understood. How low were they?"

"Matt will not be held back," she repeated as though reading from a school administrators' handbook. "With No Child Left Behind, we acknowledge there are social aspects to consider, as well as Matt's emotional well-being, and summer school is a wonderful opportunity for him to catch up before he enters fourth grade and takes the required tests again."

"Mrs. Chambers, exactly how bad were Matt's scores?"

She avoided making direct eye contact. "On top of his poor scores in the classroom, Matt failed both portions of the standardized test." Sliding a page from her folder closer to him, she pointed to a percentage and a graph. "Here are the average scores. The country's, the state's, the school's…and Matt's."

Damn. He'd had a dull headache before entering the school, and now between the fluorescent lights and the counselor's words, the ache turned into a full-blown pounding. He rubbed his eyes and tried to focus on the numbers, wishing he could don his sunglasses and pretend he was anywhere but there. "I see."

"Let me assure you, Mr. Tulane, we're going to do everything we can to help Matt."

The classroom door opened and Mr. Keener assessed the situation with a glance. The counselor gave him a discreet nod and closed her file folder, and the principal and Matt stepped inside. Matt walked over and slumped into his seat, the water bottle in his hand unopened.

Mr. Keener drew their attention. Nick noted that the older man focused on Matt, his expression kindly. "Don't be too upset about this, Matt. It's a good opportunity, not a bad thing. And we'll have fun here over the summer, too."

"What about Matt's friends?" Nick asked, hoping to find a positive. "Maybe some of them are going to be here? Did any of his classmates…" His words trailed to a halt when a sweeping glance at the two school officials made him realize Matt was the only kid in his class who had done so badly he'd pretty much failed.

"We never know who'll take advantage of the summer-school program," Mrs. Chambers said carefully, her unblinking look laced with meaning. "Matt's friends could attend, but as yet I don't believe any of them have been registered."

Matt shook his head firmly back and forth. "They're not coming. Nobody wants to come if they don't *have* to."

Nick cleared his throat and scooted back from the table to

stretch out his legs, unable to breathe any longer with his knees against his chest. "Who teaches summer school?"

There were questions he needed to ask. Things he needed to understand. Matt really *was* following in his footsteps, although much sooner than Nick might have expected.

"Marcy Woodard," Mr. Keener informed him. "She's taught here for several years now, and she's a wonderful teacher."

"Matt might also benefit from a tutor," the counselor added.

"The teacher can't teach him? Isn't that the point of Matt attending these classes?" *Whoa, sounding like the old man there, Nick.*

The woman squirmed. "The number of teachers involved in the program depends on the number of students who sign up to attend. Right now, Ms. Woodard will be teaching *all* the students from first to third grade. As one of the oldest children in the class, Matt could very well find himself left largely to his own devices."

"Then why bother making him go at all, if the teacher isn't going to be able to focus on what he needs to learn?" What kind of lame joke was that? Make the kid go through summer school for nothing?

"Are you suggesting an alternative?" The counselor slid an awkward glance in Mr. Keener's direction.

Nick took a calming breath and looked down to see Matt rubbing the toe of one battered and wheel-less Heelys shoe against the other in agitation. The back of his neck was blood-red and he was having a hard time controlling his tears.

Nick's elbows dug into his thighs. "If I take on the expense of hiring a tutor, why would Matt need to attend summer school? Why not just hire a teacher myself, who would focus entirely on Matt and get him on track?"

The counselor seemed surprised that he'd made the suggestion, as if she wasn't used to parents cooperating. That might have been true with some of them, but Nick didn't want Matt going through what he'd experienced growing up.

"That would be wonderful."

"Then Matt wouldn't have to attend summer school?"

Hope radiated from Matt's red-rimmed eyes. "Please, Dad?"

All three turned to stare at Principal Keener. "One-on-one attention is always best."

Mrs. Chambers cleared her throat, the little lines forming around her mouth as she did so, giving her a lemon-pucker expression. "That does indeed sound like a wonderful idea, Mr. Tulane. However, as good as the plan is, your difficulty will be finding a qualified person willing to take on a summer-long position. Hiring a college student as a summer tutor is one thing, but hiring a certified teacher is quite another. And the cost may be an issue. Very few teachers will be willing to give up their vacation for the kind of tutoring Matt needs, and those who are will demand a hefty sum."

"We'll make do." Money wasn't a factor. He had his share of expenses with his businesses, but he and Matt led a pretty simple life and he'd been using Uncle C.'s bookkeeper's financial guidance for a while now. Tucker Dawson might look and sound like a good ol' southern boy, but he was a genius when it came to accounting and finance.

The beeper at the counselor's waist buzzed, and she glanced at her watch again. "I'm sorry. I have another appointment I wasn't able to reschedule. If I think of anyone willing to take on the job, I will certainly give you a call. Otherwise we'll see Matt on June sixth. Summer school runs five days a week, five hours a day for eight weeks. It's all explained in here," she said, placing another folder on the table in front of them and sliding it forward. "There are medical release forms, as well as a lunch menu and schedule." That done, the counselor made her excuses to both Nick and Mr. Keener, murmured goodbye to Matt and left.

"Nick, I want to apologize for not staying on top of this."

"Looks as if we're all at fault."

"Well, I appreciate your understanding. This must have come as a shock, and I hate that it happened this way. You probably thought everything was fine, since we didn't contact you again."

Nick didn't comment. Matt was a good kid. Nick didn't want Keener thinking Matt was a problem. "Everybody makes mistakes. I didn't stay in touch with Matt's teachers like I should have. I'll be more aware of things from now on."

"Matt? Would you mind stacking the chairs we used on top of the tables?" The principal tilted his head toward the door. "Nick?"

Dreading whatever might come next, Nick followed the older man out of the classroom and shut the door behind them.

"Nick, I realize no parent wants to hear what you just did, but Matt will be fine. If you can't find a tutor, don't worry. The standardized tests the kids take every fall and spring are basic. You can tutor Matt at home, and combined with the summer-school program I'm sure he'll be ready for them."

The guilt made Nick sick. "I'd like to say it's no problem, but I'm afraid that's not really feasible for me right now, Mr. K. I'll do anything to help Matt, you know that. But I've lost two of my employees this week, and I'm filling in for Cyrus managing the restaurant until he gets back from vacation." Nick ran a hand over his hair and massaged the back of his neck. How had he dropped the ball with all this, lost control? He was a parental failure.

"Worst-case scenario is that Matt has to attend summer

school and you hire a teaching student to help him out at home. Either way, I'm sure he'll learn what he needs to learn. It'll be fine—you'll see."

Not when Matt would hate every moment of it. It was a disaster waiting to happen. Then it hit him. "Tucker's wife, Suzanne, is a teacher." *And she'd be discreet.* "Maybe she can help us out."

"Sounds like a plan. Let me know what you find out."

"You'll keep this quiet—between us?"

The older man nodded, his sympathetic expression one of understanding. The man knew what it had been like for Nick, what it would be like for Matt if people knew. "Of course. This is between you, Matt and the school."

"It's best that way. Otherwise you'll have my father, mother and grandmother all down here on a daily basis."

"Heaven help me." The older man shuddered at the thought of it. "I won't say a word."

"Thanks." Nick held out his hand. "I appreciate it." The conversation over, Nick opened the classroom door. "Come on, Matt. Let's go." His son still looked as if he'd lost his best friend, and no doubt he was worrying about his punishment.

"Don't be too hard on him, Nick. He's a Tulane through and through. Reminds me of your father, and you and your brothers. I spent a lot of years staring across my desk at you and Luke. Matt had the same look you wore every time I said I had to call your father. I can't imagine you not putting yourself in Matt's shoes, since you've been there so many times."

Nick nodded. Keener certainly had that right.

Matt pushed the classroom door wide and stepped through. He dragged his feet, his backpack sagging from one shoulder. Father and son said goodbye to Mr. Keener and a few minutes later the late May sun hit them in the face.

"So what do you think about all this?" Nick asked, unlocking the truck with a press of the key ring.

"I don't wanna go. I *hate* school. I wish I never had to go again!" Matt ran to the truck and yanked open a rear door, climbing inside and slamming it behind him.

The moment Nick was behind the wheel, Matt wiped his face and stifled a sob. "Matt…"

"Dad, please. *Please.* Don't make me go. Everybody'll think I'm stupid."

"Nobody will think you're stupid." Nick tossed the file folder Mrs. Chambers had given him onto the passenger seat, where it landed atop the latest bestseller on tape.

"I am. Only losers have to go to summer school."

Nick ground his teeth until his jaw hurt. How many summers had he spent in school without any apparent success? Three? Five? "You're not a loser, Matt. A loser wouldn't take this chance to do better. I don't want to hear you talking about yourself like that. Look, I'll check in to hiring a teacher. If I can find one for a reasonable rate, you can stay home and no one will be the wiser. Okay?"

"You promise?"

"To try? Yeah, I'll try. In the meantime, you're going to be busing tables and doing dishes at the restaurant as punishment for lying."

"But, Dad—"

"And no video games until further notice." Nick added his best father's glare. "Understood?"

# CHAPTER TWO

JENNIFER ROSE SAT IN her car and stared at the entrance to the Old Coyote Bar and Grille. The last of the sun's rays faded behind the Tennessee mountains surrounding the town of Beauty, giving everything a reddish pink tinge. She'd spent the afternoon finishing her student reports and taking care of all the details that came with the end of the school year, then she'd packed up her classroom and piled the stuff into her car. Now her hands were wrapped so tightly around her steering wheel that her fingers ached.

"You can do this," she murmured. "You can *do* this. Just go in there and tell them you're going, as if nothing ever happened. Doesn't matter if it's all a lie because your plans are ruined. They don't need to know that. What business is it of theirs, anyway? Come fall, you can say things fell through and it's no big deal. Just stop whining and do it. You can do—"

Her car door opened suddenly. *"Out."*

Jenn blinked and then glared at Suzanne Dawson, the teacher in the classroom next door to hers, and her best friend since she'd moved to town. Usually a smiling, easygoing person, her friend glared right back at Jenn.

"You've been sitting here five minutes staring at the restaurant and muttering to yourself like a crazy woman. Let's go—I'm starving."

The words brought a scowl. It *so* wasn't fair. Suzanne ate nonstop and looked like a twig. "Have you lost more weight?"

"Nice try. You're going in there. Forget about all the D-Day stuff. Let's have some fun."

Easy for her to say. Suzanne had major plans for the summer. Snorkeling. In Hawaii. Lying on the beach with her skinny body in a bathing suit that was comprised of strings and patches. If Suzanne wasn't such a nice person, Jenn definitely would hate her. "I will. I am." *I'm going to do this.*

Declaration Day was a longstanding tradition at Beauty Elementary, a way to unwind and linger with friends the teachers probably wouldn't see much over the summer. Every year until now Jenn had enjoyed the gathering because she'd actually *had* plans for the summer. Real plans, not fake ones.

"Then what are you waiting for? You can't let that jerk of an ex end your life just because he thought the grass was greener in what's-her-name's pants. It's time to move on." Suzanne reached in and began tugging on her arm. "Come on, *out.*"

"I'm coming, I'm coming! And I *know* it's time—it's not that exactly." But how could she explain? Suzanne wasn't like her. She was outgoing and funny and always ready to party. She wouldn't think twice about going on vacation alone. But Jenn?

*Stop being such a chicken. You should go. You should.*

Oh, why did vacationing alone seem so impossible?

"You're pissed because that jerk-off shouldn't have treated you the way he did. You're mad because you let him—"

"I didn't *let* him. I brought up the idea of getting a divorce first. He just beat me to filing."

"And *now* you're wondering if you'll ever feel normal again." Suzanne's perfectly arched eyebrows rose. "Am I close?"

Sort of. Actually she'd felt relatively normal for a while

now, compared to the off-kilter, how-did-this-happen daze she'd been in for most of the past year, but what if what she really had to have out of life was something…extraordinary?

*You don't ask for much, do you?*

She'd tell them she was going, then she'd go to her parents' house in Cincinnati and lay by their condo pool. No pictures? No problem. She'd say she lost her camera. Or maybe someone stole it—or she could print some pictures off the Internet. That would work.

Jenn swallowed, took a long look at the restaurant's entrance and groaned. "You left out the part about how our divorce totally destroyed my vacation plans. Forget Todd—"

"Thata girl."

"He's a jerk and I know it, but, *darn it,* I really wanted to go on that vacation."

"Then go. But watch your language," Suzanne teased. "Sheesh, are you getting wild on me or what?"

*If only.*

The thought came out of nowhere, but Jenn meant it. Wild wouldn't care about traveling alone. Wild would see it as an adventure and fun and… There were times when she *really* wanted to be wild. Wanted to know that all the doubts and insecurities about herself, instilled by Todd, weren't true. Was she having an early midlife crisis? A post-divorce meltdown?

Suzanne snickered and Jenn blushed when she realized she'd been talking aloud. What all had she said?

"Let's go figure it out inside. Come on—it's time to have some fun. Aren't you tired of moping around?"

Unbelievably so. "You know I am."

"Then smile. That's the first trait of a woman out on the town. Her flirtatious smile. Oh, *pulleeeze,* that's just sad. Fake it if you have to." Her friend's voice lowered and a glint appeared in her eyes. "You can't tell me you never faked it with I-think-I'm-a-god Todd." She raised her hand, her thumb and first finger a couple inches apart. "Come on, be honest. Little wienie?"

Jenn choked.

"Ha, I *knew* it! That smile says it all—and it looks beautiful on you. Now, follow instructions and do this." She held up a finger and tapped a front tooth.

Jennifer glanced around the shadowy parking lot to see if anyone was watching them. "Suzanne—"

"*Do it.*"

Obedient, she tapped her tooth with her fingernail. What silliness was this?

"Feel that?"

"Uh-huh."

"Good. Remember that later. Because right now you're going to go in there, smile that beautiful smile every single time you think about Mr. Little Wienie Man and have a great evening with friends. Right?"

"Wh-right," She hated that she sounded like Elmer Fudd. "But why am I doing this?" She dropped her hand in a hurry as an older couple drove by and shot her a funny look.

Suzanne grinned. "Stop it. Why are you worried about them—who cares?"

"Right." She shrugged. "Not me."

"Good. And that," Suzanne said, holding her crooked finger up in front of her mouth, "is in case I forget to tell you later. When you can't feel it anymore?"

"Yeah?"

"Then it's time to stop drinking."

An hour later, Jenn stared in wonder at Amy Warren. The

first-grade teacher danced across the Old Coyote's small dance floor completely uninhibited and, more importantly, *not* drunk.

Despite Suzanne's inane comment about knowing it was time to stop drinking when she couldn't feel her teeth, Jenn and all the other teachers present were very aware of small-town public appearances and how a wrong move would reflect badly on all of them.

The school board probably wouldn't care if their teachers got together over drinks on the last day of the school year, but all those present had ordered soft drinks or iced tea so their professional reputations would remain intact and gossip would be kept at bay.

Which meant Amy's dancing had nothing to do with alcohol or reputations and everything to do with a lack of inhibition. And that begged the question… Was Todd right?

So many reservations held Jenn back. She wanted to go to Paradise Island, but she was afraid. Who wanted to go on vacation alone?

But look at the dance floor. She wouldn't be alone there and she wanted to dance, and yet was she dancing? No.

*Chicken.*

With good reasons. The main one being her body and the extra weight she carried. Always a chubby kid, she'd long ago learned not to draw attention to herself. Since discovering her ex's infidelity, all she had done was eat her disgust with herself, to the tune of a whopping twenty—oh, who was she kidding? *thirty*—pounds. In eighteen months. On a body that was already short and already soft, thirty pounds was a lot. One wiggle and everything on her jiggled. Who wanted to look like Jell-O?

Rolling her eyes, Jenn grabbed her empty soda glass and got to her feet, unable to pull her gaze from Amy's movements and the smile her friend wore as she danced and sang along to "It's Raining Men". How did she do that? How did Amy let go and have fun, dance, despite everyone watching?

"Need another?"

Startled out of her thoughts, she looked up and found herself face-to-face with a drop-dead-gorgeous man. The bartender? "Um…"

A slow grin spread across his face. A heart-stopping, toe-curling, sex-me-down smile that mushed her insides into nothing in the split second it took the smile to reach his eyes.

*As if you'd ever stand a chance with a guy like him.*

On a scale from one to ten, she was a five at best. Maybe a six on a good day, and that was being *way* generous. He was a fifteen. And fifteens didn't look at sixes.

*Unless they were a size six.*

"What would you like, sweetheart?"

*Sweetheart?* The waiter had called her *ma'am,* not that there was anything wrong with that, but it had made her feel old. And fat. Ma'ams were typically more matronly and… substantial. Weren't they?

*The bartender wants a big tip. It's called flirting, Jenn. Remember that?* Sadly, it had been a while. "A Coke. Please. Sorry, I'm a little distracted."

His grin widened, as if he'd heard that one before and her face burned with embarrassment. No doubt he had rendered more than one woman speechless over the years.

"You want rum with that?"

She shook her head and handed over her glass, imagining she felt a tingle streaking up her arm when their fingers brushed. Yeah, right. The bartender was six-feet-plus of hard-muscled male. The tanned, outdoorsy, athletic type that put Todd's nonmuscular lean build to shame. While he got her drink, Jenn tried to picture herself out with such a guy and failed.

She hadn't impressed her ex-husband, and she didn't imagine short, pudgy and studious would appeal to a man whose biceps couldn't be contained by the sleeves of his black T-shirt. If Todd had thought her boring, she'd be nothing short of coma-inducing to a man like this.

"There you go. A Coke, straight up. Anything else?"

*How about you?* She rolled her eyes at the foolish thought. *Hey, at least you've got good taste. He would certainly be a great way to spend the summer. Maybe he'd want to go to Paradise?* "No, th-thanks. What do I owe you?"

White teeth flashed, all the brighter paired with his sun-darkened face and uniquely beautiful silver-blue eyes. Toss in the deeply etched lines bracketing both sides of his mouth and a day's worth of stubble on his chin and cheeks, and *gorgeous* was a poor description. Pure, sexual fantasy was more accurate.

"Don't worry about it. I'll let you slide this once." That said, he tilted his head toward the others who were with her, smiling lazily. "Y'all look as if you're having fun over there. Special occasion?"

His slow Tennessee drawl sounded, oh, so sexy. Was there *anything* wrong with this guy? Where was the fairness in life—why couldn't people be equally attractive? It was a question she'd like the answer to one day.

Shaking her head at her thoughts, Jenn took in the scene. Fifteen teachers, all of them women, were out on the dance floor gyrating to the music blaring from the jukebox. Some had rhythm and some didn't, but they were all having a blast and it showed. Why couldn't she just close her eyes and go be a part of it? *Just do it. Be wild.*

Jenn took a sip of her drink, her feet planted firmly on the well-worn wooden planks. "It's the last-day-of-school celebration."

The bartender's forehead wrinkled and he stared at the group, those stunning eyes of his becoming thoughtful. "The teacher thing. Uncle Cyrus mentioned that, but I'd forgotten about it."

Uncle Cyrus? She hadn't lived in Beauty all her life like Suzanne, but she'd learned enough to know pretty much anyone who called the restaurant's owner "uncle" was a Tulane, a member of one of the town's founding families.

"This is where all of the teachers reveal their master plans for summer vacation, right? You guys do this every year?"

She nodded, amazed that he'd remember or care about such a thing. "Yeah."

The bartender continued to gaze at the teachers on the dance floor, the thought of something serious pulling his eyebrows low. "So where are the ones without plans?"

She blinked. No way was she going to identify himself as the sole loser with nothing going on other than a measly graduate-level class for geeks. "Everyone plans something for summer, don't they?"

"I suppose. If you think of anyone who doesn't, let me know."

"Why? Oh, you mean, to wait tables or something?"

Mr. Gorgeous tapped the bar twice with his hand. "Something like that, yeah. Have fun on your teachers' night out. Don't get too wild."

There was that word again. Sighing, she watched the bartender walk over to a customer who was hiking her petite self up onto a bar stool. The woman wore a navel-revealing tank top stretched low across perky boobs, and her waist would have made Scarlett O'Hara turn as green as her window-curtain dress.

Jenn had had a waist. Once.

"Artificially enhanced," Suzanne suddenly murmured from beside her. "Gets 'em every time." She leaned against the bar and made a face. "'Til they get up close and personal, and realize most of them are hard as rocks." She waggled her eyebrows and grinned. "Have I ever ~~introd~~uced you to Nick?"

"Nick?"

Suzanne inclined her head toward the bartender, who was now completely engrossed with Perky Boobs. "No, but that's okay."

"What, you don't like gorgeous men?"

"On magazine covers, sure. But in real life they're not for me."

"Oh, really. Why?" Suzanne demanded, the glint in her eyes stating loud and clear that if Jenn put herself down or said the wrong thing, she was going to hear about it.

"Um…" Jenn took in Nick's thick black hair. "I prefer blondes?"

"Jerk-off had brown hair."

"Exactly. See what I got for choosing a brunette?"

"Uh-huh. You know, a little self-confidence goes a long way. You're great with your students, but put you with adults and you freeze and become a wallflower."

"Kids are more fun. And wallflowers are…important. Who else can watch everyone's purses and make sure the punch bowls are filled?"

Suzanne shook her head at her. "I'm not going to win, am I?"

"Not tonight." Jenn smirked. "I'm on a roll." *And in a mood. It takes a lot of courage to lie through one's teeth.*

"So I see. The others are saying it's time to do the deed. Kim has to leave early and finish packing."

"Me, too. Leave early, I mean. It's been a long day. Let's go tease them with Hawaii, then I should head home."

Suzanne blocked her exit. "Suck it up, chick. Escape is not an option. Come on, you can't leave us here alone. As the newbie hires, you, Amy and I have to close this party down, remember? Show the others what we've got?" she insisted, holding her hands up and dancing to the music.

"What *you've* got. How does Hawaii compare to sitting at home eating Doritos every night or…or Jane. Did you hear? She's going to Paris with her daughter. And Serena's going on a missionary trip with her husband. Amy's heading to Machu Picchu, Glenna's going on a tour of Tuscany and Jody's visiting Disney World with her family. There's not going to be anyone left in Beauty this summer." She sighed dramatically. "Guess I don't need to lie about my plans. It's not as if anyone is going to be here to know one way or the other."

Suzanne laughed. "Want a little cheese to go with that whine? Come on, it isn't *that* bad."

"Are you sure I can't just tell them I signed up for a human-development class for my master's and be done with it? It's plain, it's boring… It's me."

Suzanne made a sour face. "This summer is your first taste of freedom in how many years?"

"Five," Jenn admitted reluctantly. "Well, eight if you count two years of dating and the months until the divorce was final."

"And you don't think it's time to have some fun? Kick up your heels a bit?"

"My divorce-care class taught me that it's normal to feel anxious this way. They say it's really important not to jump into relationships or projects too soon, because newly divorced people have a tendency to do impulsive things and regret them later."

Suzanne nodded. "That's all well and good, but I don't

think by *jumping* they meant for you not to pick your feet up off the ground. Your divorce was final last December."

"Great Christmas present that was," Jenn muttered. "Besides, who would want to date me like this?"

"Okay, you want to hear me say it? Fine. I'll admit you've put on a little weight *but*—"

"A little?"

"You still look *great*. Tell them exactly what you told me at school—that this summer is the Summer of Jenn. Have a makeover, then go to class and get out and about and when you meet a nice guy, you'll realize you're worrying for nothing."

"I do like the sound of that."

Suzanne wrapped an arm around Jenn's shoulders and prodded her toward the tables. "Stick with me, kid. We'll get you through this yet."

Jenn's heart thudded in her chest, and she braced herself to face the group. She needed a nudge, something to get her sufficiently psyched to carry out her ideas about rejuvenating herself, body and soul. Trip or no trip. But *what?* Everyone knew a person had to have the right mindset to diet and exercise, and hers was seriously lacking motivation. All she wanted to do these days was drown her sorrows in chocolate.

And then she saw him.

Standing at the table surrounded by her friends, she noticed Todd at the entrance. He hadn't gained an ounce since their divorce—if anything he looked better than ever. Then Todd turned to his side and snagged hold of his beach-bunny mistress and Jenn watched as the man she'd supported through med school, the man she'd spent way too much time on, waiting for him to call, to notice her, to *care* as he was supposed to care, lowered his head for a blazing kiss from the skinny bimbo who was barely out of high school.

"Jenn, what are you doing this summer? Come on, tell us!"

She felt Suzanne's hand on her arm. "Are you okay? You look a little—"

"I'm taking my life back," she whispered, her voice growing stronger as anger and mortification coursed through her veins. She'd been such an easy mark. Someone to play mommy and take care of everything from laundry and cleaning and *bills* until the perfect trophy wife showed up. Well, not anymore. "This summer is all about me." She nodded firmly to confirm her words. The Summer of Jenn. Oh, yeah, she liked that.

She'd needed a kick in the pants? Well, this was definitely it. She wasn't about to stand by and let Todd Dixon ruin the rest of her life. "It's…it's about taking control of my life, having fun and becoming the person I want to be." *Not the fool I've been.*

"Ohh, this sounds good," Glenna said, her back to the scene unfolding by the entrance.

Thank God the others didn't see. But Jenn heard the whispers starting at the end of the long table, saw more and more of them turn their heads toward the entrance.

"What are you going to do? Are you going somewhere? One of those spas in the desert?" Glenna asked.

"Come on, Jenn, stop being so secretive," Amy teased her.

Using Suzanne's trick, Jenn flashed them all a blazing smile, remembering that Todd hadn't been all that great in bed. Ha! One good thing about dating someone so young was that the poor girl no doubt had a daddy complex and didn't realize Todd's four-minute sex-capades weren't exactly world-class.

Jenn grabbed her purse and keys and gave them a breezy woman-on-a-mission laugh. *You can do this.* "That's something you'll have to wait to hear about later. For now I've got to go or…or I'll be late."

"Late for what? Jenn, you're bad! Where are you going?"

Jenn pretended not to hear as she walked away from the table. She marched right past the bar and the gorgeous bartender and Miss Perky Boobs. Past Todd and his sleazy arm candy, with her skirt too short and tight, her back bare in a halter top, without the slightest sign of a tan line, bra strap or fat roll, and out the door.

And all the while she hoped and prayed no one would even notice.

## CHAPTER THREE

JENNIFER WAS NEARLY TO her house when she heard Todd call out her name. She stumbled briefly, but kept walking. So much for wishing she could be invisible.

"Jenn, wait up!"

She jabbed her key into the hole and twisted, but somehow the lock jammed. "Oh, come on." Things just couldn't go her way, could they?

"Jennifer, let's be adult about this."

Adult? *Adult!* She rounded on Todd. "What on earth would you know about being an adult?"

He grimaced, not even out of breath from the jog across the restaurant's parking lot and around the corner to her house. Nevermind that she was huffing and puffing and sweaty. *Ugh.* It would have been quicker to lock herself in her car, but she'd been so angry she'd forgotten that it was sitting there in the lot.

"Why haven't you returned my calls?"

She leaned against the door for support. "I don't know. Maybe because I don't want to *talk* to you?"

Todd put his hands on his hips in an arrogant pose, his dark hair and Catholic schoolboy uniform of khaki pants and navy polo shirt looking fresh and neat despite the heat. *Indicative of his cold heart.*

"It's been months since the final papers were signed, and it was over months before that. Can't we move on?"

"I am completely beyond that. What I'm not over is you showing up at the restaurant today. You *knew* I'd be there—I'm always there with my friends on the last day of school. And yet there you are with your tongue stuck down your receptionist's throat. You did that to embarrass me!"

"No, I—" He swore softly. "Jenn, I forgot about it. I didn't even know it was the last day of school. Why would I?" Todd wiped a hand over his face and shifted his feet on the grass that she hadn't had time or the energy to mow. "I'm sorry. I didn't do that on purpose. And believe it or not, I wanted our marriage to work but—"

"I'm fairly certain there isn't a single marriage counselor out there who'd have told you to fix our problems by screwing around."

His gaze narrowed. "You want me back, is that what this is about?"

"*No!*" The thought was appalling. The very idea made her sick to her stomach, even though she'd been raised to believe marriage vows were meant to be kept and problems worked out. She did *not* want him back. Some people might be more forgiving than she was, but infidelity wasn't something she was prepared to overlook.

"We were friends once. Can't we go back to that?"

"*Friends?* Oh, you mean, before you took all the money I had saved to pay off your student loans and your debt? Or before you *cheated* on me?" She should have sued him for alimony just to get even, but she didn't want that tie to him, didn't want to take anything from him. She'd won the house. That was enough. "Things weren't working. I *knew* that, Todd, but instead of talking to me, separating or asking for a divorce, you messed around and *lied* about it."

"I admit, I could've handled things better."

"You think?" Wait a minute. Was that an admission—and an *apology?* She narrowed her gaze on him. "What do you want?"

Todd gave her one of his practiced smiles. "I've been calling you because…I need a favor."

"Of course you do."

"It's important. And I hope you'll be kind enough to help me out."

She blinked at him. "Help you out with what?"

"I didn't argue when you said you wanted the house."

"I could have asked for half of your earnings, since I worked my butt off while you were in med school. Toby Richardson said I could have pressed you for a lot more, and you know it. You're out of favors, Todd."

Todd gritted his teeth. "Can we leave the lawyers out of this?"

"Get to the point."

"I just want to look at our old vacation plans. See? No big deal."

*"What?"* Why would he possibly want her… Her nails dug into her palms. "Why?"

He dropped his gaze to his feet. "Erin and I are getting married—she's pregnant. We found out today, which is why we were at the restaurant tonight. To celebrate. Anyway, I'd like to take her somewhere special for our honeymoon. You know, before the baby comes. Otherwise, it'll be a long time before we'll be able to get away and do something like that."

The ringing in her ears drowned out most of his words.

"Anyway, I told her about the trip we'd planned and she loved the sound of it. She wants to go there. Erin admires you, Jenn. I think she'd like to be more like you."

"I'm going to hurl."

"I wish you'd try to understand my side of things," he said with insensitive determination. "I needed more, and I wasn't getting it from you. I wanted to do things, be adventurous, and you wouldn't even try. The divorce was for the best."

"You got that right." Did she *ever* know that for a fact. The lying, sneaking, two-timing…Little Wienie Man! Be more adventurous? How could she be in the mood, when she knew he was out with other women? Sleeping with nurses in the on-call rooms? She'd even heard a rumor about a freight elevator.

"Look, I thought since you're not seeing anyone and obviously wouldn't be taking the vacation, I might—"

"Stop." She held up her hand, struggling to remain calm so she wouldn't end up with the police on her front lawn when her nosy neighbors called 9-1-1. "*Why* wouldn't I be taking the vacation?"

Jenn stared at the man and wondered what on earth she'd ever seen in him. Todd looked soft, not at all the handsome pre-med student she'd thought herself in love with but a spoiled boy pretending to be a man. Playing at being a grownup. Why had it taken her so long to figure that out?

"Look, Jenn, I know it's been a rough year for you, but you've got to admit you're not quite ready for fun in the sun, right?" His gaze swept over her, lingering on her rounded middle and ample hips. "Besides, I know how you are about traveling alone. You didn't even want to go to your parents' house by yourself. You said it was too far to drive."

Mostly she hadn't wanted to go because married couples usually traveled together. Especially to see the parents. Showing up on their doorstep alone would have sent her mother into a tizzy, and understandably so.

"Wouldn't it be a shame to let all that planning go to waste? Just hand the plans over and I'll mail them back to you when I've had a look."

Her palms itched. She relaxed a fist and rubbed her hand against her elastic-waist pants, afraid if she smacked his face she'd somehow give him the upper hand. Assault charges versus her trip. She wouldn't put it past him. But the audacity of the man—standing there, trying to justify his actions by making her feel bad about herself?

She often told her second-grade classes that violence didn't solve anything. At the moment, however, she greatly sympathized with little Michael Marshall. Nailing Todd with a good right hook would certainly make her feel good—just as Michael had claimed after Brad Zimmer had made fun of his stutter one too many times and he'd walloped Brad a good one. "Amazing. I can't believe you've done it. You've convinced me to feel *sorry* for her."

"Who?"

"*Her.*" And the unborn baby who would soon be more mature than its own father. What a nightmare. But Todd wasn't her nightmare. Not anymore. *Thank you, God.* Some things happened for a reason. So why not let this be another reason to turn the summer into exactly what Suzanne had called it—the Summer of Jenn. Why not let this moment lift her declaration to the next level? Exercise. Diet. Whatever it took to help her have the confidence to prove Todd wrong and take that trip! Did she dare go by herself?

*Yes!* She'd rather have company, but if she didn't—why *not* go anyway? She was only hurting herself by letting fear and timidity hold her back. Why not put her repressed emotions out there and use them to lose weight and get in shape, instead of eating more and more? Why not heal the inner part of her that was hurting so badly? Dr. Phil might just be onto something.

If she planned things well, worked hard, she could do this. Everyone knew confidence and self-image went hand in hand. All she had to do was find her courage. Grow a pair. Embrace her inner I-can-do-anything diva instead of locking her up in order to keep her off the dance floor. This was it— her moment. Her motivation. The *thing* she needed to come to terms with herself, revenge. Todd didn't think she was beachworthy? Well, he could just… He could just kiss her big, fat *butt!*

"So you're going to be like that, huh?"

For the second time that evening, she realized she'd spoken her thoughts aloud. Shrugging off the fear that her neighbors might also be listening, Jenn gave Todd a genuine smile for the first time since she'd learned the truth of his betrayal. "Yes, I am. If you want to take your…" She faltered, refusing to stoop to his level, "*Erin,* somewhere nice, plan it yourself."

Todd glared at her and turned to leave, but she caught hold of his arm. "And one more thing. For your child's sake, if for no other reason, don't you *dare* put your son or daughter through the pain of seeing their father run around on their mom. This time, Todd, be *adult* enough to honor your vows."

Todd stiffened and his face darkened, but he didn't say anything. Jenn stared him down, then turned on her heel and— thank goodness!—the key opened the lock.

Slamming the door in his face wasn't nearly as satisfying as nailing him with her fist would have been, but it had to do. Success was the best revenge. Now all she had to do was achieve it.

The Summer of Jenn had officially begun.

"HELL HATH NO FURY like a woman pissed off," Nick drawled as Jenn slid onto a bar stool beside Suzanne. "Ladies, have a good night. Yell, if you need anything."

Suzanne nodded, but didn't take her eyes off Jenn, making Jenn even more self-conscious since everything seemed a bit…weird.

"Your face is as red as my shirt. What happened?"

Jenn concentrated on hooking the heels of her summer sandals over the lower rungs of the stool. It took more work than she had thought it would—possibly because of the time she'd spent at her house searching for something sexy to wear back to the Old Coyote and then finding Todd's left-behind prized possession instead.

Revenge had definitely been sweet—and expensive. "Why not? Why let Little *Wienie* Jerk ruin my fun with my friends?" *Hiccup.* She covered her mouth with her hand. "Oh, that's rude. Excuse me."

Suzanne's mouth dropped open. "Have you been drinking?"

Jenn saw the bartender's head turn their way.

"Hello? Jenn? Oh, you have. Hon, what happened?"

Jenn laughed and looked around them.

"The worst of the gossips are gone, don't worry. Just tell me."

"What's to tell? He followed me home. Like the sick, little puppy he is. But I got the last kick, er, laugh in. I wouldn't give it to him."

"Give *what* to him? What did he do? Say? Tell me!"

"He's been calling me." She nodded to confirm her statement. "But I wouldn't phone him back. So he came over."

"Why?"

"Because he wants *my* vacation."

"What? *Why?*"

"That's what I said. It's not fair, you know." She pointed

to Suzanne's empty dessert cup. "You lost weight after your divorce and you're losing weight *now*—don't say you're not. All I've done is gain it, and…and he pointed that out."

"Correction. I lost weight when I was dating Tucker. I was so sure it was too soon to get involved that I felt sick every time he came around me."

"I didn't know that."

Suzanne propped an elbow on the bar. "A girl has to keep some diet secrets." Her gaze settled on the bowl of peanuts nearby and she pushed them in front of Jenn. "Eat. It'll help absorb the alcohol. Now, what else did Todd say?"

"Just the usual. I can't *stand* him. That, that—"

"Need me to supply an expletive?"

"*Oooooooh!* He actually had the nerve to say he wants to take his girlfriend on my vacation before they spawn."

"You mean, she's—"

"Pregnant," Jenn blurted out, nearly overturning the dish of peanuts. "The cheating liar has a baby on the way. Believe it or not, I don't care. I don't," she repeated. "It's beyond over, but he stood there on my uncut grass in front of the house he said we'd fix up together and told me he wanted to take her on *my* dream vacation, since it's obvious I'm not going because I'm not…beachworthy."

"He said that? What did you do? Please tell me you told him to shove it where the sun don't shine. *Jenn?*"

"I wanted to."

A plate of fries appeared in front of them, along with coffee and two glasses of water. "On the house. Enjoy, ladies." Nick smiled at Jenn before walking away. She eyed his backside and shook her head.

"*But?*"

"Yeah, it is nice, isn't it?"

Suzanne giggled.

She blinked back to the present. "What's so funny?"

"You. And yes, it is, but finish your story. What did Jerk-off do next?"

"I told him to plan his own vacation and have enough parenting skills not to make his child watch him cheat on its mother."

"I suppose it could've been worse. You could have given your plans to him."

"I told you I didn't." Jenn snorted, picked up a fry and popped it into her mouth. "I'm pathetic, but that's my vacation and I'm not giving it up. Not after all the work I put into planning the thing. I know *all* the little places to go see. Where I want to eat, shop, swim… The insider stuff that regular tourists won't know about."

Suzanne raised her brows. "But you said you aren't going now. Unless you've changed your mind?"

"I have. I *am* going. I'm going to—" She dropped the fry she was holding and shoved the plate away. "I'm going to lose weight and take that trip. I have to for me and all womankind."

Suzanne beamed like a proud parent. "Good for you. It's about time you pulled yourself out of this funk."

"Todd's right about one thing, though. I'm not beachworthy. I had to buy a whole new wardrobe of shapeless dresses to get me through the school year. Look at this," she said, plucking at the denim jumper she had on now. "I tried to find something sexy to wear here and… This is *not* sexy."

Suzanne couldn't hide her smile or the laugh she poorly disguised with a cough.

"It's not funny, either."

"Oh, sweetie, I know. But it's not that bad, either. If you've decided to diet, I have no doubt you can lose the weight you've gained."

"Really?"

"Really. Don't let Todd get to you. If you do, you let him win." Suzanne made herself more comfortable on the stool. "Jenn, I'm worried about you. Everyone deals with stuff like this in their own way, but you don't drink."

No, she didn't. It just proved how unnerved she was with her life at the moment. When she'd discovered the bottle, the only thought in her head was to hurt Todd the way she'd been hurt, and the only thing he'd ever seemed to love during their marriage was that stupid champagne. "Do you know," she said softly, "I packed my lunch for an entire *year* to save money to buy the chandelier in the hall, and the weekend I bought it Todd went out and bought that bottle of really expensive champagne? He said it was sexy and sophisticated and it made him feel like James Bond. As if Todd could ever be 007."

They both rolled their eyes.

"It was such a slap in the face."

"But it's finished. And you've decided to fight back, right?"

"Right. I just don't know where to begin. It's easy to gain weight, but how am I going to lose all this before the end of summer?"

Suzanne was quiet and thoughtful, then a grin formed on her face. "I've got it. I know exactly how you can do it."

"Really?"

"Admit it. You probably couldn't lose a lot if you tried on your own, but if you had help you could kick butt, right? Jenn, Nick's looking for a tutor for his son, and since the two of you seemed to hit it off earlier—"

"Hit it off?" That drew her out of her daze. "Get real.

He asked me where the teachers were who didn't have any plans," she muttered morosely. "That's not exactly hitting it off."

"Maybe he was checking to see if you'd say you were spending the summer with a boyfriend or something. Ever think of that?"

"I'm not that drunk."

"Look, he wants someone who'll keep things discreet. Are you interested or not? He brought you food, too. On the house."

Fattening food. For the fat girl. She fingered the plate of fries, wanting another one. "Why can't you do it? You'll only be gone a couple weeks, not the whole summer. Is the kid such a problem?"

"No problem. Matt is wonderful, very sweet, with a heart of gold. And what better way to spend your summer than hanging around with a sexy bad boy with a body that would give any woman inspiration to look her best? You never know what might happen."

"You've got to be kidding me." Jenn glanced at the hot bod in question and sighed. "Guys like that don't notice women like me. We're not even a blip on the radar."

Suzanne waved the complaint away. "I disagree, because Nick is the best. But that's beside the point. The point is, he needs a tutor and he asked me to only mention it to people I knew would be discreet."

"What's the big deal?"

"Matt's shy and embarrasses easily, and Nick doesn't want people talking or kids making fun of him. You know how gossip works."

That she did. "People suck."

"My, my, you are in a mood. But why not consider it? You could help Matt, earn some extra money, and you never know.

Maybe being around all that hard muscle and sex appeal would be just the thing to distract you from..."

Jenn looked up in time to see Suzanne indicate the fries. And lo and behold she'd picked up another, had been nibbling on it and hadn't even noticed. Jenn stared down at the fattening treat, then thought of her faulty marriage and the rest of her life. "Why do I do this?" She said, tossing the fry down. "Why do I let him get to me? I know I'm only hurting myself, but I can't seem to stop. I don't even want these fries. I didn't want the champagne, either, but he made me so angry and I just...I hate the thought that I failed."

Suzanne patted her on the back. "You didn't fail at anything. Cheaters cheat. It's as simple as that. Listen, about the weight, if you want I know a doctor who prescribes..."

Jenn shook her head firmly back and forth. "No drugs. They give me heart palpitations, and I'd only gain it right back once I quit taking them."

"Then what you need is someone who'll take charge and get you exercising. Too bad it won't be me."

"Why not? Suzanne, you *have* to help me."

"Can't. Hawaii, remember? And...I'll be a bit restricted in what I can do when I get back, too."

Jenn shoved aside the fries, suspicious of Suzanne's curiously bright eyes. "What's going on?"

"Are you ready to be an aunt?"

# CHAPTER FOUR

"AN AUNT? You're pregnant? Oh, I'm so happy for you!" Jenn nearly fell off the stool trying to hug her friend.

Suzanne laughed with delight. "It's about time, huh? I didn't think it would ever happen again, especially after all that treatment failed to produce any results. But don't worry, *you* are still going to have a fantastic summer. I'll come home from Hawaii and support you any way I can. I promise. The doctor just wants me to limit strenuous activities and avoid heavy lifting."

Jenn hugged her again, then looked down at Suzanne's impossibly flat stomach. "That's why you've lost weight? Morning sickness?"

She nodded.

"You're having a *baby*."

"Tuck is over the moon. He says I wasn't giving his *boys* enough credit."

Jenn nodded, dazed. Thrilled for her friend and a little jealous, too. A good jealous though. She wanted kids. And had things gone as planned, she would've been pregnant soon, too. The trip was where it was supposed to have happened. But plans change. "Do I get to host the baby shower?"

"Absolutely. Maybe you can toss it into the mix and use it for added incentive? Maybe wear your Paradise dress?"

"That stupid dress wouldn't fit my thigh at the moment."

"Stop exaggerating. The material has a bit of stretch, and with a little dieting you'd be good to go in no—" Her mouth dropped and she stared at Jenn, a grin slowly overtaking her features.

"What?"

"I cannot *believe* I didn't think of this earlier. It's *sooo* obvious! It's the perfect solution to your problem."

"Liposuction?"

"Do you really want to go through the risk and pain of surgery?"

"No."

"Good. Because this is better. In fact, if you both agree, it won't cost either one of you a thing. Gym fees aren't cheap, so why not offer to tutor Matt in exchange for a membership at Nick's Gym? Hello? See what I mean? No, wait. We'll ask for a *trainer!* A personal trainer who'll kick your butt if you don't stay on track. Jenn, you could take that trip to Paradise at the end of August, right before school starts, and come home looking like a million bucks, all tanned and slim. The girls at school would *die!* Come on, say something. You've got to admit that would be quite a comeback."

Yes, it would. But could she do it? Hope soared for the second time that evening, even as her nerves positively hummed. Was she ready to do this? With her muddled head, she couldn't think straight.

"Nick? Nick, come here for a sec, will ya?"

That got Jenn's champagne-blurred attention in a hurry. "What? You mean, he's— *Now?* "

"Yes, now. It's almost closing, so he's not as busy, and you've got just enough alcohol in you to not be so shy. Nick!"

NICK GLANCED OVER to where Suzanne and her friend sat and smiled at the women. Suzanne wore a broad, happy grin, as any expectant mother should, while her friend glanced at him beneath her long lashes and looked as if she wanted to crawl under a table. He frowned, noting that the brunette's gently rounded cheeks were looking unusually pale. Tucker's wife whispered something to the woman in encouraging, coaxing tones he couldn't make out.

Finishing off the order, he placed the last of the drinks on the tray for the waitress and made his way to the two women, leaning against the bar in front of them. "What's up?"

"We need to talk to you about the tutoring thing."

"Okay." His gaze shifted to Suzanne's friend. Surprisingly, he'd been thinking about her ever since he'd seen her leave in such a rush. He hadn't been able to get her pretty gray eyes out of his head, and he'd felt compelled to find out what happened to send her off in tears. Tuck had filled him in on all the gory details of her divorce and the scene at the door. "Just to warn you, your ex is still here."

"Doesn't matter," Suzanne stated bluntly. "We're not going to worry about him. Nick, Jenn has a proposition for you."

He waited, watching as Suzanne elbowed her friend in the side when she didn't immediately speak up. "What's that?"

Jennifer Rose fiddled with the strap of her purse and nibbled her lips, distracting him in a way the perky twentysomething with the belly ring hadn't been able to do.

"I wanted to ask you… Suzanne mentioned… Um, you know, I think I'd like that rum and Coke now."

He caught the alcohol on her breath when she exhaled and wondered what had happened between her and Dixon. He'd overheard enough of her conversation with Suzanne to know that drinking wasn't the norm. "Sorry. I can't serve you that."

"Why not?"

She sounded so indignant, he smiled. "Because I've decided you're not really a rum-and-Coke kind of woman."

Her head lowered once more. "Figures. I'm not a lot of things."

What did that mean? He shook his head and added a teasing grin. "Don't take it so hard. I've been tending bar since I came of age and I can usually tell a person's drink within a few minutes of talking to him."

"Oh?" She perked up a bit. "So what do you think I'd like?"

Enjoying himself, he looked her over. Her dark brown hair curled around her face and neck in thick waves, the tips ending where her cleavage began. She was what some people would consider full-figured, but he was a man who appreciated a woman's curves. "I think you'd like…A Kiss on the Lips."

"I—I don't… I mean, um…"

Nick glanced discreetly over at her ex-husband and found the guy still glaring at them. Todd Dixon had always been a loud-mouthed idiot, way too full of himself. Back in school, Dixon had called Nick stupid, snickered at his D's and F's, and laughed and made fun of him because he'd been held back to repeat a year.

The way Nick looked at it, he and Jennifer Rose were on the same side. Payback wasn't out of line, not in this case. Especially after hearing what the guy had done to her.

"Come here." Nick smiled at her look of shock and was glad her ex couldn't see it from where he was. But without more than a gulping swallow, she leaned toward him. "Your jerk of an ex-husband is watching you as if he owns you. Wanna have a little fun with him?"

Her eyes flared wide, leading him to believe she wasn't used to being flirted with. Knowing that made him want to do it more.

"What k-kind of fun?"

Nick nuzzled his nose aga... hers, heard her sharply indrawn breath and caught sight of Suzanne's delirious grin with his peripheral vision. But he didn't stop. He felt compelled to help this woman out, even if he wasn't sure why. Was it because of what Todd had done to him in school? Because she was a friend of Suzanne and Tucker's? Or because there was something about her pretty face and sad eyes that told him she was a nice person whose confidence needed a boost?

When Jenn didn't protest or pull away, he brushed the corner of her mouth with his lips, giving her a slow, sweet kiss that held more heart-thumping heat than anything he'd experienced in quite a while.

She smelled like heaven. The scent of her skin was earthy from the muggy night outside and whatever perfume she'd put on that morning was just strong enough to be intriguing. When he drew away, she sat there, face beet-red and looking more than a bit dazed. "Nice to officially meet you, Jennifer Rose. I'm Nick Tulane."

"I knew it. You two *did* hit it off."

"*Suzanne.* It's not like that." Jennifer peeked up at Nick, a question in her eyes.

"Really?" Suzanne turned to him. "Nick?"

He winked at Suzanne, but didn't offer up any excuses or explanations. Jennifer seemed…sweet. And after being hit on by too many women with enough sexual experience to give the pros tips, sweet appealed to Nick. A lot.

"Jennifer, what are you doing?"

Dixon surprised them all when he grabbed hold of Jennifer's arm and tugged, as though to pull her away from the bar.

She yanked free. A good thing since Nick had already straightened in order to separate them himself.

"What are *you* doing?"

The pretty boy continued to glower at Nick before shifting his attention back to her. "You're making a fool of yourself."

"What did I do?"

He leaned over and sniffed. "Have you been *drinking?*"

Her spine stiffened and she sat straighter on the stool. "Actually, I've been celebrating. Have to admit, Todd, your precious champagne was good, despite the fight it caused when you bought it."

Dixon's eyes bugged out and his mouth dropped open. He gasped, and Nick thought the guy was going to have a heart attack right there. Clearing the space in front of him, in case he had to go over the top of the bar, Nick grinned. "Champagne, huh? You should've invited me to the party, sweetheart." He lowered his voice. "But I guess we can continue it later," he said, to egg Dixon on.

"You *drank* the Bollinger?"

Impressed, Nick whistled. "Mighty fine taste there, beautiful."

Dixon shot him a killing glare. "Don't you have a glass to wash somewhere?"

Both women gasped at the insult, but Nick simply braced his hands on the bar and rejoiced in the fact that now, unlike the days in school when he couldn't hit a ball or shoot hoops to save his life, he could lay the guy out in his burying suit if he wanted to. Owning a gym and lifting weights had a way of evening the odds. "What's the matter, Dixon? You get your kicks from bullying women instead of kids now?"

"She's my wife."

"*Ex*-wife, and thanking God every day for it," Jenn murmured.

Nick smiled at her, letting her and everyone else know he agreed with the statement. Dixon muttered obscenities under his breath.

"Todd?" A young woman came up behind Dixon and tugged on his arm. "Can we go? I'm feeling queasy."

Todd didn't break eye contact with him. "It's the lousy food here." He put his arm around his girlfriend's and glared at Jennifer. "You owe me for the Bollinger."

"Mmm, 'fraid not. I think this makes us even," Jennifer said, her gaze shifting to Dixon's date.

He sneered at Jennifer before stalking away, dragging his overly made-up doll two steps behind him.

Jenn bit her lip and groaned. "I'm so sorry. That was… Oh, that was mortifying and totally uncalled for."

"That was Jerk-off being a jerk-off," Suzanne corrected. "I hope she pukes in his lap." Tucker's wife swivelled back to face them. "Now, about that kiss."

Nick chuckled. "Lay off, Suz. I had to do it—especially when I saw Dixon glowering that way."

"You know Todd?"

A guy down the bar raised his mug for a refill and Nick took care of business while keeping a close eye on the women. "We went to school together. He was a bully then, too."

Suzanne looked around then moved closer to Jennifer. "The bully is now by the door chatting up some old guy in a suit. You know him?"

Jennifer glanced that way. "That's Harold Pierson, the hospital president. Todd wants to be chief of surgery."

Dixon? Nick bit back a groan. That was the position his eldest brother, Ethan, had his sights set on.

"Idiot. I wouldn't want him operating on me."

Nick silently seconded the statement.

"He would be awfully busy looking at his reflection in the shiny instruments," Jenn added with a low giggle.

Nick smiled and filled several more orders, his ears straining to hear their conversation. Finally he was able to rejoin them.

"Just in time. We need to talk to you about our plan." Suzanne's eyes sparkled. "But first how about both of you do me a favor?"

"What?" Nick asked, ignoring Jennifer's groan.

"My birthday is next week and I won't be here to celebrate with you two because I'll be walking on the beach in Hawaii, *but* you can give me my present right now. Nick, take her into the office like you two are an item and you can't wait to get her alone. Please?" She batted her eyelashes. "For my birthday?"

Jenn slid him an I-can't-take-her-anywhere glance and shook her head. "She's teasing. Ignore her."

"Am not. At least kiss her again and give that creep something to stew over."

*"Suzanne."* Jennifer released a throaty laugh, one that made him think of tangled sheets and hot sex. He checked out what he could see of her above the bar. Was her skin as soft as it looked? He found himself wanting to touch her and find out.

"You didn't like the first one?" Suzanne asked not-so-innocently.

Nick stilled and waited for Jennifer's response, a grin hovering on his lips because he found he was having fun. Given the way the evening had begun, fun was quite a surprise. "You didn't like it?" he repeated, wondering if she'd give him a second chance. This time he'd go for a real kiss. Just one, to see what she tasted like.

Jenn fisted her hands around her purse and groaned. "It's not *that*," she said with a low, embarrassed moan. "I just refuse to let her drag you into this—whatever this is with Todd—when everyone in town would know better than to think we're an item. It's so obvious we're not compatible."

*Compatible?* Disappointment took hold. So that was it. But why had he expected her to be different? How many times had people taken one look at him and relegated him to the dumb-jock department because of his build and his professions? A grease monkey and a weight lifter. Great combination. Nobody needed brains for those jobs, right?

"The kiss was sweet, and I appreciate the gesture. But we all know why Nick did it."

*"Sweet?"* Suzanne's brows rose. "Nick, you're losing your touch. Wait until I tell Tuck."

He straightened and established some distance. "Stop teasing her. We were playing around because of Dixon, that's all."

Jenn bit her lip again, her teeth worrying the flesh and making him want to do the same, even though she'd made it clear she didn't find him…what? Worth the price of her teacher's reputation? He couldn't blame her, though. How many college graduates would date a dropout? She might not know he didn't have a diploma. But how long would it be before someone filled her in?

Suzanne sighed dramatically. "Gotta tell you guys, from back there it looked as if you two were pretty compatible to me." She stared hard at her friend. "At least compatible enough to work for a common goal as we discussed."

That got his attention. "What goal?"

"Nothing," Jenn said abruptly. "I've changed my mind. This probably isn't a good idea."

"It is." Suzanne nodded firmly. "You know it is."

"The champagne is wearing off. I can't do this."

"You don't need it to ask Nick a question." Suzanne

squirmed on her seat in excitement. "Why *not* use this opportunity to really put the screws to Mr. Little—"

"*Suzanne.*"

"Fine, whatever. Mr. LWM, that better? Nick kissed you because Todd was staring, but why *not* use Nick's animosity toward you-know-who's-an-idiot to your mutual advantage? It's obvious those two don't get along," she said, indicating Nick with a sweep of her hand. "What better way to rub your success in his face?"

"*If* it's a success. *If* the plan works. *If* I can do it." She indicated Nick. "*If* he agrees to do it, which is doubtful."

"Agrees to what?" He fought his impatience. They were talking in circles.

"With Nick's help, you're sure to succeed. Picture Todd's face and tell me you don't want him eating crow after that beachworthy crack."

"You two going to fill me in on the womanspeak going on?"

"Jenn, come on," Suzanne wheedled. "*Ask him.* Please do this. For yourself, for me and every other woman out there who's ever been screwed over by a jerk. You do this, and you give all of us the last laugh. What do you say?"

## CHAPTER FIVE

NICK WATCHED as Jennifer Rose inhaled, her full breasts rising and drawing his attention to them before he managed to force his gaze upward. He stared at her and waited.

"Um…I don't know where to begin."

"How about the beginning?" he urged, noting that two more groups of customers were heading out. Less than twenty people remained, Dixon included.

"Well, Suzanne suggested… She thought we could help each other."

"I'm with you so far. How?"

"I'll tutor your son for the summer," Jennifer said in a rush, as if she had to get the words out or choke on them.

"Great." The din of the jukebox, the big screens in the billiard area and the rapidly emptying bar and restaurant faded as they leaned toward one another across the broad expanse of polished wood. "But I get the feeling we're not talking money here, are we?"

"No." She gulped, glanced at Suzanne and got the other woman's nod of encouragement in return. "Instead of paying me—" she paused long enough to take another breath and close her eyes briefly "—I'd like membership to the gym and a personal trainer. I—I want— No, I *need* someone to kick my butt in gear so I can lose the weight I've gained since my divorce. But I have to do it quickly. Like, by the end of summer."

Nick didn't blink. "That's it? You want a membership and a trainer in exchange for tutoring?"

"N-no. I mean, yes, I do, but… I have a dress. A really beautiful dress that I want to wear on a trip to Paradise Island. It's important because the dress is… The dress is me. Who I want to be. And I *have* to fit into it."

"I see. Those are your conditions?"

"No," Suzanne interjected quickly. "We also want more of the same thing you displayed tonight."

Jenn turned toward her friend, her confusion apparent. "What do you mean?"

"Nick has to be your guy friend." Suzanne quickly held up her hand. "Not boyfriend, guy friend. You know, so other guys will take notice."

Jenn gaped at Suzanne.

"You know how people are about checking out the girls who are hanging out with cool guys. Well, Nick's not dating anyone right now so he, you," she said, looking him in the eye, "have to pretend to like her. Well, not pretend. The real thing *would* be nice."

That wouldn't be a problem—except for what she'd said earlier. If Jennifer Rose thought she had the right to insult his intelligence the whole time they were together, they wouldn't be hanging out long. He'd find another tutor.

"Suzanne…"

"I'm not asking for a marriage proposal here. Just point out her good qualities to the guys who ask, and do that whole 'We're just friends, but she's hot' thing that guys do. At least until Jenn reaches her goal or cuts you loose because someone comes along that she's interested in."

"*Suzanne.* I didn't— That's *not* my idea. We didn't discuss any of this."

"I'm improvising." Suzanne waved a hand to dismiss Jennifer's protest. "In exchange for tutoring Matt and getting him caught up over the summer, Jenn becomes *your* personal project. You can't give up on her when she balks and tries to quit—which she will do. And she," Suzanne continued, ignoring Jenn's mutterings, "will get Matt up to speed."

"That's not reasonable. Nick has things to do. Responsibilities."

"It's fair," Suzanne insisted. "You're giving up a big part of your summer for Matt, and you'll need intense workouts to lose the weight so quickly."

Jenn studied Nick, as though wanting to gauge his reaction. "And…"

"There's *more?*" Jennifer buried her face in her hands. "Oh, help me."

Nick fought a grim smile, not thrilled with the idea but able to see its merits.

"Jenn reserves the right to add to her demands later, when she has more time to think with a clear head. Tutoring isn't cheap, as I'm sure you've heard."

Neither was personalized training, but he didn't mention that fact. Like it or not, he was too excited at the prospect of saving Matt and himself from a summer of listening to his parents rail about Matt's grades and the whole summer-school fiasco. If it became public knowledge, all hell would break loose. Again.

Even though Jennifer Rose looked horrified at her friend's stipulations, Nick nodded without hesitation. She'd learn pretty quick that the last thing she wanted to do was anger her trainer and she'd keep her comments to herself. Short of that, he consoled himself with the knowledge that the summer would only last so long. "Deal."

"*What?* You're not even going to argue? *Think* about it?" Jennifer rubbed her temples, the tiny lines around her eyes indicating a headache.

Nick shrugged, wondering if by not thinking about it, Jenn would find him even more dense. "What's to think about? I need a tutor, you need help, and Dixon has it coming."

"B-but the other… What about that?"

Ah, so that's what worried her, being seen with him. "Being your guy friend?" When he'd talked to her earlier, he wouldn't have guessed her to be a judgmental snob. "What about it? People are going to notice us spending time together. What conclusions they draw are all their own. It's not a big deal to me. Is it to you?"

She sat there, wide-eyed and pale. "Oh. Um, no. Not at… No."

"So it's a deal?" Suzanne pressed.

Jennifer's beautiful dove-colored eyes didn't waver. "I want you to be sure. You're sure?"

Glancing around the bar and noting that the two older men who remained were watching the game and paid them no attention, he shrugged. "Business is business. I'm sure."

"But…"

"No buts." Suzanne nudged her friend. "You want that trip? This is your chance. Are you brave enough to take it?"

Nick leaned down and opened the minifridge, pulling out three water bottles. No more champagne for Ms. Rose. Caps off, he lifted his bottle in a salute. "Here's to the start of an interesting summer."

He and Suzanne both stared at Jennifer, waiting for her to commit to the plan.

Finally she lifted her bottle. "To, um, wearing my dress and…and taking my dream vacation to Paradise Island."

"And last but not least," Suzanne said with a snicker, "to dancing on tables. She wants to do that, too, you know."

*"Suzanne!"*

THE POUNDING in her head went on and on.

Jennifer opened her eyes the following morning only to gasp and groan, squeezing her lids shut in a feeble attempt to counteract the shards of pain shooting through her brain. Three glasses of champagne did this? Or was it four? Everything had gotten sort of fuzzy after two.

"Drinking sucks." She flung her arms over her face and moaned. What had she done? Had she really told Nick Tulane she lacked the ability to control her eating habits? Maybe she hadn't said that in so many words, but close enough. She hadn't gotten this way by eating healthy, that was for sure. "What must he *think?*"

*Thud, thud, thud.* She paused, listened and wasn't sure if the sound was the jackhammer pummeling her brain or something else. Then the doorbell rang. Jenn pushed herself up onto an elbow and glared at the clock beside her bed. Nine o'clock. On the first day of summer vacation? "Go away."

The words emerged as a whimper. She gingerly lowered herself and rolled over onto her side, pulling the pillow over her head.

"Jennifer? Open up." *Thud, thud, thud.* "Rise and shine. Time to get moving."

Her second-storey bedroom window was located over the front door and the muffled sound of Nick Tulane's voice reached her like a shot. She jerked upright, held her head together with her hands and scooted to the edge of the bed, pausing long enough for the room to stop pulsating before she stumbled toward the window. The morning sun was blinding and she groaned long and loud when she finally pried her eyelids open and absorbed the fact that this wasn't her imagination. Nick Tulane really was standing on her porch looking like a fantasy come true in workout gear, sex appeal oozing from every corded muscle revealed by his sleeveless shirt and loose knee-length running pants.

"Shoot me now. I'm having a *nightmare*." Her head thumped against the glass and Nick looked up at the sound. She pulled herself away but it was too late. Their eyes made contact the split second before the sheer curtain fell into place.

"Ahhh, feeling the pain this morning, eh?" He released a devilish chuckle.

Jenn's shoulders slumped. What had she done? What had she agreed to? Enlisting Nick's help had sounded like a wonderful plan last night, but in the light of day she saw a whole host of problems. She didn't want a guy like Nick watching her and looking at her while she worked out. Didn't want him seeing her sweaty and smelly and out of breath or…or jiggling in places that shouldn't *jiggle*.

"Deal's a deal," he drawled. "Do I need to come up there and get you out of bed myself? Come down, or I'm coming up."

"Oh, no. Please, no." He couldn't hear her through the glass, but Nick probably got the point when she stumbled away from the window. She grabbed a robe along the way and took the stairs very gingerly, so that her head wouldn't implode. She made it all the way downstairs before she thought to look into a mirror.

"Oh, crud." Frantic, she rubbed at the eyeliner smudged beneath her eyes, attempted to tame the rat's nest that was her hair and breathed into her cupped hand. "Ugh. Oh, my. Oh. Oh, that's *bad*." Hangover breath was not a good thing.

Giving up on the impossible, she flipped the dead bolt to the side and cracked open the door. "N-Nick, thank you for coming by, but…I've changed my mind."

He tilted his head, his expression assessing. "How bad is it?"

The irritating man looked determined—and amused. She disliked him even more. "You're a morning person, aren't you?"

A thick black eyebrow arched at the accusation. "You're not? Isn't it a job requirement, doing what you do?"

She leaned her head against the cool wood and sighed. "Look, I appreciate you coming over here, but I've changed my mind. Last night…I had a little too much to drink, as you could probably tell, and I shouldn't have been making any decisions at all. I was in a mood and… You can go home now and enjoy your weekend."

She tried to close the door but Nick pressed a hand beside her head and gently but firmly pushed the door inward. Jenn backstepped and grabbed the belt of her robe. "What are you doing?"

Those eyes of his—what man had eyes like that?—looked her up and down. "I'm getting tough. Exactly like I'm supposed to. And let's get something straight. We have a binding contract, sweetheart. You're not reneging."

"It's okay. *Really.* I'll still tutor your son." *It's not as if I've got anything better to do this summer.*

Nick crossed his arms over his broad, extremely well-defined chest and stared her down. Every gorgeous inch of him was tanned and toned and rippled with muscle. His arms bulged below the dark blue-and-white shirt, and who knew the thick muscles along the side of a man's neck could be so sexy? Nick put The Rock to shame, for pity's sake. And there she stood, looking like something the cat coughed up. Twice.

"As of right now, you are in boot camp."

He made the statement with a perfectly straight face although his eyes held a fiendish glint, as if he actually meant it. Awkwardness combined with her post-champagne queasiness, and her stomach rolled and threatened to mutiny.

"And I'm your drill sergeant. Got that?"

She swallowed firmly. Puking in front of this man was not an option. "This is ridi—"

"This is me getting tough, so that you'll fit into that dress of yours. Now, get your butt upstairs, shower and put on workout clothes. You've got fifteen minutes. I'll fix you something to knock out the headache I see in your eyes, and after that we'll talk about your fitness and diet regimen before we go for a walk."

*Diet regimen? A walk? Workout clothes?* She scrambled for an escape, clarity, something besides the big, fat nothing she had in her head. "But I didn't mean for *you* to train me. I meant I'd tutor your son in *exchange* for a gym membership and a personal trainer. I thought we'd do the see-and-be-seen thing at the gym. You know, when we're there at the same time. Don't you have other people who'd help me?"

He stiffened as though she'd insulted him. "Why not me?"

How exactly did she put this? Especially when he already looked as though she'd hurt him? "Because you're…the owner." And gorgeous. Drop-dead, movie-star gorgeous. A man who belonged on a billboard advertising sleek sports cars—or *underwear.* Guys had to look really, really good to model underwear. But Nick? He could do it.

*Whereas my Victoria's Secret days are* so *over.*

Jenn tugged on the belt of her robe again. Did it make her hips look even bigger? Maybe she should leave it loose, so she didn't emphasize the obvious?

"I am the owner," he agreed. "Which means my people run the gym. I realize you might not remember all of our discussion last night…"

"I remember it." She wished she didn't, but she did.

"Good. But let's clarify some things. Your deal is with me in regard to my son, which means, if anyone trains you, it'll be me."

She got the impression that he wasn't happy about the decision, but he was sticking to it. Why, she didn't understand. If he was the owner, couldn't he make one of his trainers take on the job?

Nick looked around the entry, over her head, then headed down the hall to where her kitchen counter could be seen. She followed blindly, stumbling and wincing because every step made her head hurt more. "But—"

"You're wasting time. Get your act together, Ms. Rose. Fourteen minutes."

She lost patience. "No! Oh, geez." She grabbed her head and held fast. "I *can't*. Not today. Not after last night. I just told you, this was a mistake."

He swung around. "We have a deal. Unless you can come up with a life-threatening illness to explain why I can't train you, you're out of luck."

She faltered, unable to find the words she needed. Who could argue, hungover and looking so horrible? "I've *changed my mind*. That's good enough reason to me. I don't want to do this. I don't know what I was thinking. Obviously, I wasn't thinking clearly, or I would've known better than to think it was possible to lose thirty pounds in two months."

"It's possible."

That caught her attention and her rambling excuses came to a halt in her brain as she focused on his comment. "It is? Really?"

"Really. I don't recommend it, because slower is better, but it can be done. Especially if a person is morbidly obese, which you're not. Your loss will probably happen more slowly. But it won't happen at all if you don't want to work with me. And why is that?"

Did he really have to ask? "You want the truth?"

"I'm not leaving without it."

She inhaled shakily and tried to pretend she was talking to an errant second grader instead of a forceful, dynamic man bent on making her keep her word. "Fine, I'll—I'll tell you. I don't want you training me because, well, it's obvious you don't have a clue what I'm going through." She couldn't maintain eye contact. "I mean, look at you. We're two totally different people and it'll never work because you can't possibly understand where I'm coming from. And when I don't lose fast enough, I'll be disappointed and when I'm disappointed or upset, I eat. So then I'll binge and all I've managed to accomplish will be for nothing and then—"

"Damn. Stop to take a breath, why don't you?" He crossed his arms over his chest. "Let me get this straight. You're afraid of—"

"Please, just *go*."

He didn't budge. "So that's it? You're giving up before we even get started?"

"Listen, I know what it's like to fail, and I don't want to fail at this, too. I can't…I can't take another failure right now, okay?"

Nick stared at her, his expression softening a tad. No, that had to be her imagination. Nothing about Nick Tulane was soft.

"Huh."

She waited for the punch line, but when it didn't come, she gritted her teeth. "Huh, *what?*"

"I thought you had more spunk, that's what. Especially

after last night. It's sad to think that the only way you have a backbone is if you have some alcohol in you."

Her mouth dropped. "I have a backbone." It was just semi-crushed and alcohol-saturated at the moment.

"Then prove it. I saw it last night when you talked to your ex, but I'm sure not seeing it now."

Doubts overwhelmed her, and with good reason. "I wasn't myself last night."

"I guess not." Nick stepped close and surprised her by sliding a hand under her chin, lifting her face toward his before he dropped his hands to his hips and glared at her, his expression every bit as intimidating as the drill sergeant he claimed to be. "What about that dress? The vacation you mentioned? Where was it to—Paradise Island?"

She glanced down. "What about them?"

"You going to hand them over to Dixon and the woman he tossed you aside for?"

Anger filled her. "No."

"What was that?"

"*No,*" she stated more firmly, ignoring the corresponding thud in her head. "I'm not handing Todd anything, but—"

"You give up now, before we even take *a walk,* and that's exactly what you're doing, Jennifer Rose."

# CHAPTER SIX

HE SAID HER FIRST AND last name as if he were calling her by her first and middle name. Smooth, fluid. His voice low and husky. Soothing and coaxing and, oh, so tempting. Did she dare to believe him?

"You can work out and be healthy. But you have to *want* to do it."

"I do."

"That's not true if you can give up so easily."

He was crazy. She wasn't drunk now and she knew good and well it was going to take a lot more than spunk and backbone to get the weight off her. She wasn't a picky eater. If only. No, she *liked* to eat. Her father used to tell her that she was on a see-food diet. Whenever she saw food, she ate it.

As if in response to the topic, her stomach now growled long and loud. Heat crept into her face and she cursed the stupid tears that were stinging her eyes. Her gaze shifted to where her fantasy gown hung at the mantel edge, there for her to admire as she'd sucked down her champagne.

Following her stare, Nick whistled. "That it?"

She nodded, mutely.

"I gotta tell you, sweetheart, that's one sexy dress."

Yeah, it was. That was the point. To feel sexy and to *be* sexy. Act it, live it. Did Nick have any idea how embarrassing it was that he now knew it didn't come close to fitting her body or her state of mind? That she wanted to be the woman who'd wear that sexy dress, but inside she felt like the chunky burgundy-red couch beside it?

"Give me the summer and you'll see some great results. If you're not happy, I'll buy you another new dress that shows off every one of your luscious curves. It's the least I can do if you get Matt back on track with his schoolwork. What do you say?"

*Luscious curves?* She knew it was the flirt in him. Guys like Nick Tulane did that, especially in his profession. He had to flatter his clients, get them motivated so that they'd continue to patronize his gym. But he actually seemed to believe he could do it. That she could do it. And that was powerful, to have someone who believed in her.

Her heart beat too fast, making her head ache still more. She breathed deep and sighed, feeling as if she was teetering on the edge of a cliff. One wrong move and she'd fall, but if she made the right one… Could she really change? Succeed? She was so tired of being the way she was. Tired of her clothes not fitting, of eating her way through the evenings in an attempt to make herself feel better, only to discover she felt worse. Tired of feeling like such a failure.

*You can do this. You know you can do this. You* want *to do this! Here's your chance! Take it!*

"Well? Are you up for the challenge?"

Swallowing, she released the air in her lungs and nodded once. "Where do we start?"


"Do you have plans tonight?" Nick asked just before noon.

Jenn lowered the cold water bottle she'd been holding pressed to her head and frowned at him as they made their way inside her house. "Huh?"

"Do you have plans tonight? A date?"

"Um… No." She tried to ignore the trickle of sweat that was slowly making its way down her neck onto her chest, lower, into the *V* of her T-shirt. Was it her imagination or was Nick watching its descent?

She turned away on shaky legs, unable to believe she'd walked three miles instead of spending the morning in bed. Between all the water Nick had forced into her, the pain relievers she'd downed and the concoction he'd given her to "cure" her hangover, her headache was gone. But her body was ripe and soaked with sweat. Ick. A second shower was definitely on the agenda.

"I thought we could fix dinner here together. Let Matt get to know you. Next week I'll be overloaded at the garage when everyone decides to bring their cars for a checkup before vacation. I figured we could kill three birds with one stone."

"Three?" A bird sounded good right now. Roasted turkey with all the trimmings. Mashed potatoes and gravy. Stuffing. What was it about saying the word *diet* that immediately made her crave food? She headed for the kitchen. Dinner was a long time away.

Nick shut the front door and followed her. "Yeah. Remember Suzanne's stipulation? We need to be seen together and Beauty is small enough that parking my truck outside your house for an hour or so will definitely stir some interest. With Dixon, if no one else."

"You don't have to worry about honoring Suzanne's stipulation. You know how she is."

Nick grinned, the flash of the smile breaking over his tanned features wreaking havoc on her heart rate. She stumbled and nearly bumped into the wall.

*You're not known for your grace, Jennifer. Megan is the dancer in the family.*

"That I do, which is exactly why I'm upholding my end of our deal. Is it a date?"

Her face burned with embarrassment over her clumsiness and also the memory of her father's comments, and she hoped he blamed the excess color on their morning trek.

Would it really hurt for Todd to think she could attract such a gorgeous man as Nick? Even as a friend? "Yeah, sure. If you like."

Why not? She needed to meet Matt, and thanks to Nick's relentless prodding and demands he'd already seen her at her worst. First, this morning fresh out of bed, and now covered in sweat and trembling from exhaustion. Three miles. Her legs felt weak and rubbery, but that was a good start, right?

"We'll pick you up at four."

"But I thought you said you were coming here for dinner?"

"We are. But first we're going grocery shopping for healthy food to replace all the unhealthy stuff you'll be getting rid of."

"Um… Getting rid of?" For the first time since she'd entered her kitchen she noticed the bagged groceries that were covering her countertop. "You did that?"

"Yeah. I did a little snooping in your fridge and cabinets while you showered earlier. We've got some purging to do."

"But that's my food."

"We'll get more food this afternoon. Healthy food," he said pointedly. Then he walked over and gathered up the bags, eleven in total.

Sugar, flour, cake mixes, cereal. Not the pasta! "But—"

He gave her a look that forbade any protest. "It's a life choice, Jenn. This—" he held up the bags, his arms straining slightly from the weight "—or that dress. Which do you choose?"

She'd always known that life wasn't fair, but this bit the big one. She was a smart college-educated woman. She *knew* the food in those bags wasn't good for her and that she needed to eat healthier, but one glance at that packaged chocolate cake and she felt the pull of familiar comfort. And she wanted it. What about the times when she needed a friend and was too embarrassed to call Suzanne or her mother to talk about Todd's behavior? Food had been her friend. And seeing Nick carrying those friends out the door brought more than a little spike of panic. "But shouldn't we take this slow?" She ceased her protest at his piercing stare. "Fine. Whatever. I choose the dress."

"What? I couldn't hear you with your teeth clenched."

"The *dress*."

"Thata girl. Now, say goodbye to processed foods."

She closed her eyes, as if that would make it easier.

Then her stomach growled. And growled. And Nick kept going, carrying her best friends out the door.

Her hands fisted. *You can do this.*

NICK FROWNED as he watched Jenn try to draw his son into a conversation. Matt had barely said a word to either of them since he'd been introduced and told that he wasn't going to have to attend summer school. He'd seen the relief in his son's expression. So what was the problem now? The kid still wasn't happy.

"Oh, come on. I won't make your *whole* summer miserable."

Jenn smiled at Matt, the teasing curve to her lips drawing Nick's attention away from the road to the ripe fullness of her mouth.

She wasn't his type. He preferred his women a little less uptight and a little more active, but there was something about her and the wounded look in her eyes that got to him. Maybe because he saw that same hollowness in the mirror every morning. Knew what it was like to not appreciate the image that stared back.

Jenn didn't like her physical appearance, but Nick didn't like the part of himself that never measured up to his family's standard, to his brothers and sister and their well-educated careers. A grease monkey didn't compare to physicians, a globe-trotting travel writer, an attorney and whatever it was Luke did so well with computers.

*Somebody's gotta be the black sheep. Might as well be you.*

Jenn leaned over the seat of the truck and nudged Matt's shoulder. "You'll only be miserable when I make you eat worms and snails and stuff like that."

For the first time Nick saw Matt struggling to hold back a grin.

"Oh! I just thought of something. Your dad mentioned that you like guitar and country music. Is that true?"

Matt gave her a hesitant nod and a shrug. "Sort of."

"Well, I was on the university campus the other day and saw a Keith Ashton poster. He's going to perform there."

Matt's eyes widened, duly impressed. "He's *good.*"

"I know. I have a few of his CDs. It's a small venue, too, and it makes me think that a field trip might be in order. Going to see his performance live might be the reward you could earn after working and studying hard all summer, don't you think?"

"I wouldn't mind hearing him in concert myself," Nick added, not about to let Jenn fork over the money required for those tickets. They wouldn't come cheap, and he could afford it better than she could. Everyone knew teachers were underpaid for all they put up with in a day.

"But what if I don't do good on the papers and stuff you make me do? Do I still get to go?"

"Will you—"

"No," Nick stated firmly, watching Jenn's expression change from coaxing to mulish.

"But Dad—"

"The concert is a reward, like Ms. Rose said. It's something you have to earn. If you don't earn it, you don't get to go."

Jenn shifted on the seat beside him, obviously upset by his decision. But he didn't care. Matt needed something to prod him along and telling him he'd get to go to the concert either way wasn't incentive in his opinion.

Nick pulled into the grocery-store lot and parked.

"Why were you on the campus?" Matt asked as he climbed out of the truck.

Nick rounded the vehicle in time to hear Jenn's response.

"I'm taking a psychology class to put toward my master's degree."

"But you're already a teacher. Didn't you graduate?"

She laughed softly. "Yes, I did. But I like going to school and I love learning, and the degree would mean a pay raise and more options for the future."

Jenn fell into step beside Matt and the three of them headed toward the entrance. Nick saw their image in the reflection of the windows. They looked like a family. Dad, Mom and kid. The sight branded itself in his head.

He'd known last night that the next couple months would be hard. She was a brainy teacher, whereas he was a high-school dropout. Spending so much time together meant that he'd have to find something to talk to her about because work-out techniques and diet changes could only take up so much time. But he'd already figured out that Jennifer Rose had a wicked sense of humor, which came out in her dry wit. She had personality. *And hips that swayed with every step.*

He smiled again. No doubt about it, Jennifer Rose was curvy and soft and womanly, definitely appealing. But too smart for him. Facts were facts. Who signed up for a psych class on her summer off? Who wanted to study and spend hot, lazy summer days with her nose in a book? When he'd asked what her schedule was like for the summer, he hadn't considered the possibility that she'd be in school. Voluntarily to boot. Who *did* that?

"I hate school."

"Now, don't say that. School is *fun*. And so long as a person tries to learn new things, their possibilities in life are limitless. With the right education and hard work, you can be anything you want. Go any place you want. I take classes most every summer."

"But why?"

*Good question.* Nick waited for her answer, the divide between them widening.

"To keep busy."

*Every* summer? She couldn't find anything better to do?

"You *want* to go to class?"

She laughed, the sound throaty and feminine and full of humor. "Yes, I do. And you want to hear something more amazing? I *pay* to go to school."

"Nu-uh."

"Yes, I do. It costs a lot of money to go to college, but I think a good education is worth it. And it's a great way to meet people. My ex-husband and I actually met in class a long time ago."

"Not a great recommendation there," Nick murmured low so only she could hear. But it was true. How had she wound up with someone like Todd Dixon?

Jenn made a wry face and acknowledged that with a nod.

"Why don't you do that, Dad? Don't you like school? You could meet people. Maybe even a girl. Paul's had three moms so far, but I haven't had any. Maybe if you went to college you'd meet me a mom."

Nick's gut clenched, but whether it was over the fact that he'd always thought Matt handled his mother's absence well or that the topic was education, he wasn't sure. He felt Jennifer's curious gaze and faltered. It was no secret that he'd dropped out of high school. But this was the first time the subject had ever come up with Matt. The last thing he wanted to do was discuss it in front of a woman who took college courses for kicks. "I'm too busy, Matt. Running two businesses has a way of swallowing a person's time."

"Plus your dad wants to spend time with you," Jenn added. "If I had all of that going on, I probably wouldn't be taking classes, either. Kids are only young once and parents don't want to miss a second of it."

Matt seemed satisfied with her answer and Nick was glad the subject was dropped as the door to the grocery store opened automatically. Inside, he ignored the smiling, flirtatious whispers and stares of the checkout girls and grabbed a cart. They were in a public setting now and he had to pretend to be Jennifer's guy friend. But their conversation had just proved Jenn was right and they weren't compatible on any level. Could people with such differences be friends? This wasn't going to be easy. And what exactly did guy friends *do*?

"Did you *have* to throw out all my food?"

Nick smirked. *Guy friends* did that. He might not know Jenn well, but he cared enough about people and the crap they put into their bodies that he didn't want to see her harm herself—no matter how good certain foods tasted. "I didn't throw out *all* of it."

"Dad said your sweet tooth is bigger than mine. That you were a junk-food junkie."

Nick frowned. "You weren't supposed to repeat that, Bub."

Jenn released her lower lip with a rueful sigh. "That's okay. I know it's true. But it's such a waste."

"I dropped the unopened stuff off at a church on the way home," he informed her. "They have a soup kitchen and will put everything to use. Now, listen up. The first trick to eating better is to open your eyes and look for a rainbow."

She stared at him, clearly befuddled. "Huh?"

"When you think of food from now on, think rainbows. If it doesn't have a color, you probably don't need it or want it because it's not particularly healthy. You want reds, yellows, oranges. Lots of greens and blues. Things high in antioxidants and vitamins."

"Vegetables?" Without missing a beat she looked at Matt in horror. "He makes you eat *vegetables?*"

That did it. Matt giggled a little-kid giggle, the sound happy and carefree, a first since finding out about the whole summer-school thing, and Nick found himself laughing, too. He stared at Jennifer as she scrunched up her nose and eyed the spinach with the look of a vampire sighting a cross, and that got him chuckling louder.

People poked their heads around the corners of the aisles to see who these shoppers were, what they were laughing about. More than a few left with their eyebrows raised high at the sight of the three of them together and with Matt in tow. And then and there it happened.

"Nick? Nick, is that you?" Mrs. Bumgarner approached them, pushing her cart, her eyes alight with curiosity. "It's good to see you again and sounding so happy. Matt, how are you? And…Ms. Rose, isn't it? My granddaughter had you for her teacher last year. Emily Cyrus?"

"Yes, Emily. How is she?"

"Fine, fine." Mrs. Bumgarner looked at Nick, practically beaming. "Saw your mother at church on Wednesday evening. She didn't say anything about you dating our wonderful Ms. Rose."

Nick rubbed the back of his neck. "Mrs. Bumgarner—"

"You should come to church more often, Nick—and bring Ms. Rose, of course," she said, smiling delightedly at Jenn as she pushed her cart past. The gleam in her eyes stated clearly that she was going NASCAR as soon as she turned the corner, so she'd be the first to spread the news. "You've picked a nice girl to date this time, Nick. Your mother must be thrilled."

Mrs. Bumgarner turned the corner and, sure enough, Nick heard the squeaky wheels pick up speed. The gossip would start within minutes. After being seen together on their walk and now this, word would spread like wildfire. The gossips would bring up the past and mention his dropping out. Wonder at the irony. They'd comment about her being smarter than he was. How many college-educated women would even consider dating a high-school dropout? A graduate, maybe, but not a dropout. Even though he stayed current on the issues— talk-radio was great for that—truth was, people habitually stayed within their own crowds and cliques, education levels. It was the way the world worked.

"Great, now we'll be the primary topic at the next potluck." Jenn ran her fingers over her hair and tucked one side behind her ear, a frown on her face. "I'm sorry, Nick, but I still wonder if this is a good idea," she murmured, keeping her voice low. "I remember that woman. Every time she came in to pick up her granddaughter, I had a roomful of mothers trying to get out the door all at once."

Nick grimaced. Yeah, Mrs. Bumgarner was known for that. But his worry wasn't so much about his so-called relationship with Jenn but that with all the talk, Matt was bound to hear something. He had to have a chat with Matt soon. Maybe tonight, if he could work up to the topic. Why had he put it off for so long? He didn't want Matt hearing the news of his past and lack of education from anyone else, but the timing couldn't have been worse with Matt struggling in school. How would Matt react after learning his old man had hated school, too? That he'd quit the first chance he'd had? It wouldn't set a good example at all, and Matt might think he could quit. *Great example you've set there, Nick.*

Then there was Ms. Rose. What would she think?

He grabbed a head of lettuce and spun it in his hands. *You wouldn't be where you are today if you cared what others think.*

True. But as he watched Jenn tilt her head back and chuckle at something Matt said, watched her smile at him and share the warmth of her laughter, Nick wondered how she'd look at him when she discovered her trainer hadn't had the brains to finish high school.

Then again, when it got right down to it, he already knew.

## CHAPTER SEVEN

ON THE WAY TO NICK'S apartment above the gym Monday afternoon, Jenn found herself tapping her fingers along with the radio. It was a beautiful day. The sun was shining and everything outdoors was green. If only she could figure out the deal with Nick. They'd gone to the grocery store on Saturday, both of them in decent moods, but after the run-in with Mrs. Bumgarner he'd turned quiet.

*As if he was embarrassed to have been seen out with a fat chick?* She rolled her eyes. They were two grown adults. If he still had the mentality of a high-school freshmen and thought "fat chicks" were bad for his image, well, shame on him. She didn't think that was it, however. He seemed fine the rest of the time, treating her with respect but… Something was just off.

Jenn stopped at the traffic light and took a steadying breath, gaining perspective from the scenery around her. There was a quaintness to Beauty, the mixture of old-fashioned storefronts and brick streets mixed with modern-day upgrades. After her divorce she'd considered moving back to Cincinnati, but couldn't bring herself to leave. She could certainly see herself spending the rest of her life here, but whenever she thought about the four empty bedrooms in her fixer-upper she knew she didn't want to do it alone. Still, until she was happy with herself, how could she expect anyone else to be happy with her?

"That's what the summer is all about. *You*. Make Nike proud and 'just do it'." She nodded to herself, then jumped when the driver behind her honked because the light had turned green and she hadn't noticed.

Five minutes later Matt opened the door to Nick's apartment with a glum expression on his face, dragging his feet to the table where Jenn proceeded to unload her three-ring binders, books and papers. Preparing herself for a long afternoon, she explained what they were going to do and got to work.

"Go ahead, Matt. We'll answer the questions after you read the passage. It's very short." Matt stared at the worksheet a long time, but made no move to begin reading aloud. "Matt?"

"I don't want to." He shoved the paper away from him.

"Matt—"

"I don't *want* to. This is stupid! All my friends are having fun today. They're at Bryce's house, swimming."

Having asked for something to drink soon after they'd begun, Jenn set the glass of milk she'd poured for Matt on the table and took her place beside him. "I'm sorry about that. I know it's no fun to be here when your friends are out playing together. But we have to do this, you know? The good news is the sooner we have our tutoring session, the sooner you can join your friends."

"I'm not allowed."

"Why not?"

Matt clammed up. His lower lip trembled slightly but his eyes were dry. Thank goodness. She didn't think she could handle his tears when she felt so much like shedding a few of her own. If she even breathed wrong, her body ached. She'd been okay in the car, but climbing the stairs had brought back various pains incurred during their high-intensity walk. *No pain, no gain.* "Come on, talk to me. What's going on? Did your dad not want you swimming somewhere without him there? Parents worry like that."

No answer.

"Okay, then. Well, we're wasting time, so how about you read that first—"

"I hate reading. Reading is stupid."

"Why do you think that?"

No answer again. Jenn inhaled and switched tactics. Given Matt's attitude and test scores, reading was definitely something they needed to work on. But his cooperation was key. "Tell you what. How about we leave the reading for a little later and do some practice sheets in math instead? Sound good?"

Nodding once, he swiped a hand under his nose.

Jenn placed a timed practice sheet in front of Matt and felt her heart lurch as the boy straightened his shoulders as if he faced an entire classroom of bullies. Unlike the reading assignment, the math sheet was full of white space, but still the same reaction. Something was off here, but Jenn wasn't sure what. Children loved learning—when it wasn't problematic for them and didn't cause them stress. Did that mean Matt was having problems comprehending?

Figuring out the trouble wouldn't be easy, especially not when he shut down and refused to speak, other than to say he hated this or that. She had to help him, but how?

Her mind shouted out a warning, but she knew it was useless. She loved all her students, wanted the best for them and wanted them to succeed. It was impossible for her to spend nine months with a class and not care for every child. But a summer of one-on-one? She'd have to be very, very careful here. Pretending to be Nick's friend, spending so much time with Matt… She was in dangerous territory and she was intelligent enough to know it.

"THAT WASN'T SO BAD, was it?" Nick watched as Jennifer sat in his spare office chair, her face blazing ten shades of purple because he'd made her step on the scales. "This is to have a base line. I don't want you weighing yourself everyday. This isn't about numbers." He picked up a pen and tapped it against the desk calendar, feeling awkward with her embarrassed silence because he didn't know how to help her get over it.

He didn't understand women and their obsession with weight. If their clothes fit, if they felt good and were healthy, that was all that should matter. What was it about wanting to achieve some magic number? "I, uh, wanted to thank you for not saying anything to Mrs. Bumgarner on Saturday. I probably should've given you a reminder about keeping things quiet, but I didn't think about it. Anyway, I appreciate you watching out for him. One of Mrs. Bumgarner's grandsons is in Matt's class. The kid's a bully and he'd have a field day if he knew Matt needed help."

"I would never do anything to deliberately embarrass one of my students."

Her lashes hung low over her eyes, and her tone was sharp. Indicating he'd put her on the scale to embarrass her? "How'd today go?"

She shrugged, still not making eye contact. "Matt's not happy about missing out on events with his friends. He told me about the swimming thing. We could've postponed the session until tonight."

"He shouldn't have brought it up at all. He knew he wasn't allowed to go regardless of when you two met." But at least Matt hadn't told Jennifer *why* he wasn't allowed to go, or that he was grounded because of the forgeries. The less Jennifer Rose and everyone else knew about that, the better. Nick shook his head. How had things gotten so complicated?

"We made a little progress this morning, but we're going

to have a long summer ahead of us. Especially if Matt doesn't open up a little more in order to help me figure out the problem areas."

Problem areas? Nick shifted uncomfortably. Jenn was criticizing his kid. Had she ever struggled in school—did she know what it was like? *You're on the same side, remember?*

He looked up, found her face still hot with color. Dressed in a T-shirt and calf-length yoga pants, Jenn's arms were soft and smooth-looking, her belly gently rounded and not quite disguised by the loose clothing. But then he took in the luxurious hair, pulled into a ponytail for convenience's sake, and her smoky charcoal-gray eyes and the tempting texture of her skin. Ms. Jennifer Rose was everything womanly and feminine. While she was overweight for her height and optimum health, she wasn't obese. Exercise and sensible eating would trim her down. It was her attitude that held her back.

"Yeah, well, about your program. You have to give it time. You're not trying to train for a triathlon or a body-building competition, just shaping up which means—"

"Like I could even do the other."

"Anyone could, if they set their mind to it," he corrected her. "I've heard of seventy-year-old guys who've done it with heart attacks in their medical history. But for this summer your focus needs to be on lifestyle changes, eating intelligently and exercising every day. If you do that, the weight will come off."

"Before the end of summer?"

Nick got up and rounded the desk, leaned his hips against the edge of it in front of her. "Don't put so much pressure on yourself. Studies have shown that stress can cause changes in the body that make it easier for fat to collect around the middle, which is another reason why exercise is so important. Exercise helps us destress and keeps us active. Muscles, bones, body chemistry. It all responds to exercise. We weren't meant to sit around doing nothing. Jenn, you're smart and beautiful. All you need is to—"

"Stop." Her lashes lifted and her gunmetal gray eyes pierced him, dark with hurt and determination. "Just stop. You can yell at me about working out. It's your job and it's what I agreed to. But don't lie to me. That's not part of our deal and I don't appreciate it."

"You think I'm lying to you because I said you're smart— or beautiful?"

"I'm smart, I know that, but I'm also…*big*. Bigger than I ought to be." She made a face. "America is the land of the supermodels, but unless super-sizing my fast-food order counts, I'm not one of them."

His gaze swept over her body, lingering on all the interesting places where "big" was pure temptation. "There are different kinds of beautiful. Maybe you're not so skinny, but that's not a bad thing in my opinion. That's not a bad thing to a lot of guys."

"I asked you to stop. Don't *do* that."

"Don't do what?"

She lifted her hands, a frustrated expression on her face. "Talk to me that way. Compliment me. Todd did that. And my father. They'd both tell me I was pretty and then they'd tell me what was *wrong* with me. They'd start with the good then point out that I'd eaten more than I should have, or that my pants were getting too tight and… Oh, why am I telling you this?" Her face flamed once more.

"Your father said those things to you, too?" That was something he identified with, being put down by one of the people who should have built him up and told him he could be anything, do anything. Or in Jenn's case told her she was fine the way she was. The thought of them having that in common stunned him.

"Yeah. And I know what you're going to say. I *know* it's over and it doesn't matter in the least, but—"

"It's not over if you haven't moved beyond it. And the fact you're bringing it up proves that you haven't dealt with the past." A muscle ticked in his jaw. Why did some people need to make themselves feel better at the expense of others? "Jenn, if I say something to you, it's the truth. And if I have any concerns about your weight, it's only because it's not healthy for a body to carry too much of it. Diabetes, heart disease, hypertension. I'm sure you've heard all this before."

She gave him a reluctant nod. "I'm just saying that I'd rather you not say those things to me as if you're…flirting or something."

"Because you think I'm lying if I do?"

She shrugged. "Forget I mentioned it, okay?"

Nick fought his frustration. There was more to Jennifer Rose and her weight problem than the obvious. And they had more in common than she might think. He knew what it was like to be on the receiving end of insults. "I won't say anything to you I don't mean. Now, can we get on with the session? You're stalling."

A person's ego could only take so much damage. And Jenn's had obviously taken as much as it could bear. The blushes, the way she couldn't maintain eye contact. It all became clear. The meat guy, the cashiers at the grocery store on Saturday. Jennifer had kept her head down in that unmistakable don't-look-at-me, I'm-not-worthy stance of the walking wounded, her body paying the price for her psychic pain because she was too kind to take her misery out on anyone else.

Her chin lifted. "I'm not stalling. Not deliberately, anyway. Look, Nick, all I'm saying is that this summer I want to concentrate on me. The *real* me that isn't sugar-coated with false words or lies or side trips away from reality, where I pretend dessert hasn't been my best friend for half my life. Don't you get it? If I'm going to do this, I need someone to be as honest with me as I am with myself. Suzanne is a wonderful friend, but she isn't that person. She's too afraid of hurting my feelings. Which leaves you and this deal we've made. You have to be the bad guy and good guy rolled into one and tell me the things I need to hear—whether or not I want to hear them and whether or not they're nice."

She was describing a boyfriend. A spouse. *A guy friend?*

"But I can't do this if you're messing with my head. Pretending to be friends is one thing, but you don't have to be all—" she waved a hand in the air "—'you're beautiful' in private, you know? All I need and want from you is the truth, nothing else. Ever. Okay?"

Narrowing his gaze, Nick silenced the dark thoughts roaring through his head. *Pretending to be friends?* If that's what she wanted, fine. Obviously, all she was doing was pretending they had a friendship going. But why did the statement make him angry?

Because he didn't measure up to her? Because she'd judged him and he'd come up lacking? Maybe she knew he hadn't graduated. Who knew, but he wasn't going to bring it up. That topic wasn't up for discussion or review. It rankled, though, because she wasn't giving him a chance to prove to her what kind of man he'd become without any diplomas or fancy titles after his name.

"So, are we clear?"

He nodded, unable to do anything else since Matt's future

was at stake. "No sugar-coating. No lies. Just the truth and nothing but."

"Good." She breathed a sigh. "You can really be that honest?"

He waited for her to look at him, anger giving his voice an edge. "You're overweight. About thirty-five pounds," he added when he realized she silently dared him to say it.

She immediately looked away. His heart stalled in his chest and he hated himself for making her feel bad. Nick leaned over and nudged her chin toward him.

Jennifer Rose was sweet and strong, but she was also too damn smart. Vulnerable from her divorce and definitely not his type with her intelligence and education. But he didn't want to see her hurt and he definitely didn't want to be the one to hurt her. "For the record, though, if I feel you deserve a compliment I'm going to give you one."

Jenn blinked at him, then gave him a tenuous, beautiful smile. "Thank you."

"You're welcome."

"I'm sorry I keep waffling. But I really want to do this. Really."

He smirked and drew back. "Then get off your butt and let's get started. Write down what I tell you in the boxes."

"MATT, STOP FIDGETING, please." Seven days after her first lesson on the weight machines, Jenn placed her hand over Matt's to keep the boy from moving his math paper back and forth and shook her head.

He slid her a look from beneath his long lashes and did as ordered. "Sorry."

"No problem. Now, number four? What's sixty-four plus thirteen?"

"Seventy-seven."

"And number three? Try that one again."

Just like all the times before, Matt stared at the page, his forehead wrinkling in a frown of concentration and his mouth moving as he read the numbers. Then it began again. Biting his lip, he began to fiddle with the page, moving it back and forth with his right hand.

If she quoted the problems aloud, Matt got the answers after doing the calculation in his head. But if he read them… Could it be something as simple as needing corrective lenses? He could read, knew his numbers and wrote them correctly. But the process was long and agonizing. So where was the problem?

"Matt? Do you see the numbers on the page?" she asked, just to clarify.

He nodded firmly, stopped and tucked his hand under his leg, but after a few seconds of looking at the problem and not coming up with the answer, he began to rock on the seat. Back and forth, then front to back. Finally diagonally side to side.

Developmentally, she knew that girls were more apt to sit still while they studied or read, and that boys often associated movement with learning. They played imaginary drums while they studied, fiddled with their pencils, zipped out a chord on air guitar. Wriggled and squirmed and rocked. But was Matt's constant fidgeting that or something else? A variation of ADD?

"Seventy-two?"

His answer blew her visual impairment theory to pieces. He could see the numbers and the answer was correct. "Very good." The rocking stopped and Matt released a ragged sigh. Her heart contracted, and she was saddened by his behavior. She didn't want to subject Matt to the rigors of testing if there was no need, but why couldn't he figure out the answers on paper as quickly as he did when she asked him out loud? She was becoming frustrated trying to match his behavior to the learning impairments described in her books. Toss in the tension and strange awareness that existed between her and Nick after their talk in his office and she had a chronic headache.

Nick was polite, always, but he was a quiet brooder, as well. The more time they spent together, the worse it became. Jenn rambled whenever she got nervous and these days she pretty much kept up a steady stream of chatter about her class at the college. Maybe Nick didn't think she would give Matt her full attention.

*Like now?*

She blinked her thoughts back to the present. "I, um, think that's enough math for today. Did you read the story I asked you to read?"

Matt nodded, but the effort was lackluster at best. The tension behind her eyes increased. "Matt?"

He pulled the three pages of a short story and the sheet of questions he was supposed to answer from a SpongeBob folder, his head down as he slid them toward her.

Jenn picked up the stapled sheets, then flipped to the question page. Her heart sank. Matt had tried, she could see that from his many eraser marks, but his responses to the questions about story order, characters and plot were more or less nonexistent, the printed letters a mess. She forced a smile and set the papers on the table. "I can tell you worked hard on these. Did you ask your dad to go over the pages like I suggested?"

"He's busy."

"I know he's busy, but I'm sure he'd take the time to help you. He knows how important this is."

"I got an F, didn't I?"

She patted his back and tried to ignore the smell wafting in the window from the Old Coyote Bar and Grille down the street. "We're not working for grades, Matt. You know that."

"But I got 'em all wrong, didn't I?"

"That's the best thing about stories, they're all open to interpretation so you're allowed to have your own opinion. But the question about order? What came first, next and last? We need to work on that."

"Why do I have to read when Dad doesn't?"

"Honey, your dad must read all the time. He has to read to run his businesses."

"But he doesn't read books. We listen to them in the truck and on the CD player. Why can't I do that? I don't like to read."

Remembering the many audio books she'd seen lying about their apartment, she sighed and reminded herself that Nick really was a busy man. So what were her options? There was a system called Carbo Reading, where the student listened to a story numerous times and followed the book visually. After repeated sessions, the student was required to read from the book without the audio aid. Critics believed the process was simple memorization, and didn't result in true learning. But right now she'd like to see Matt make some progress. "Tell you what. Let's take these papers over to the couch and get comfortable while we go over them. Okay?"

Matt shrugged and Jenn searched her mind for something to ease the hurt and pain she saw in him. "Once we get them finished and go over your assignment for tomorrow, maybe we can go for a walk in the park and play some Frisbee or toss a baseball or something."

He perked up at that. "I'm not very good."

"I'm not, either, but so long as we have fun what's it matter?"

"Do I have to read the story again?"

"Yup, but I'll help you. We'll read it a couple times and practice your vocabulary words because you know—"

"Practice makes us better," he grumbled with a long-suffering sigh. "Yes, ma'am."

"How'd it go with Matt today?" Nick asked the following Thursday.

Jenn inhaled then sighed, lowering the weights onto the base with a soft *clunk*. She knew better than to feel frustrated after such a short period of time, but she couldn't help it. Between always feeling on edge around Nick, Matt's pouting over his summer of schoolwork and her stomach constantly growling, tensions ran high. "Fine."

"Nice try. What's going on?"

She opened her mouth to respond, but nothing came out. Instead the room whirled for a second. "It's, um…fine."

"I'll talk to him."

She blinked away the fog. "What? No. No, I'd rather you not say anything." She lifted her hand and smoothed it over her hair, hoping Nick didn't see the way she was trembling.

After their talk in Nick's office, she'd really dedicated herself to the training program. And she'd done well. She'd watched every rainbow-colored bite that went into her mouth, measured her portion sizes and ignored her stomach. Sugar-free gum had become her constant companion and she was sore all over, but she could already tell a difference in how her pants fastened around her waist. Kind of made it worth the belly grumbling she was putting herself through.

*And it only took nine packages of gum to get you here.*

"Matt needs to know how important it is that he works toward doing better on that test he has to take this fall."

She strove for focus and calm, but came up short. Irritability was a constant companion these days. *Sugar withdrawal, anyone?* "Matt knows perfectly well how serious this is. He doesn't need any more pressure. What he needs is your help. Nick, I know you're busy, but I can't stress how important it is for you to sit down with him for a little while every day and listen to him read. Help him with the words, ask him questions about the story. Parental involvement is *key* to a child's success."

He scowled at the reprimand. "Like I said, it's been a hell of a couple weeks. My uncle extended his vacation to make it a second honeymoon for my aunt, and we're working flat out at the garage."

"I know, but can't you spare a few minutes?"

"Get on the spin bike and get going."

Jenn stifled a groan and did as she was ordered, grumbling beneath her breath because Nick was pushing her so hard. *It's because you gave him a two-month deadline and he's trying to get you to meet that goal.*

But even if she lost a pound to two pounds a week, no way was that dress going to fit. "You're mad at me because I'm bringing this up, aren't you?" She put her feet in motion, glaring at him.

He'd paced away but now he returned to stand in front of her. "Do you think it's easy being a single parent? I'll do anything for Matt, but I'm running both my businesses and the Old Coyote. I'm barely sleeping as it is, plus I'm training you. Your *job* is to help him. Remember that part of our deal?"

Having dealt with plenty of parental situations over the years, Jenn recognized a defensive tactic when she saw one. "I know this may sound harsh, but shouldn't Matt come first?"

Nick's blue eyes churned with anger and disbelief.

"*You're* supposed to be tutoring him and doing what I don't have time to do. Those were the terms of our arrangement."

"I remember," she said tightly, losing patience. "But it's been weeks and you haven't read with Matt *once*. Nick, come on, what's up with that?"

# CHAPTER EIGHT

"I'VE BEEN BUSY. GO FASTER."

"I am!"

"A turtle could outrun you."

Jenn gritted her teeth and pedaled as fast as she could go, glaring at him the entire time. Sweat covered her body, her lungs burned with the effort of keeping up the pace and still she pedaled. She hated her relationship with Nick. He built her up during her workout sessions, told her she could do it, she was doing great. But bring up anything to do with Matt's education and the barriers came up, as if it was a personal affront to him that Matt struggled. As if it was his fault?

But that was ridiculous. Children struggled in school all the time. They had some subjects they did better in than others. But what about her arrangements with Nick? In public he was usually attentive and easygoing as a *guy friend* should be, but whenever they were alone, there was an unbreachable wall between them. Why did he run so hot and cold?

"All I'm saying…" *pant* "…is that Matt needs you. He needs to know…that reading and math…are *important*." She closed her eyes briefly and fought the frustration rolling around inside her. Combined with her hungry state, her head pounded. "I didn't say…anything. When you took my idea for the concert. And turned it. From an incentive to a punishment."

"Here we go."

"If he doesn't— Oh, good grief! Do well on. His tests. But what you do, how you behave, what Matt *sees* in you. Influences him. And if. You're too busy. Too *whatever*—" she gulped in air "—to *help him* with this, or by letting him *see* you reading some *yourself.*"

"This isn't about me, dammit."

"Then who? What do you think. He thinks? He has to consider himself. And reading. Worth the effort."

"You're one to talk about thinking something is worth the effort."

She opened her burning eyes wide to discover Nick now stood with his hands on the lower handle curve of the bike, his gaze too close, too knowing. Jenn shook her head. "This isn't. About me."

"Matt's worth it. We both agree on that. But you? I don't know about that. I think so, but why do you want to lose weight?"

Jenn struggled to draw in more air. Oh, her legs burned! "You know. Why. The trip."

"But it can't be just the trip. If it's just the trip, then once the trip is over so is your drive to succeed. Is that what you want?"

"No."

"Then why are you doing this? Why are you here? Don't slow down, keep pedaling. *Faster.*"

"Oh, help me." Her heart pounded in her chest and she saw Nick as the drill sergeant he'd claimed to be. "Because I want to—" She panted. Her lungs were on fire. Thank goodness the gym was virtually empty at this time of day, otherwise she was sure everyone would be watching.

"Want to what? *What?*"

"Feel better. And…lose weight!"

"*Why?*"

For the same reason she wanted to prove to Matt he could read. It was necessary. It was healthy. It was a good thing. But the truth was most of all she wanted to be skinny, and she knew if she said that Nick would jump on the comment and tear her to shreds in the mood he was in. "To be. Healthy."

"Why?"

What was *with* him?

"Why?"

Nick lowered his head until he was nose-to-nose with her, those amazing eyes of his squinting into hers. With every pedal and huff she felt weaker, more vulnerable, and she knew he saw it.

"You want Matt to know a good education is worth it. But what about you? Is your body *worth* being treated with respect? Is your health and well-being *worth* being kind to yourself? Are *you* worth it?"

"Yes." It was a weak, lackluster response and she knew it. The desperate bid made that much worse because she couldn't maintain eye contact.

"What was that? Say *I'm worth it.* Don't stop. Don't slow down, keep pushing."

"You're pushing. Me. Because you're mad. About what I said. Punishing. Me. *Why?*"

"You can't say it. Why are you slowing down? Don't stop."

"I'm *tired.*" Sick and tired of not being who she wanted to be.

"Trainers push. It's what we do. Say it and you can stop. Say it, Jenn. *I'm worth it.* Three little words."

"I. Hate. You."

He grinned. "I know. But say it anyway. *I'm worth it.*"

A rough sound caught her by surprise and horrified her because it was almost a sob. Almost. She clamped her mouth shut and prayed hard. What was the problem? Three little words, like he said. Why couldn't she say them? And to say that she hated him? She pedaled hard, but she wasn't going anywhere near as fast as she had been. Why wouldn't he leave her alone?

"It's hard, isn't it? After people say the things they do to help us *try harder,* it's almost impossible to believe we're worth anything. I know, sweetheart. I know exactly what that's like."

"How?" Maybe if he could trust her enough to tell her how he knew, maybe then…

"I just do."

Their eyes locked and she saw the same hurt, the same pain in him that she felt, and she knew his words were true. On this, they connected. "I'm—" Her head spun faster than the wheel she pedaled, pounding with the rhythm of her whirling feet. She felt so weak and shaky and dizzy, that she might—

"Jenn? *Jenn!*"

She didn't pass out, but she came close to it. One minute she was on the bike and the next she was in Nick's arms, everything swirling as he lifted her off and carried her into his office.

"Put…put me down."

"Hold still. Stop squirming. Did you follow the schedule?"

She nodded weakly.

"Don't lie to me." Nick seated himself on the couch with her sprawled across his lap.

Was he trembling—or was she? She tried to move herself off his hard thighs, but she couldn't budge even though he barely restrained her. She was so weak.

"Jenn? Sweetheart, I'm sorry for pushing you this hard." His lips brushed her forehead, her eyebrow. "Hear me? Sweetheart, I'm sorry. I'm in a lousy mood and I took it out on you."

"I'm okay." Maybe if she said it enough, her body would believe it. Why couldn't she stop shaking?

"Did you eat?"

She sighed, recognizing his tone. How can he be so different? Yelling at her one minute about Matt and working out, and the next minute being so caring? Concerned? His about-faces made her head spin almost as much as the lack of food.

"I'm fine."

"That's a no."

"The only way I'm going to fit into my dress is if I lose weight quickly."

His arms tightened around her. "Where do you think the energy to work out and burn calories comes from?"

He growled the words, and the sound of his heart was rapid in her ears. Angry on Nick looked...intense.

*Intensely delicious.*

Where did that come from? That's no way to think about a friend. "I'll, um, eat when we're done."

"We're done."

"I barely did anything today. I'm *fine.*"

"We're done," he repeated. "Don't argue with me. I don't want you skipping meals. All that does is shift your body into survival mode, so that it stores everything you do eat." He shook her gently. "You nearly passed out on me."

"But I didn't." She lifted a hand and rubbed her eyes. How embarrassing! "How many people saw me?"

Nick's mouth tightened. "That's not important."

"It is to me. I can't believe you carried me in here. I'm too big. Why isn't it working? It's been weeks and I've barely lost anything. Just a couple pounds. How come the stupid scales aren't moving faster, when all I'm doing is eating *grass* and exercising?"

He squeezed her to gain her full attention. "Listen to me and listen good. You are *not* to skip another meal. You do what

I say and you'll lose the weight, but regardless of what the scales say, this isn't worth doing at all if you end up making yourself sick. Do you hear me? Throw away the damn scales."

She stared into Nick's eyes and realized with a start that she'd scared him. His pulse beat rapidly in his throat and his gaze was… Caring? For all his bluster, he did care. It was right there for her to see and she stopped being upset with him. "I don't want to fight with you. Please, let me up."

A knock sounded at the door, then a man with dark hair and striking features stepped inside. His forehead wrinkled when he took in the sight of Jenn on Nick's lap. She tried to scoot off, but once again Nick stopped her.

"She okay?"

"She didn't eat." Once again he growled out the words. Coming from such a big man she should've been highly intimidated, but having spent nearly every day either in Nick's company or his son's, she now understood that Nick's bark was way worse than his bite. She hoped.

"I figured it might be something like that. I brought you some orange juice and crackers." He opened the juice before handing it to Jenn. "Drink up. It'll help bring your blood sugar back up."

She bit her lip and stared at the information block on the back of the bottle. "It's got a lot of sugar in it."

Nick grimaced. "I've created a monster. Drink the damn juice."

"There's no need to swear at me." She rubbed her temple, feeling sluggish and shaky and moody. Her head hurt, too, and the room was wobbling in front of her, everything off-kilter. She took a small sip, sliding the man who'd brought the juice a glare when he took her hand and pressed his fingers to her wrist.

"More," Nick said. "Doctor's orders."

"You're not a doctor."

"But I am." The man in front of them grinned. "Don't let the workout gear fool you. Drink it all. And since Nick has yet to introduce us, I'll introduce myself. Ethan Tulane, Nick's brother."

She stared at him, suddenly able to see the connection. "I should've known."

"What?" they asked simultaneously.

Practically sandwiched between them, she couldn't miss the male energy. They were both gorgeous, and they both stared down at her as if they'd actually do her bidding if she just snapped her fingers. And they asked *what*? "Nothing. I'm—"

"Jennifer Rose," Nick added grudgingly.

"Nice to meet you, Jennifer Rose."

"Oh, it's…it's just Jennifer or Jenn. Rose is my last name, not my middle. Nick calls me that sometimes. Mostly when I irritate him."

That statement earned her a glare, but Nick made no move to shove her off his lap or to offer any explanations as to why she was still there. And apparently she wasn't the only one to think it strange because Ethan nodded toward the empty space beside them. "Would you be more comfortable lying down?"

"She's fine."

Amusement sparkled in Ethan's gaze. "I see. Well, she's obviously in good hands so I'll leave you to give her a lecture—or mouth-to-mouth."

She gasped sharply. "I don't need a lecture. And we're just friends."

"Shut the door on your way out."

Jenn twisted her head around to glare at Nick. "That's rude," she informed him in a stage whisper.

Ethan laughed harder at Jenn's bid for manners. "See you

around, little brother. Don't be such a stranger. Jennifer, it's nice to meet you. Don't worry about Nick's grumbling. Tulanes have a tendency to be possessive, and Nick never did play well with others." He winked at her before smirking at his brother. "Don't forget that lecture."

Ethan Tulane was gone in an instant, the door closing softly behind him with a *snick* of sound.

Jenn tried hard to ignore the way it felt to be surrounded by Nick. On his lap, in his arms. "*Why* did you do that?"

"Do what?"

"Act so…so whatever." Aware of his frowning displeasure, she took another nervous sip of juice to give herself something to do. Was it possible? They spent a lot of time together and she'd continually warned herself not to make more of the situation with Nick than there was, but… She needed air, time to think. Sitting on Nick's lap like that was making her lose her mind. "Let me up."

"No. Ethan isn't the guy for you."

"Why not? He's a doctor and handsome and you should've been nicer to your brother." She rolled her eyes, and regretted it when the move made her head pound harder. "Ow." Fingers to her eyebrow, she rubbed. "And I don't *need* a lecture. You're just trying to change the subject from the fact that you know I'm right and you need to spend some time with your son, reading with him."

"Drop it while you have my sympathy after nearly giving me a heart attack. And listen up. Ethan hooks up with women who know the score. He's all about casual relationships and two-to-screw dates. That's it."

"Two-to-screw?"

"Two dates, a night in bed and he's done."

She pondered that for a long moment, whatever it took to

keep from looking directly at Nick. "What makes you think I can't do casual?"

His entire body tensed and hardened beneath her. "You been with anyone since Dixon?"

Of all the— "That's none of your business."

"No, *that* says it all. Drink some more." He lifted the bottle and pressed it to her lips.

Jenn swallowed to keep from having the orange juice all over her shirt. "Is that really why?" A horrible thought occurred. "Oh, no."

"What?"

She smoothed the hair that had escaped its band, and wiped the cool sweat from her cheek and forehead. Had her mascara smeared? She couldn't come work out without at least a little makeup on. She'd scare the guys away for sure then. "I'm a wreck. That's it, isn't it? I'm a wreck and too big, and he's only into skinny, little—"

"Shut up."

She gaped at him. "Don't tell me to shut up."

"There's absolutely nothing wrong with the way you look."

"Yeah, right."

"You don't believe me?"

"Of course I don't," she stated bluntly. "I look like a big, sweaty *blob*."

He took the juice from her hand.

"What are you doing?"

Nick set the juice bottle aside and slid his hand along her jaw, palmed her face and stared into her eyes, as if he wanted to look into her soul. But that couldn't be right, because how silly was that? It was her low blood sugar. She couldn't think straight. Nick liked women who resembled Ms. Perky Boobs, not an overly plump—

"Following doctor's orders by learning to play well with you. Look at me." He waited for her to make eye contact. "You don't look like a blob."

That said, Nick lowered his head, oh, so slowly toward her. His gaze dropped to her mouth along the way and she had the urge to wet her lips. Her heart galloped in her chest, an overweight racehorse struggling to keep up with the sleek thoroughbreds way ahead of her, and she didn't move. The moment was so surreal she was afraid to breathe, do anything, for fear of screwing it up. Was he really going to kiss her?

The door opened abruptly, this time without a warning knock, and an older woman took two steps inside before coming to a halt. Nick groaned and buried his face in her neck so he didn't see the amusement and curiosity lighting the woman's wrinkled features.

"Go *away*, Ethan."

The woman chuckled and Nick tensed, his entire body going rigid beneath her once more.

The elderly woman smiled at her, the look positively beaming. "Well, hello, dear. I see Marguerite Bumgarner was right. I'm Rosetta, Nick's grandmother. And you are…?"

"Going to die of embarrassment," she whispered.

OF ALL THE MEMBERS of his family who got on his nerves or drove him crazy, Gram wasn't usually one of them. Until today. What was he thinking? What had he been about to do? He had as much chance of getting a diploma as Jenn did of climbing atop his desk right then and dancing for them. "Gram, now's not a good time. Can't it wait?"

His grandmother didn't so much as blink. No, she smiled expectantly at Jenn and ignored him entirely. He knew that look and bit back another groan.

"Don't be embarrassed, dear. Not at all. I know very well how one can get carried away by passion. Why, all Nick's grandfather had to do was—"

"*Gram.* Did you need something?"

"An introduction would be nice. Where are your manners, dear?"

"Gram, Jennifer Rose. Jenn, my grandmother."

"A pleasure. Have we met before? You look familiar, dear."

"I'm not sure. I'm a teacher at the elementary."

"Ah, that's it. You bring your students to The Village to sing for us."

Jenn nodded at the mention of the assisted-living facility and the two chatted about the previous year's program.

Nick had hoped to avoid meeting up with Gram because of the guilt trip he knew he'd receive about the upcoming family gatherings. It had been happening a lot lately. His brother Garret would call and ask him to do something first. After Nick turned him down, his mother's invitation would come next. And when that didn't work, Mom called in reinforcements in the form of Gram, knowing that Nick couldn't tell his grandmother no very often. If at all.

"Um…I feel a lot better now, Nick. Why don't I leave you two to talk?"

"Don't be silly, dear. Of course you can stay."

His gut clenched. "Gram—"

"Mrs. Tulane—"

"Rosetta, dear." Triumph glowed on Gram's face. "Or Gram," she added, her purpose clear.

"*Gram.*"

Jenn's face pinkened. "Rosetta, please don't misunderstand what you s-saw. Nick and I are just friends. I felt dizzy in the weight room and he helped me." She elbowed him in the ribs then shoved herself off his lap and onto the couch before attempting to scramble to her feet. Moving so quickly must have sent her head spinning because she closed her eyes briefly before latching on to the back of the nearest chair.

Nick jumped up and steadied her with a grip on her shoulders. When she regained some of her color, he reluctantly let go.

"Well, I should hope so. On both counts. Friendship is a necessary aspect in a relationship, otherwise they never last. And men are supposed to be gentlemen and help those in need. But when I walked in…" Gram turned her gaze on him. "Have you invited Jennifer to the wedding festivities?"

That brought Jennifer's head up once more. "Wedding? Oh, I couldn't possibly impo—"

"I'm not going." The blunt response slipped out before Nick could stop it, earning Jenn's wide-eyed disbelief and his grandmother's down-the-nose glare of disapproval.

"Excuse me?"

"I don't want to fight with you, Gram."

"Then don't. You'd miss your brother's wedding—the first wedding in the family? Matt is in the ceremony. If for no other reason, you should be attending the events because of that. And what about tonight? You'll be at the rehearsal dinner, won't you?"

He locked his jaw.

"Nicholas?"

Gram stared at him. Jenn, too. His hands fisted. The last thing he wanted to do was go a round with either one of them—or go to the rehearsal dinner. But he could feel the tide turning, the sand shifting beneath his feet. He knew it was expected, that he'd cause a whole other battle if he skipped it, and he was outnumbered but…

"I see."

How was it possible to put so much impact and disapproval in two little words? "It's just a dinner. Look, I'll come to the wedding. Okay? I'll be there for the ceremony. That's the important thing." He could drop Matt off tomorrow afternoon for all the photos, leave and go to work. Then show up late, just before the ceremony began, and take off as soon as it was over. That counted as being there and no one would even notice if he wasn't at the reception. He'd cause more of a stir if he actually showed up. Didn't they get that?

"Of course it's important, but that's not good enough."

Gram's voice shook slightly. Was she that upset about this?

"Nicholas Tulane, you are a member of the family whether you acknowledge us or not."

Awww, crap. "Gram, it's not like that and you know it."

"Jennifer, it was nice to meet you."

"Likewise." Jennifer glanced at him, her expression urging him to speak up and say something. To agree to go.

He didn't.

Gram's mouth was a hard, flat line, disappointment clouding her eyes. He and Luke had inherited their blue eyes from her, but right now it was kind of eerie having her look at him like that. Shaking her head, Gram turned to leave without giving him a hug, something she'd done from the time he was born. *No one* left her presence without a hug.

"Jennifer, dear, it was good to meet you." Gram stepped forward and hugged Jenn close. "Come see me sometime. I'd love to chat with you."

"Oh, um, sure."

Gram dipped her head. "Nick."

"Gram…"

The door shut behind her. Nick waited for her to burst

back into the room with a list of demands, but seconds passed and there was no sign of her.

Damn.

"I cannot believe you did that! She's your grandmother and she only wants you to come to rehearsal dinner. What's the big deal?"

Given Jenn's uncompromising tone, he chose his words carefully. "The big deal is none of *your* business." Nick walked toward her slowly, intending to round the desk and seat himself behind it, but along the way he was aware that Jennifer inched backward with every step he took and that just made him angrier. She knew he'd been about to kiss her. There was no mistaking his intent. Obviously that wasn't what she wanted. "The *deal* is that if I don't want to go to my brother's wedding, I don't have to go."

"Did you see her face? Nick, she loves you so much! Why *not* go to the dinner?"

## CHAPTER NINE

"I JUST TOLD YOU. I don't *want* to go." The words emerged as a small roar that Nick couldn't quite control. "Besides," he continued, lowering his voice, "there will be so many people there they won't even notice I'm not at the dinner. They won't miss me."

"Not miss their brother? Their son? Their *grandson*? Of course, they'll miss you!" Jenn stopped backstepping and held her ground. Nose to chest with him, she planted her feet, stubborn determination etched on her features. "What did your brother do to you that you don't want to go to such a special occasion?"

"I'm not arguing with you about this."

"Do you not like his bride?"

"Darcy is a sweetheart."

"Your massage therapist?" Her eyes widened then narrowed to almond-shaped slits. "She's very pretty."

"I'll tell her you said so."

"Maybe you like her too much. Is that it?"

He had to count to five before he could speak. "I'm not a backstabbing cheat like your ex. Darcy is an employee and my future sister-in-law. Garret is a lucky guy, but I'm not going because of any intimate feelings for his fiancée. We were all a little surprised that he broke off dating his girlfriend at the time and fell for Darcy, but the two of them couldn't be happier."

"So you claim the family even though you don't want to spend time with them?"

"We don't get along. It's as simple as that. Put me in a room with my brothers and father and we argue. Period."

"But you love them?"

"Of course."

"Then you're going."

"No, I'm damn well not."

"Fine, you want to be difficult? I can be that way, too."

"You already are!"

Jennifer lifted her chin. "We're going to the dinner and the wedding together," she informed him blithely. "Despite my nasty divorce, I *love* weddings, and I want to go. So I'm making it part of our deal—one of the stipulations I retained the right to add, thanks to Suzanne's forethought."

He slid a hand over his face and muttered something Gram would've smacked him upside the head for saying in front of mixed company.

"It's your brother's wedding to one of your employees," she continued in a rush. "Think about how bad it will look if you don't go. People expect you there, and part of our deal was to be seen together like Suzanne said. You agreed to the terms. *Remember?*"

He had agreed, but of all the things he'd expected her to ask of him this wasn't one of them. He thought of the tension and the conversations that would take place. Crap!

His gaze dropped to her mouth. Jenn wet her lips nervously, reminding him of what he'd been about to do before Gram had so rudely interrupted. Stupid move on his part, but tempting all the same. And it would shut her up. Maybe then she'd change her mind and not want to go?

"S-stop that."

"What?" He crossed his arms over his chest. "Maybe I should add a few conditions of my own to our deal."

Her eyes took on a wary glint. "Like what?"

"You want this summer to be all about you? Learning how to have some fun? Finding your inner—" he couldn't help but smile at the words "—table dancer?"

Heat spread through her cheeks and her eyes closed briefly. "I can't believe Suzanne told you that."

"Answer the question."

"Yes, what about it?"

"Let's find her."

"Wh-what do you mean?"

"You want me to be blunt?" Jenn's face had more color than the Red Hots Nick had eaten as a kid.

"I—I think you might have to be. Just so I know what you're saying."

Uh-huh. He moved close, his gaze sweeping over her from her brand-spanking-new Skechers to the lightweight pants and tee that had Teachers Rule spread across her very generous chest. She had a great rack. "My dates have a tendency to…want more at the end of the night."

"You mean, they want you to put out."

"If you insist."

She nearly choked. "You don't mean that."

He lowered his head until their noses almost touched, his eyes locked on hers. No sense in stopping now. It was bad news to get involved with Jenn, but he couldn't seem to help himself. And what better way to have her back off? She'd chicken out, freak out or—*Take him up on it? And then what?*

"You still want to go?"

"I don't put out on the first date. Or the second."

He smirked. "No two-to-screw? That sounds like a challenge."

"I believe in deep, emotional commitment on both sides before…well, going to the next level."

Yet another thing to admire about Ms. Rose. "I don't doubt you do. But still, it sounds like a challenge." And one he would have liked to explore further, if she wasn't the way that she was. Sad to say, most of his dates didn't have her intelligence, and while that was a major turn-on, it was also a turn-off. What man wanted to feel stupid compared to the woman he was with?

"You're just saying that to…to… *Why* are you saying things like that to me?"

Good question. Deciding that was a subject best left for later, he lifted his hand and smoothed a stray tendril that had escaped her ponytail. "You ever hear of Mara Corday?"

"No."

"Gina Lollobrigida?"

"No. Are they your old girlfriends?"

He smiled as he thumbed her cheek, the tempting curve of her mouth. "When I moved out of my parents' house, I lived in a little room above my uncle's garage for a few years. My uncle has a collection of pinups my aunt made him store there to get them out of the house." He stroked her face again, unable to help himself. Her skin was so soft. "Those pictures dated from the early 1900s to the 50s and 60s. Models back then were a far cry from the anorexic models and actresses of today. Women then were more…womanly. Curvy and soft and beautiful. Bathing suits cover a lot less now, but dressed as they were in those discreet suits and gowns, those other women were sexy as all get out and I stared at magazines and pinups for hours on end. You remind me of them."

Jenn's lower lip trembled. Nick rubbed his thumb across

the flesh and looked into her astonished eyes, wondering how any woman Jenn's age could be as sweet and naive as she appeared. Did she think guys thought more about a little extra weight than they did breasts and hips and the strength of their thighs? AC/DC's "You Shook Me All Night Long" sounded in his head. A smile curled his mouth at the corners. Jenn could shake him, all right.

A sound filled the room, low and rumbling. Jenn gasped and clamped her arms around her belly, and despite Nick's best intentions, he smiled at the absurd noise before anger rolled in to stomp on his humor. She wasn't going to starve herself. He'd see to that.

Jenn needed to eat before she passed out, and he needed a chance to get himself together and think about things. Was he really going to mess with a woman who blushed and stammered and had been emotionally abused by a jerk like Todd Dixon? "Go grab a healthy lunch and have your tutoring session with Matt before you go home to get ready for this dinner."

She swallowed hard. "You'll go?"

"It's a condition of our agreement—you said so." It was a lousy excuse and he knew it. But he felt guilty about not going and the only way he'd get through the evening was by having someone else there to focus on. Someone like Jenn.

"But if you expect—"

"I keep my word. I said you could add conditions and you've made this one of them. I'll do it."

"But what about the whole dancing-on-the-table summer thing and your, um, dates?"

"What about them?" Before his mind could interfere, he dropped his head and brushed a kiss across her mouth, heard her sharp gasp just as the cinnamon gum and orange juice taste of her registered. "What better way to spend the summer than to discover the woman you are away from your ex? Even for an evening. I'll pick you up at seven."

Jenn opened her mouth as though to protest—or back out completely, Nick wasn't sure which—and then took off across the office floor as quick as a shot. She paused by the door, looked at him again, but didn't utter a word.

Nick held her gaze until she turned around and then he watched her generous hips sway as she bolted for safety. Images filled his head and he lifted both hands to rub his face, easily able to picture her in the poses of the pinups he'd admired for so long. He saw her sprawled across his bed, dressed in satin and lace, her big gray eyes watching his every move with a flirtatious smile on her full lips. Or like Ingrid Bergman's famous 1945 haystack pose for *Yank*.

But nothing could alleviate the dread he felt at the night to come. This was it. Before the evening was over he had no doubt one of his family members would fill Jenn in on what she obviously didn't know, and then…

*End of story.*

Was that why he'd allowed himself to agree—to end things and get it all out in the open without actually having to be the one to tell her? Because he knew the night would end any chance of her wanting him for more than a friend?

*You reap what you sow, Nick. Your lies about school caught up with you, just like your daddy's anger caught up with him. It happens to all of us at some time. The trick now is making amends.*

His fists clenched. The memory of him and his grandfather sitting on the ground by Grandpa's favorite fishing hole was as fresh today as it was back then. The smells of the water-soaked earth, flies buzzing in his ears, mosquitoes biting and the sound of the reels whizzing over the water.

He hadn't made amends, though. The more people talked, the angrier he'd become, until the five-mile distance between the family home on the mountaintop and his compact apartment in town seemed like halfway around the world. Maybe if his grandfather had lived longer, the damage could have been repaired. But as it stood, nothing had changed.

Nick moved to a photo on the wall by the door. Stared into his grandfather's face. Granddad had passed away a year after that fishing trip. "I miss you, you know that? I wish I'd been smart enough to listen." Too much time had gone by, and too much had been said that shouldn't have been said. All of it in anger.

And as of tonight, Jenn would see him exactly the same way his family did. Once the truth came out, he wouldn't have to wonder about getting to know her better. Boundaries would be set and lines drawn. They always were.

NICK'S MOOD was just as dark later that afternoon when he entered the apartment to check on Matt. From the garage's office he'd watched Gram drop Matt off after the boy's final tuxedo fitting and he knew the moment Jenn pulled onto the lot to begin Matt's tutoring session.

He'd kept to himself, returned phone calls, placed orders and generally had done everything he could think of to stay out of the apartment and away from Jenn. On the one hand he was aware that he was using her as a scapegoat for his anger because he didn't see eye-to-eye with his family, but on the other hand reality was what it was. People stayed with their own kind, defined by their likes, interests and so on. Jennifer Rose would be no different. But he didn't like it because it lead to an even more important question. When had it started to matter to him what she thought?

"It. Was. A. Cro-cro—"

"Crocodile," Jenn supplied.

"Crocodile. The crocodile… Can I have a drink?"

"Finish reading this section first, please."

"But I'm really thirsty."

Nick hesitated in the short hall outside the kitchen where they sat, able to see them thanks to the pass-through into the rest of the open apartment. Jenn had tutored Matt five days a week since the start of summer vacation three weeks earlier. Shouldn't they have made more progress?

"Wait just a little longer, please."

Matt inhaled and sighed. "The crocodile…c-c— What's that word?"

"Crawled."

"Can I stop?"

"Just a little bit longer, Matt. You're almost done with this story."

"But I don't want to read right now. Can we do math?"

"We've done enough math for the day. Let's try to work on your reading for a while. You're doing great. You just need some more practice."

"But math ''

"Matt, honey, your math skills are coming along really well. You know your times tables and you can follow patterns. But we can't shrug off reading. You're having some trouble and we need to figure out why and focus on that."

Nick's keys bit into his hand.

She ruffled his hair. "What's five times three minus one?"

"Fourteen."

"See? That was the gist of the word problem you missed earlier, but this time you didn't even have to think about it. Try the passage again. Take your time."

Matt inhaled, his head lowering over the page. "The crocodile— Dad!"

Nick stifled a groan when Matt flew across the room and hugged him as if he'd been gone for years. "Hey, bub. How's it going?"

Matt glanced at Jenn, almost too afraid to speak in case she countered his response. "It's okay."

"Matt's already come a long way with his math. We're working on reading now."

Nick squeezed Matt tight, hesitated, and then grabbed the flashlight from the kitchen bar, pretending he'd come to retrieve it and not because he'd been unable to stay away. "That's good. Go get back to work, okay? You're doing great, Matt."

Matt sighed heavily and shuffled back to his kitchen chair, head down and a bleak look in his eyes.

Nick knew that look all too well. Back in school, he'd tried hard, too, but he'd stumbled over the words on the page, had a hard time getting them to make sense and strained so hard to read that finally he'd gotten fed up with the headaches and embarrassment and had stopped trying. The day he was able to quit without his parents' permission, he had.

Nick met Jennifer's gaze momentarily before he turned and left. Matt's frustration fed his own, but it was the proof that Matt was now going through what he'd experienced that kicked his anger into high gear. He didn't want to identify with his father. Alan Tulane was a man revered by this town, and especially at the hospital, but throughout Nick's early years, his father had stood over his shoulder and shouted at him in frustration. Ordered him to do better, as if that would make it happen.

He'd spent hours and hours studying. Every night. Weekends. All for nothing, because he'd go to school and fail anyway. *Just like Matt.* This was what it was like. The anger, the frustration… No wonder his father yelled.

*Matt's not you. He just needs a little help.*

And he didn't want Matt to quit. He wanted Matt to have a good education. Be whatever he wanted to be when he grew up instead of having to work so hard to juggle everything to make ends meet. Nick made a good living, liked fixing cars and was proud of his work, *good at it,* but there were times when he saw Garret drive by in his expensive Cadillac and tailored suits and he wondered what might have happened if he'd stayed in school and figured things out.

"Matt, let Ms. Rose help you, all right? You do what she says."

"Yessir."

Nick turned and stalked out the door, maneuvered the stairs without really seeing them and tossed the flashlight into the office before leaving the gym for a run. He wouldn't shout at Matt. Wouldn't call him lazy or stupid. Wouldn't suggest that his son was "slow on the uptake" as his father had so often pointed out.

No, he'd do none of that. He'd punish his body instead. Punish himself for not being able to help his son, because it was no less than he deserved. This was still more proof that he and Jenn were on two totally different playing fields and that he'd made a huge mistake today when he'd mentioned the summer ahead. They had nothing in common.

Which made taking Jenn to the rehearsal dinner tonight and introducing her to the rest of his family a really good idea.

THAT EVENING Jenn pulled her best outfit from the closet and prayed it would zip. She'd stayed with Matt longer than she'd planned to, trying to help the boy with his reading, but as a result, she'd lost what little time she'd have to shop for a dress to wear to the rehearsal dinner. If the suit didn't fit she'd be forced to cancel, and if she did that, Nick wouldn't go. That much she knew for a fact.

"I've lost a few pounds. I'm lifting weights. I'm eating grass. *Please fit.*" The suit was her Easter outfit from two years ago. A beautiful skirt with a fitted waist, an A-line shape and a flirtatious hem. The jacket was meant to button, but she could wear it open over a camisole. The look was figure-flattering, something she desperately required at the moment. "Please, please, *please* fit."

The jacket and matching skirt were a beautiful dove-gray color that brought out her eyes and paired with matching pumps and hose—her best dinner-at-the-country-club getup. But now that the time was drawing near, she was becoming ridiculously nervous. Why had she insisted Nick take her? If her sister was at the club, would Jenn have gone? No. Because she knew what family tension felt like.

*Nick's relationship with his family is not the same as yours with Megan or your father.*

She hoped. Old bitterness welled deep within her and paired with more recent memories of Todd's betrayal and deception. Was it any wonder she doubted her ability to attract a man? To feel desirable?

*Nick kissed you. Obviously you did something right.*

But *why* had he kissed her? And that talk about pinup girls… Could she really be compared to women like that?

Jenn glanced down and gave herself a critical once-over. Despite the extra weight, she still had a shape and her legs were nicely solid, not too cottage-cheesy. Her skin was smooth and her breasts full without the aid of a push-up bra. Guys appreciated that, right? But did men like Nick really fall for girls like her?

*He didn't say anything about falling. He said* nothing *about falling in love.*

"The real question is whether or not you're going to take him up on the romantic offer."

Did she dare?

No, no, no. She was the responsible one. Casual sex was like Russian roulette with six bullets instead of one. That wasn't for her and it wasn't who she wanted to be. If she were really honest, she'd say it was more like something Megan would do. Act out and pay the consequences later.

Lacking any insight or answers, Jenn glanced at the clock beside her bed and gasped. Murmuring another prayer, she lifted the suit from the bed.

*Please fit.*

# CHAPTER TEN

NICK GRIPPED THE WHEEL with both hands. The run had left him tired and soaked with sweat, but now he was showered, dressed and in the truck, and still wondering why he'd agreed to this. Suffering through a wedding with a crowd he could get lost in was one thing, but a dinner where the majority of the guests were family members he barely spoke to…

"Why aren't we going?" Matt asked from the backseat. "When Gram took me to try on my tux she said to make sure we weren't late. She said it a couple of times."

"Yeah, I'll bet." He'd bet Gram had had a lot more to say than that, too, considering he'd just told her he wasn't going at all. "Did you…mention the summer-school thing?"

"No. I don't want her or anybody to know. Is that okay?"

"Yeah, Matt, that's fine. I haven't said anything, either. We'll keep it between us, okay?" Matt nodded and Nick breathed a sigh of relief. One worry down, five billion more to go.

"She asked about Ms. Rose, though."

Nick froze. *Five billion and one.* He forced himself to let go of the wheel long enough to turn and face Matt. "Gram asked about her? What'd you say?"

Matt shrugged. "Just stuff."

"Like what?"

"I don't know."

"Try to remember."

Matt scrunched up his face and rubbed his freckled nose. "She just asked if I liked her and stuff. I said I did. And I told her that Ms. Rose watches TV with me sometimes. Ms. Rose likes the big screen as much as Darcy does when she babysits me."

Which meant Gram knew Jennifer had been upstairs in his apartment, an area he kept pretty well off-limits to everyone but Matt and himself.

Suzanne had wanted other guys to notice Jenn, but he'd never considered his family getting involved. Things were becoming complicated.

"Dad? We're gonna be late."

Maybe if he stalled long enough they wouldn't have to go at all?

"I betcha Ms. Rose looks pretty. Have you ever seen her all dressed up? Last Halloween she was a fairy princess with wings that flashed. She was *really* pretty. The teachers voted her the prettiest."

*No doubt she would be pretty tonight, too.*

Even though Nick wanted to kill the engine and go back inside, he put the truck into gear. "Seat belt on?"

"Yup."

"Then I suppose we should go get our date."

SHE FELT LIKE a stuffed sausage. Jenn struggled to breathe normally as she hurried down the stairs after someone laid on the doorbell as if it were a game-show buzzer in the final seconds. Nick was five minutes late, but Jen had needed every one of those minutes to make up for the time she'd lost wriggling herself into body-shaping underwear guaranteed to make her look ten pounds thinner.

Surprisingly, the skirt had actually buttoned and the jacket had fit—but only because it was left open over the cami. She couldn't take a deep breath for fear of popping the button at her waist, but she'd packed a safety pin in her purse just in case. Silently, she praised the makers of spandex.

Jenn crossed the hardwood floor, her three-inch heels already pinching her toes. *Doesn't matter. They make your legs look longer.* The key to looking slimmer, according to the fashion magazines, was lengthening the body.

*If that's the case, you should try stilts.*

Jenn grabbed the knob with one hand and the lock in the other, swinging the door wide. "I'm sorry I'm—" Her mouth dropped before she caught herself and forced it closed. *Oh. My. Word!* "You look…um, hi."

To say Nick looked gorgeous was such an understatement. He was…*delectable.* A mixture of *GQ* and Ralph Lauren on six-foot-plus of brooding male. Nick's jet-black hair had been gelled into the kind of finger-mussed disorder that actors paid big bucks to achieve. A black shirt stretched across his chest beneath a charcoal suit jacket lined with fine black pinstripes, all of which molded his broad shoulders to perfection.

Sooty black lashes lowered over his eyes and Jenn watched as Nick studied her from her hair right down to her feet. Conscious that he was taking in every detail of her appearance, she sucked in her stomach as best she could and prayed it worked.

"Matt said you'd look pretty."

"He did?" How sweet! She'd come to love Matt all too easily. He was smart and funny, with old-fashioned manners that made her smile. His *yes, ma'ams* and *no, ma'ams* went straight to her heart.

"Sorry we're late."

"No problem."

"Are you ready?"

"Yes, I—I just need to lock up."

Nick turned to get out of her way, but then stopped and swung back to face her. "Jenn, I'd appreciate it if you'd keep the tutoring thing quiet. I don't want anyone, especially in my family, to know."

She frowned at the intensity she heard in his voice, but since he'd admitted he and his family didn't get along the last thing she wanted to do was say something awkward. "Of course. I wouldn't want to embarrass Matt or reveal a confidence. And I hope you'll extend the same courtesy to me. About the training." She swallowed and smoothed her hand over a hip to wipe away the moisture on her palm. "Nick, I'm sorry about today. Forcing you to do this. I could just tell it meant a lot to your grandmother and I hate to see families fight. I know what that's like." She made a wry face. "A little too well, to be honest."

He gave her a grim smile. "Then you'll understand and not argue when I say I've had enough?"

A laugh bubbled up. "Absolutely."

Out beside the truck she waited patiently while Nick moved two audio bestsellers off the seat and helped her into the cab. Nick was quiet the entire drive to the Beauty Ridge Country Club, while she and Matt talked about the merits of the latest Nintendo Wii game and how he hoped to get it for his birthday. Finally they arrived and Nick's scowling countenance grew even darker as he escorted her inside, making her wish she'd kept her mouth closed and allowed Rosetta Tulane to be disappointed.

Nick *really* didn't want to be there, but why? What was so bad about their relationship that he couldn't spend a few hours with his family? Jenn didn't get along with her sister, but it didn't stop her from going to see her parents.

*But Megs usually isn't there when you go, either.*

True. Come to think of it, her parents hadn't heard from Megan in a while. But self-centered people are all about them. Meg's behavior was the norm. Typically, the Roses only heard from Megs if and when she needed something.

Shaking her head, Jenn frowned and hurried to keep pace with Nick's longer strides. He walked so fast that she wondered if his plan was to enter the building, walk through it, and keep right on going out the back door.

Inside, Jenn resisted the urge to roll her eyes. She noted she'd been correct in assuming that genetics had been kind to the Tulanes. They were easy enough to pick out of the crowd, every member tall, dark-haired and striking in looks, just like the grand dame herself. Rosetta cheerfully took over the job of introducing Jenn to the others, who were gathered around a long table, leaving Nick to his brooding by the bar.

"And this is Luke."

Jenn automatically smiled as she heard the new name and turned away from Nick's younger sister only to gasp in surprise. Two? There were *two* of them?

Nick's identical twin smiled and winked at her. "I love that expression. You didn't know?"

Nick hadn't said a word. "N-no." Did he look hurt to find out that Nick hadn't mentioned him? "But we haven't talked about family much," she hurried to reassure Luke.

His gaze shifted momentarily to Nick before he refocused his attention on Jenn and smiled. "Well, it's nice to meet you, Jennifer."

She murmured a polite response, but couldn't stop staring at Luke in amazement. He and Nick were identical, but Nick, thanks to his many hours in the gym, was broader and more solid, with a harder edge to his features. Sexier than any of his siblings.

"How did you and Nick meet?"

"I was about to ask the same thing," Alexandra, Nick's sister, chimed in. "Nick hasn't brought a girl to meet us in... What?" She glared at Luke, who'd nudged her and was now giving her a brotherly glare.

Rosetta patted Jenn's arm with a chuckle. "Don't mind them, dear. It's just that Nick hasn't brought a girl to meet us for a long time, which makes you something of a novelty. I hope you'll forgive our curiosity."

"Of course." She paused, then realized that they were waiting for her to continue. "Oh, um, Nick and I met at the Old Coyote," she said, searching the room for Nick and finding him just behind her left shoulder. One glance told her that he was listening to every word. So why didn't he join them?

"How long have you been dating?" Alexandra asked. A small, feminine version of her brothers, Alex—as she preferred to be called—was slim, with sleek black hair and amazingly beautiful violet eyes.

"Oh, um...We're just friends."

Marilyn Tulane joined them. "Jennifer, I'm so glad you could be here this evening. I don't mean to interrupt, but has any of you seen Ethan? I've tried to call him all day today, but he hasn't returned my calls."

"Having fun?" Nick murmured from behind her while his mother went on to discuss the possible whereabouts of the missing brother.

She started, not aware that he'd moved close until she felt the moist heat of his breath in her ear. A shiver ran over her body and she hoped no one noticed.

Nick did. Amusement warmed his cool blue eyes before his gaze dipped to the fullness of her breasts and the dip of the camisole where her body instantly responded in blatant detail.

"What are you doing? Stop that." She glared at him, careful to keep her voice low, so that the others wouldn't hear. She was keenly aware of their interested glances.

"Stop what?" A smile layered his voice. "Are you cold?" he asked not so innocently.

Heat shot through her. *"Yes."*

"Really?" His voice was mischievous.

So that was the game? He would distract himself from his family issues by flirting with her? Jenn glared at him, but couldn't quite ignore the chuckle rumbling up from his chest. The sound was low and rich, and, oh, those eyes… It was a wonder she hadn't melted into a pool at his feet. A girl could certainly forget herself around Nick.

A blush continued to warm her cheeks, and Jenn bit her inner lip and prayed Nick's relatives wouldn't make too much of their byplay. But then a group of people came into the country-club dining room, laughing and talking loudly, behaving like prep-school chums and drawing everyone's notice. It took the Tulanes' attention from Jenn and Nick, especially when the crowd of men parted. Jenn moaned when she spotted Todd in the middle of them. Was he the one being congratulated? And by the head of the hospital, no less.

"Oh, no." Apparently Nick had come to the same conclusion, because his expression lost the teasing warmth it had held and changed to a dark and dangerous-looking scowl.

She placed a hand on his arm. "Oh, Nick, I'm sorry. Ethan must be so disappointed."

"He had to do it today," Nick snapped. "Pierson had to get the last word in and ruin things, didn't he?"

Behind her, Nick's family whispered among themselves and Jenn saw Garrett's bride-to-be grasp his arm to detain him when he moved forward as if to speak to the group by the door.

"What's going on?" she whispered to Nick. "Besides the obvious?"

"The woman Garret dated before Darcy is Harold Pierson's daughter. When it became obvious things were on the rocks with Garret's old relationship, Pierson threatened to scuttle Ethan's chances of becoming chief of surgery if Garret wouldn't stay away from Darcy and propose to his daughter as expected."

Her heart sank. "So he announced the promotion on the same night as your brother's engagement celebration and then he brought Todd here? How petty."

Nick shifted his weight toward her, without taking his eyes off his family. "Your ex and Pierson are a lot alike. They're both—"

He broke off. Jenn turned to see Alan, Nick's father, and Luke trying and failing to stop Garret. The groom headed toward the newcomers with a menacing stride.

Handing her his drink, Nick stepped in front of his brother.

"Get out of the way."

Garret was tall, but Nick was taller. He was also broader and more powerfully built. Nick stood toe-to-toe with Garret, as the rest of the family gathered round.

"You go over there and Pierson wins. Is that what you want?"

"Ethan—"

"Is a big boy. He'll get over it and he'll extract his own revenge—if he wants it. You go over there and rip Pierson's head off and you'll be in jail instead of getting married, and Pierson will be telling everyone how he thinks he's made the right choice."

Jenn watched from two feet away, her attention torn between Nick and Garrett and Todd's smirking expression of superiority, which was matched by Mr. Pierson's. They really were two of a kind.

Then Ethan Tulane entered the room. Jenn was one of the first to spot him, and it seemed as if every person present caught their breath at once. A knot tightened in her stomach. What would happen now?

Ethan took in the scene with a swift assessing glance, his chest lifting and falling with the wry look of a know-it-all older brother when he spotted his siblings' battle-ready stances. Ignoring the hospital president and the new chief of surgery entirely, he joined his family with a lazy, deliberate stride that had more than one woman there giving Ethan interested glances.

"Down, boys."

Garret lifted a hand to the back of his neck and rubbed hard. "Dammit, Eth, I never thought he'd actually do it. He threatened to go to the board and recommend someone else but—"

"It's done. It doesn't matter now, and Darcy is wringing her hands and worrying herself sick. Go take care of her, and leave Harry to me."

"You've got a plan?" Nick asked.

"Let's just say the news has helped me to make some decisions." Ethan's gaze locked on Jenn. "Hello again, Jennifer Rose. You look lovely."

Jenn tried to smile despite the fact that everyone was watching her. "Thank you. I'm sorry about what happened."

"So, how about doing something to make me feel better?"

A low rumble erupted from Nick's chest, surprising everyone who was near enough to hear it—including Nick himself, if the ruddy hue creeping into his face was anything to go by.

Ethan laughed. "Take it easy, little brother. We all know who Jenn came with. But I'm going to beg a dance to soothe my battered ego, all the same. Jenn? Shall we show them how it's done?"

She glanced at the Tulanes and studied their expressions, ranging from concern to humor to curiosity. "Um, I-I'd love to, but that's probably not the best idea. I don't dance."

Tobias Richardson, Garret's best man, chuckled. "Turned down again today, Eth."

"No, I—I didn't mean that. It's just…"

"We'll keep it to a slow dance. Come on, make a guy's day a little brighter?" Ethan held out his hand, and after a quick glance at Nick, Jenn accepted, unable to say no when it might seem to Todd or anyone else who was watching that she had rejected him. As if any woman would pass on a dance with such a gorgeous doctor.

Aware of Nick's gaze on them the entire time, Ethan led Jenn out onto the dance floor, where the band was playing an old Sinatra song.

"So," Ethan murmured, as he drew her into his arms, his mouth by her ear and a smile in his otherwise low voice, "are you and Nick serious?"

# CHAPTER ELEVEN

NICK SWALLOWED THE LAST of his drink and studied the gentle curve of Jennifer's face as Ethan led her across the dance floor and held her way too close. If his brother's hand drifted down her back one more time...

"You look good in a suit. You should wear one every day." Alan Tulane walked over to join Nick at the table closest to the dance floor.

"The dry cleaner wouldn't be too happy with all the grease and sweat stains." As it always did, the reminder of Nick's professional life made Alan Tulane scowl. Some things never changed.

"I'm surprised to see you here tonight. Your mother said you weren't coming."

"Gram wanted us to be here. Take it up with her."

"I wasn't complaining, Nick—we all wanted you to attend. Mind if I sit down?"

"It's your club, not mine." Nick took in his father's Brooks Brothers suit, picturing his old man among the white shoe boys out on the golf course with their plaid pants and embellished polo shirts, fat Cuban cigars in their mouths.

Without a thought, Nick's gaze shifted to the rest of his family and the uncomfortable lump in his stomach grew. Alex was wearing designer heels and a too-sexy dress, and Luke,

Garret and Ethan all sported suits that cost more than his well-paid employees earned in a week. His family fit in here, and they were perfectly comfortable. But not him.

He was an exception to the Tulane majority. Normally, the club wouldn't let someone like him through the door without a hefty contribution and a background check, but with his father's name attached to his, the valet had parked his truck and called him "sir". Same with the host who'd shown him and Jenn to the table located in the center of the large dining room as if he wouldn't have been able to find it himself.

"Matt's wound up."

Nick focused on his son. "He's only excited about being in the wedding."

"It's more likely due to him being in the punch bowl all night. That probably hasn't helped."

Nick's grip tightened around his glass. "He's fine."

"Just thought you might want to have his blood checked, if he's that thirsty all the time. Can't be too careful."

His father was just looking out for Matt. That's why he was so critical. But what would his father do if Matt's summer plans became public knowledge? How many lectures had Nick sat through because of his own grades and behavior?

"Matt doesn't get a lot of sweets. When he has access to them, he enjoys them while he can. That's all." Which made it sound even worse. As if Matt was out of control and on a sugar binge. And his father didn't care. "I think I'll go save Jenn from Ethan's four feet."

Nick stood, more than ready to walk out the door. How long was the damn song going to go on?

"I'm glad you came, Nick. Christmas was six months ago."

Nick didn't remind his father that he knew where Nick lived and worked. That the phone lines ran both ways. He'd given up on Alan Tulane acknowledging anything positive he did a long time ago. If he screwed up, yeah, his father would be there to criticize and point out what he'd done wrong, but when he succeeded? Never that.

Nick stared down at his father's thinning hair. Would his father like him better if he knew the net worth of Nick's garage and gym?

"Talked to Cyrus. He and Dorothy are heartsick that they're going to miss the wedding on Saturday. They appreciate you taking care of things for them at the grill while they're gone."

Nick smirked. His father liked to refer to the Old Coyote simply as the grill because he hated the name Cyrus had chosen. He said it reflected badly on the family and called to mind their less than distinguished beginnings in early New York, where their great-great-somebody had owned a pub known for the wild and wanton behavior of its patrons. Nick figured it was better than being a stick in the mud. "It's not a problem."

His father tugged at his ear. "Your mother and I worry, though. Matt's out of school now. Should you be working such long hours over the summer?"

"It never stopped you."

"Yes, but I had your mother at home to take care of things."

"And I don't," Nick muttered softly. "Matt gets all the attention he needs. He isn't neglected, and I know where he is at all times."

"But he spends too much time alone. Under the circumstances I understand why— I think it's amazing you do all that you do. You should be proud, Nick…."

He would be. If his father hadn't just turned his accomplishments into a backhanded insult.

"But he's getting to an age where boys like to stray."

Nick barely managed to control an angry retort. Meaning

boys like *Nick*? Was he amazing because he ran a business without a degree tacked to a wall? Where did his father get off making that kind of statement? He'd tried so hard to be the son his father had wanted him to be, and here he was, thirty years old and still trying to measure up. And failing. The same with Jennifer. He could flirt and tease, but facts were facts, and the truth was, she wasn't for him no matter how cute she looked in her snug camisole and those heels that he could picture around his waist.

"Sorry to interrupt, but I find myself without a partner. Nick, would you make an old woman happy?"

Nick glanced down. Gram had placed a hand on his fist, the one he'd clenched in preparation of… What? Decking his own father? That would be a new low.

Recalling the events of the afternoon and thinking about how he'd felt after listening to Matt's reading, Nick's throat tightened into a knot he couldn't budge. Was that what he'd turn into—someone critical and judgmental and shortsighted? His father?

"I love this song. It was one of your grandfather's favorites. Nick?" Gram's hand squeezed his and tugged.

Without a word, Nick led her out onto the dance floor. Ethan and Jenn were dancing, as well, which made two songs in a row. For someone who didn't dance, she appeared to be having a lot of fun with his well-educated brother.

"Take a deep breath," Gram ordered.

Wry amusement left him shaking his head. That's what Gram had always said whenever one of the kids had gotten upset. *Take a deep breath, think, and* then *react.*

He did as ordered, his gaze fixed on Ethan and Jenn. So what if Jenn was having fun? Wasn't that the point? She'd been married to a doctor. A jerk, but a doctor. Maybe she and

Ethan had some things in common. Nick glanced down, struck by the fact that Gram was starting to show her age. She was still beautiful, but she wasn't getting any younger.

"I'm sorry I was short with you today at the gym," she said. "I let my upset get the best of me. But it makes me sad to think you don't feel comfortable with us—sad that you don't want to spend time with us because of that."

He dropped a kiss onto her forehead, careful of her styled hair. "I'm sorry I've been such an ass over the years."

Gram's rich, warm chuckle filled the air. Nick's Grandpa had had a way with words and he'd often said when people behaved like a donkey's behind, they couldn't be called anything *but* an ass.

"Oh, I've missed you, Nick. So many years have passed and I've *missed* you. You were always into so much and I was guaranteed to get a laugh from your antics."

"It's…awkward. After everything that happened."

The lines on Gram's face softened. "I know. But regardless of what was said, we didn't stop loving you. Life has moved on, but you're still one of us."

"Sure about that? According to Dad, I'm a bad father because I'm working two businesses and not hovering over Matt twenty-four seven."

Gram's fingers tightened in his hand. "Alan is concerned for you both. Things went too far all those years ago. You two have made a *habit* of taking things too far. I'm sure your father didn't mean to imply that. Nick, you're both protective and hardworking. Both of you are perfectionists who want the absolute best for those you love. And you're both blind as bats because of your pride."

Nick prepared himself for the lecture that was sure to come.

"You butted heads over whether or not the sky was blue."

Her expression turned thoughtful. "Maybe he sees you making some of the mistakes with Matt that he did with you, ever think of that?"

Was it possible? "I don't want Dad criticizing Matt's every move, the way he did mine."

"I understand. But Alan has mellowed with age."

"Have you informed him of that?"

Gram lifted her hand from his shoulder and swatted him gently. "Don't sass your grandmother."

"Yes, ma'am." Nick slowly led her around the dance floor, his thoughts full of difficult memories. Embarrassing trips to the principal's office, and his father's dramatic rants about Nick's many F's. Cajoling, reluctant words of support that soon turned into shouts and punishments.

He looked down and saw Gram watching Matt with a sad expression on her face. "What's wrong?"

"He'll be a teenager soon, and you know good and well what pressures lie there. That's what's wrong. Drinking, partying. He needs to know he can come to any one of us for support and help—but how can he when he barely knows us?"

Nick suppressed a curse. "Gram, not tonight. You got what you wanted. We're here now. Isn't that enough?"

"No. No, it's not. While I have your undivided attention on this dance floor, I want to discuss the matter. Matt's getting older and I can tell he's picking up on the tension in our family. He's more watchful, more aware of the goings-on when you join us on these rare occasions. How long before he begins to ask why?" Her gaze narrowed shrewdly. "Or has he asked already?"

Somehow Nick managed to unlock his jaw. "I've made some excuses."

"I see."

"Cut me some slack, Gram. I don't want Dad doing to Matt what he always did to me."

"Why would you worry about that, unless…"

And there it was. Nick kicked himself in the behind as he saw the knowledge form in his grandmother's eyes.

"When I came to get Matt for his tuxedo fitting he had papers spread across the table, as if he'd been studying. A child doesn't do that on summer vacation. He said it was a special summer project, but I should've known better."

Nick understood his son's need for privacy, but lying to Gram wasn't right. Even though he'd made it clear to Matt that he didn't want the family to know. As if he was ashamed of Matt? *Aw, crap.* "He knows how gossip works. If people find out, chances are, his friends will, too," Nick explained.

The older woman looked sad, her eyes still on Matt as he sat at a corner table with another boy, watching as the kid played a handheld game. "Poor thing."

"He'll be fine. He just has some catching up to do."

"And I'm sure he will. Jennifer seems very nice and quite capable. Thank you for trusting me with the news. I won't say anything to the rest of the family, although I want you to know they would only be concerned."

And interfering. "Yeah. But thanks for keeping it to yourself."

She sighed, and they continued to dance with an awkwardness and tension that hadn't been there before.

"I think you should go now."

Nick stiffened. "What?" Gram wanted him to leave? She was that upset over things?

"It appears as if your Jennifer might need you. You should go to her."

Nick looked around at the mention of *his* Jennifer, and found Dixon trailing her to the bar. Ethan was nowhere to be seen and none of the other Tulanes were close enough to offer Jenn backup. "You're the best, you know that?" He kissed Gram on the cheek.

"And you're a Tulane," she shot right back, her words firm and direct. "It's about time you remembered that."

JENNIFER STROLLED UP to the bar to get a diet soda and stared through the French doors lining the patio, waiting for her turn with the bartender. Outside, a beautiful carved stone railing overlooked the golf course, and she could see the lights from the homes lining the greens twinkling through the leaves.

"What are you doing?" Todd demanded as he came to a stop in front of her.

She stifled a groan. Barely. Talk about ruining a perfectly good view.

Jenn glared at Todd and stepped out of line, her gaze searching the huge room until she spotted an unoccupied spot nearby. She headed that way, all too aware Todd dogged her heels. "You've got two seconds. What do you want?"

His hands settled on his hips. "Aren't you going to congratulate me?"

"No. The better man didn't win."

His face tightened. "You're being petty."

"I have good reason."

"Why are you suddenly hanging out with that overgrown busboy?"

"Why do you care? And for your information, Nick is a *very* successful and honorable businessman."

"If not for his last name and family connections, Nick wouldn't be anything in this town. I grew up with him and he's dumb as dirt, and nothing but a troublemaker who could barely string two sentences together. I thought you were a fairly intelligent woman, Jenn. Why would you go out with someone like him?"

"Because he's a man and not a jerk?"

"Back off, Dixon. You got a problem with me, take it up with me and not Jenn."

Nick appeared out of nowhere, walking right up to Jenn and wrapping an arm around her shoulders. He snuggled her close and pressed a soft kiss to her temple.

"You okay?"

Appreciating the supportive gesture of her *guy friend*, Jenn slid an arm around Nick's waist and held tight. "Yeah, Todd was just leaving."

"Nice try. I'm not going anywhere. I'm here to celebrate my promotion."

"Then get to it. On the other side of the room."

"Or what?"

"Is there a problem here?" Alan Tulane joined them, followed by Luke, Ethan and Garret. All of them scowled at Nick while Todd simply stood there and smirked.

Jenn wanted the ground to open up and swallow her.

## CHAPTER TWELVE

"SIR," TODD GREETED Nick's father with a smile, but the grin became more mocking when he turned it on Ethan. "Maybe next time, eh, Dr. Tulane?"

"Congratulations on being named chief," Ethan murmured, his face carefully blank.

"Thank you. I'm thrilled, just as I'm sure you would've been."

Jenn winced at the slight.

"Well, enjoy your dinner." Todd's gaze locked on hers. "Jenn," he murmured, nodding once before turning his attention to Nick. "You haven't changed a bit since school, Nick. Not a bit." That said Todd walked away, but Nick's family remained, silent and imposing.

Jenn glanced at Nick and waited, thinking he'd remove his arm from around her shoulders since they faced the others and had told everyone they were just friends. But he didn't.

Alan Tulane inhaled deeply and sighed. "You're determined to wind up in a fight tonight, aren't you?"

Jennifer blinked. "No, Dr. Tulane, Nick wasn't… He was just showing his support for me. Todd…Dr. Dixon…is my ex-husband and things have been… I'm sorry. Nick was just standing up for me and being a friend. It's not his fault."

Alan Tulane's gaze shifted to Nick. "Maybe not, but you know your brother's celebration dinner isn't the place for such scenes."

From across the room Todd inclined his head toward her with a deceitful smile and it dawned on her that Todd had done it deliberately, drawn Nick to her side to start trouble so that Nick's father would be upset. Of all the manipulative— She wiggled her fingers slightly and saw Todd's gaze drop to the movement. Having his attention, she pinched her thumb and forefinger together and held them about an inch apart. Todd's face flushed a dull burgundy as he caught on to what she was silently indicating. He downed the last of his drink with a glare and turned away.

Nick's father and brothers remained, staring at them with a mixture of expressions. Disappointment and upset from Alan Tulane. Curiosity and protection from Luke. Then her gaze moved to Ethan and her eyes widened when she saw him barely suppressing a cocky grin. Surely he hadn't caught her hand signal to… Oh, but he *had!*

She bit her lip to control her embarrassment as Ethan winked, his expression one of whole-hearted approval and appreciation.

"Dinner will be served soon," Alan Tulane continued. "I expect we'll have all cooled off by then."

One by one Nick's family left them standing there in the corner of the large dining room like two errant children. Ethan was the last to depart, pausing long enough to squeeze Nick's shoulder before he walked away.

Now that they no longer had an audience, Nick released Jenn and stalked out the nearest door. Jenn considered the group assembled around the table but she didn't want to face them alone. So she sucked in a calming breath and prayed for the best.

Outside, a starry sky glittered above their heads. The sound of crickets and frogs thrummed from the wooded area surrounding the golf course. Nick strode to the edge of the rectangular patio, his hands knuckle-down on the long railing as he stared distractedly at the foggy greens.

The door had barely closed behind her when Nick's fist punched the rail and a raw oath left his lips, more potent than any of the few she'd ever heard him say aloud.

"Nick, I'm so sorry." She moved to stand beside him, taking his hand in hers when it looked as if he might lash out again. Hitting that wrought iron had to hurt.

She smoothed her fingers lightly over his rough knuckles before lifting his hand to her lips for a kiss. It was something her mother had always done, and Jenn did it automatically, not thinking about how intimate the gesture was until it was too late.

Determined to offer him the same support he'd shown her, she lifted his battered hand to her chest and held it close. "Nick, Todd did what he did to embarrass you, because of me. I saw it on his face after he'd walked away."

"You're not responsible for either one of us."

"I am when I'm used as a catalyst. Todd wanted to act like a big shot in front of everyone, and he knew you'd react when you saw him harassing me. Which in turn would draw your father and brothers over and make a scene. I'm so sorry. We fell right into his childish game."

Nick shook his head, his eyes dark and turbulent as he stared down at her, his hand warm against the bare skin above her camisole. She told herself to let go, but for some reason she felt the need to maintain the contact. Nick *needed* contact. Couldn't any of them see that?

"It doesn't matter. This just proves I shouldn't be here. I shouldn't have come."

Oh, the look on his face. She'd seen Matt wear the same expression so many times recently, a mixture of pain and anger, as deep as his soul. "This isn't about Todd, is it? Not all of it."

Nick was silent a long moment.

She didn't know what to say. She'd certainly sensed the tension between Nick and his family, and Nick had *told her* that they didn't get along, but to reduce a man like Nick to his current state? That comment about Nick acting out… Alan Tulane should have taken Nick's side and not put him down in public. In front of *her*. Didn't his father see that Nick was worth a hundred Todd's?

"It's always been like that," Nick said, his voice low and soft. "When I was Matt's age, my father would call me into the study and stand over me, lecturing me loud enough that everyone in the house heard what he was saying. And he gave me that same damn look. Sometimes it was my fault, but other times…"

"Fathers expect a lot of their children, and even though Todd provoked you, maybe your father thought… I don't know, that you should've ignored Todd or something." It's what her father had always expected of her. "I shouldn't have asked this of you and I'm so, so sorry I did. I know exactly what it's like to feel as if you don't measure up."

Nick turned and fixed her with a disbelieving stare. "I'd like to meet the person you don't think you measure up to."

Jenn tried to smile and failed. She hoped Nick never met Megs. One look and he'd probably fall at her feet like all the others, and she didn't want that. "You're not the only one with family problems. Some of my insecurities may have been of my own making, but some are the result of how people treated me. How my sister treated me. I could never compete."

She watched as his gaze swept over her, lingering close to her heart where his hand rested.

"She couldn't possibly be better than you."

"She's everything I've never been," Jenn corrected him. "A

beauty queen, prom queen, homecoming queen, cheerleader. Miss All-around Everything. And if she wanted something I had…?" Jenn rolled her eyes and laughed. "She stopped at nothing to get it or something better. That included my… People in my life."

Nick's gaze met hers. "Including Dixon?"

Unable to help herself, Jenn smoothed her thumb over the texture of Nick's jacket sleeve. "No. Todd and I met at college and we didn't travel to my parents' house much because of his schooling and his schedule. When we did, I was smart enough to make sure my sister wasn't going to be there. But my father… No matter what happened, he expected me to forgive her. Just like that. It became the saying in the house that my sister was Daddy's girl and I was my mom's. Mom was the only one who ever took my side. You were right," she forced herself to admit. "This morning when I couldn't say I was worth it…I couldn't say it because I've never felt that way."

Nick pulled her against his chest and held her close, his chin resting on her head. "You're worth more than Dixon or your sister put together, and I'm going to keep saying it until you believe me."

Inhaling the musky, tantalizing scent of him, she ignored the warnings her brain was giving her to pull away, to doubt him. Nick smelled so good. Man and musk and spices, the warmth of his body enveloping her, comforting her.

"What did they say to you? Your sister and dad?"

She closed her eyes and thought of those days at home. "Dad had a habit of comparing us, and I always came up short. He said he was being helpful by pointing out problem areas so I could work on them, but…"

"He picked you apart in the process. That's a lousy thing to do to a kid."

She nodded. "Megan was the only one he didn't talk to that way. She looked more like him, whereas I took after my mom. Anyway, he always said how pretty she was. How Megan was his princess.

"Maybe I took the comments too seriously. Anyway, I grew up. Got to a point in my life where I just tried to ignore them both, and then I met Todd and… He did the same thing. I thought it was normal. Except then I realized that he was worse—and there was a difference."

Nick's arms tightened around her. "What?"

"I think in his heart my dad tried to be helpful, but Todd pointed out my flaws simply to be mean. He did it when we were arguing about something or he wasn't getting his way. I felt like a failure all the time, because no matter what I did I didn't do it right. Didn't *look* right."

"According to Dixon or your father," Nick said. "I'm sure you were fine, better than fine," he soothed her. "Just like you are now."

"Just like *you* are, Nick." She lifted her head and stared up at him, able to see the pain in his eyes. "There's a difference with your father. I see it, even if you don't. Your father and mine are alike. Both might get upset with us, both might point out our flaws, but they still love us. Anger didn't bring your father over to talk to us a little bit ago, love did. Concern."

"You feel that way about Dixon?"

"No. I think I was convenient for Todd and that was all. I'd just graduated, so I was out of school and could work and take care of our home, pay the bills. I think for Todd I was a stand-in, until he found the woman he really wanted. I just wish I had seen it before I married him, so I wouldn't feel like such a failure now."

"You're not a failure." He squeezed her gently. "Hear me?

If anyone is a failure here, it's me," he said with a heavy sigh. "I'll never be what my father wants me to be. It's impossible."

"What does he want you to be that you aren't already?"

Nick went silent, his expression becoming guarded. Jenn tried a different tactic. "Nick, you don't have to be anyone but yourself. You're an adult, a successful man people admire. Maybe the answer lies in you and your father having an honest heart-to-heart. Have you ever tried that with him?"

A look of longing flashed across his face and then it changed to resignation. "That work for you?"

She couldn't hold the eye contact. "I've forgiven my sister, but some things can't be forgotten. It would be foolish to turn a blind eye to them when I'm the one who's usually hurt. Trust is…fragile."

Nick lifted her face with a hand under her chin. "I meant with your self-image. You ever look in the mirror and decide to deal with what you see? The majority of the world isn't a size six, sweetheart."

Her shoulders sank. "I know, but—"

"No buts. Exercising for health, or to relieve stress, is one thing. Doing it because you have some impossible, unhealthy image in your head that you're hoping to achieve is another. You do that, and you still tear yourself down. Just like Dixon and your father."

"Is that why you were so insistent today? Trying to make me say that I…was worth it?"

"Not was. *Are.* You are worth fighting for. You need to exercise and eat right for *you,* because you want to do it for yourself, no one else, and not for some image." He leaned back a bit as if to get a better look at her face. "That inner diva you're looking for? The one who dances on tables?"

"Do you have to keep bringing that up?"

"Yeah, because to find her, you have to acknowledge your good qualities. That woman is a combination of things—health, happiness and inner strength. Attitude," he said with a knowing expression, "takes self-confidence. Self-confidence means believing in yourself and your abilities as a woman. That takes strength, both physical and emotional and all of *that*," he murmured, his finger sliding up to her temple to stroke it, "is right here." A wry smile pulled at his lips. "And trust me, sweetheart, you've got more than enough brains to do this. All you need is the right attitude about yourself and you'll be able to dance on any table you choose."

"You make it sound easy."

"It's not. But it is a decision. You have to make a choice, once and for all, to think, behave and *be* a certain way. We reap what we sow, that's what my grandfather always said. If you're negative, it shows. If you're happy and feeling good about yourself, that shows. But you have to believe you are worth fighting for. You have to be able to say it, too."

"I'm worth it," she whispered softly, thinking of Todd, Megan, letting their cruel words fuel her drive to succeed. "*We're* worth it, Nick."

As Jen spoke, Nick's gaze lowered, became hooded, silver-blue, fastening on her mouth until she felt compelled to part her lips to draw in more air.

Nick stilled at the sight, the tension between them rising like a flash flood, all rush and noise and chaotic thoughts before he lowered his head as if he simply couldn't help himself, and gave her a serious open mouthed kiss.

A low groan escaped him, rough and seductive, bone-meltingly hot. She shivered in response, her hands slipping beneath Nick's lightweight suit jacket to the expanse of his back. The heat radiating off his body warmed her like no blanket ever could. Nick's big, calloused hands slid down her neck to her shoulders, wrapped around her and moved lower to her hips. He cupped her behind, lifted her slightly, until she felt the hard length of him against her.

"A confident woman turns me on," he whispered against her mouth.

*Oh, baby.* She gasped, then held him tight as Nick kissed her. He had all the experience of a man familiar with women, but there was also a heartbreaking tenderness there, indicative of a tortured soul. Thanks to his father, Nick understood the hurt and pain that loved ones had the power to inflict; understood Jenn better than just about anyone, despite their differences.

In that moment, Jenn wasn't big or overweight or fat. She was simply the woman Nick wanted. Honest with him and hot because of it. The hard length of his arousal pressed against her belly was proof of that. She might be above average in dress size but he was bigger, taller and broader, all hard muscle and man. Nick made her feel small and feminine. Made her appreciate her softness. Made her believe he appreciated it because she was worth appreciating.

Tears burned her eyelids, but Nick's tongue stroked hers and distracted her from her thoughts. Molasses-slow and lazily erotic. Her senses reeled as her lower body heated and came alive with desire.

Their noses brushed, their breath mingled, but all she could focus on was the feel of Nick's touch on her body. His taste. The stroke of his tongue on hers, the nip of his lips and teeth as he played with her mouth before ravishing it with the sort of piratical delight she'd only read about in books and magazines. This was what she needed. Him.

Farther down, the patio the doors burst open and a laughing

group of people emerged, loud and boisterous. Young. Jenn froze and broke away from the kiss, embarrassed to have been caught in such a public display. A quick peek at the group had her stifling a moan and praying the group didn't look over their shoulders, but thankfully the parade of local teens disappeared down a set of stairs on the far end.

"Um…" She cleared her throat and slid sideways along the railing. She couldn't look at Nick. If she did she was afraid she'd throw herself into his arms and beg him to continue. But where would that leave her at the end of summer, when his kisses made it nearly impossible for her to remain standing?

*You know perfectly well he's out of your league. He always has been. You want a summer of fun, not a broken heart.*

"We should probably go back inside. Your family will be waiting for us."

"They can wait."

Nick might not care that his family loved him and wanted him to celebrate with them, but she did. She missed her parents. At times she even missed her sister. When they were little, they'd been close, and it wasn't until they'd gotten older that the battles had really begun.

Nick took a few deep breaths. His profile was cast in moonlight, the harsh angles and planes sharpened by the shadows.

*Out of your league.*

The door opened nearby and Matt walked through. "Dad?"

Nick sighed, the sound rough and exhausted. "Over here, Matt."

"Everyone is waiting for you and Ms. Rose."

Nick looked at her, his expression growing dark again. "Half an hour. Then we're out of here."

## CHAPTER THIRTEEN

NICK DROPPED INTO THE comfortable leather recliner opposite his TV and stared at the blank screen, amazed he'd survived the night with his family.

When Jenn had finally said she was worth it, something had changed between them. He saw her fighting spirit, her determination, and he'd liked it. Jenn was a sweetheart, the kind of woman who'd say that having a diploma didn't matter. But it would, it did. And he couldn't expect anything from her other than a casual friendship/acquaintance, because she'd pity him and his lack of abilities when she finally learned the truth.

He wouldn't have gone to the dinner without her, and he was man enough to admit that with Jenn there things had been a lot easier. They'd stayed longer than a half hour, too. Jenn had restarted the conversation whenever there'd been a lull, and more than once she'd looked at him with her sweet girl-next-door face. He'd found himself unable to look away. Found himself smiling, talking, not only to her but to his brothers. Occasionally to his parents, too.

"Dad?"

Nick got up and walked down the hall to Matt's bedroom. He leaned against the doorway, noting Matt had chosen a T-shirt and basketball shorts over a pair of his traditional cartoon pajamas. His son was growing up too fast, just as Gram had said. Being a father wasn't easy, but Nick had done it. And yet Gram had a point. Matt needed others to talk to, people Matt could trust. And despite his differences with his father, Nick knew his family would do anything for Matt. His son needed to know that. "Yeah, bub?"

"Do you like her? Ms. Rose?"

He stepped into the bedroom and walked over to sit on the side of Matt's bed. "Why do you ask?"

"I heard Gram and Grandma talking about her. They said she was nice."

"Jenn… Ms. Rose is nice. Do you like her?"

Matt nodded, his expression serious. "But…"

Nick braced a hand on the other side of Matt's legs and waited patiently. "But what?"

"She's nice 'n' all, but what if I can't do it? You know, learn all the stuff she's trying to teach me? Then she won't like me 'cause I'm a loser."

The words struck deep and made a gaping wound. Matt's fear was very real to Nick, one he understood. As a child, Matt still had the ability to overcome the problem with Jenn's help. Nick didn't—and it was a humiliation he'd never be able to change. Not even for her.

"Ms. Rose isn't the type of person to do that, Matt. You can tell by the way she looks at people, especially kids. You saw those girls earlier tonight. They came over to give Ms. Rose hugs when they didn't have to. They did it because they like her. She wouldn't treat you any differently."

*But what about him?*

"But she's really smart, though and…I'm not. If I was, I wouldn't need so much help."

"Ms. Rose is smart, but so are you, and I don't want to hear any more talk like that. Everybody needs help every now and again." Thank God Matt was smarter than Nick had been at that age. He'd be fine, Jenn would see to it. Nick smiled and squeezed Matt's shoulder. "She's so smart, she knows a good thing when she sees it. That's why she'll like you no matter what."

"What about you?"

"What about me?"

"Will you like me if I can't do it?"

How many times had he asked that question in his head? Afraid to say it to his father? Afraid the answer wouldn't be the one he needed to hear?

Nick pulled Matt into his arms and hugged him tight. "I love you, Matt. No matter what."

Matt sniffled and buried his head deeper against Nick's chest. "But what about Ms. Rose? Do you like her?"

There was a question in Matt's eyes that Nick didn't like. A hope and expectation. "Ms. Rose and I are just friends. You wouldn't be trying to matchmake like Gram, would you?"

Matt ducked his head, a bashful grin on his lips. "She liked Ms. Rose an awful lot."

Gram liked any woman who had the ability to get Nick to a family dinner. "No scheming with Gram, you hear me? Ms. Rose and I are friends, nothing more. She goes for guys like…like your uncle Ethan."

"Oh. Why not you? Why wouldn't she like you like that?"

Nick eased Matt back onto the bed and tucked the covers in around him. "People can't pick who they like, son. They just do. And Ms. Rose has a lot in common with guys like your uncle Ethan—not guys like me. Good night, Matt."

"'Night, Dad."

Nick ruffled his son's hair before leaving his bedroom, going into his own and dropping onto the mattress to stare up at the ceiling. He needed to go lock up, set the alarm. But he didn't move.

Images flashed through his head. Jennifer's smile, the lush feel of her full breasts against him. Her earnest expression and the dazed passion-glazed look she'd had right after he'd kissed her. He hardened at the thought, but then just as quickly his body cooled. Matt worried that he wasn't smart enough for Ms. Rose. As for Nick, he knew he could stop worrying—he definitely wasn't. And it was only a matter of time before she found that out. He'd thought he'd suffered enough humiliation in his life, but what happened fifteen years ago when he'd dropped out had only been the beginning.

"SO, GIVE ME AN UPDATE," Suzanne ordered as soon as Jenn pressed the phone to her ear and murmured hello. "How are things going between you and Nick? The diet? Matt? I want all the details—just skip the boring parts."

Jenn rolled her eyes and searched for a decent pair of socks. Finding a set, she pulled them from the drawer. "It's going. How was Hawaii?"

"Absolutely amazing. I'll bring pictures over to show you in a day or so after I get some laundry done. You won't believe how green and lush everything was. Now, about your gorgeous trainer?"

"I've lost a few pounds, I can walk three miles without keeling over and my suit fit from two Easters ago."

"That's *great!* I knew you could do it. But why are you being so quiet about Nick—did something happen?" Her voice took on an edge of excitement. "*Did* it?"

"Sort of. He, um, kissed me."

"A *real* kiss?"

"Yeah."

"You say that so calmly. Spill! And don't leave anything out."

"First off, I don't think he meant for it to happen. Which makes it horrible and *not* a good thing."

"How do you get that? Nick is a gorgeous hunk of male and he's nice to boot. Oh, I was so hoping the guy-friend thing would turn into something more."

"Yeah, you were pretty obvious about that. But kissing me was a huge mistake, Suzanne. He just did it because he was upset and angry at his family. And me."

"Why was he angry at you?"

Jenn took a deep breath and sighed, then related the story of how she'd met Rosetta Tulane and pressured Nick into going to the rehearsal dinner.

"Oh, honey. *Why* did you push it when he said no? Nick gets along with his family the way you say you get along with your sister."

"I know that now, but I didn't realize it at the time or think it could be that bad. It didn't take long to figure out Nick wasn't kidding. To make it worse, Todd showed up."

"What did he want?"

"To be himself. Todd got the promotion at the hospital, instead of Nick's brother Ethan."

"*No.*"

"Exactly. And since the family was all there for a wedding celebration, Todd just had to make a scene."

"Where did the kiss come in?"

She sighed heavily. "Outside on the balcony."

"Under the moonlight? How sweet!"

"It was…We were talking and…and connecting. And he kissed me. But then it ended and I realized I don't stand a chance. Suzanne, get real. We have *nothing* in common."

"Opposites attract."

Opposites maybe, but polar opposites? Jenn held the phone between her shoulder and head as she struggled to pull on a pair of pants. "Weren't you listening? He kissed me because he was angry and upset over what happened with his family and Todd. Not because he wanted to."

"Did he say he didn't want to kiss you? Because I'm not hearing it. And I've never known a man to kiss a woman he didn't *want* to kiss, except maybe a grandma with a hairy chin. Go back. What, exactly, did he say? When did this happen?"

Jenn did her best to fill in the gaps in her story and waited for Suzanne's response to Nick's suggestion about finding her diva side.

"He talked to you about that?"

"Yeah. But just for the summer. And I'd like to but…"

"Do it. There's only one way to find out if it could lead to more."

"You don't get it. You weren't there. Suzanne, after Nick kissed me we had to go back inside and sit through dinner, and when he took me home, he didn't say a word. Not a *word*."

"Was Matt with you?"

"Yes, but…"

"Well, there you go. Getting involved is one thing, but getting involved with kids who'd get attached is another. He probably just wanted to be discreet."

*Could it be?*

"You don't have to decide today, you know. Why not hang out and take things slow? If it's meant to happen, it will."

"I know, but… Maybe you're right. I just don't want to make another mistake like I made with Todd. I married one guy and then he became another. When people started calling Todd 'Doctor', he developed this God complex and started acting like a jerk. Lying and cheating, like it was okay because it was him."

"Nick's not Todd."

"I know that, but I'm afraid. I don't want to get my hopes up over a man who's already setting limits on the relationship. Nick specifically talks only about the summer. Why would he do that if he was open to more?"

He wouldn't and Jenn knew it. So did Suzanne, if her silence was anything to go by.

"So what's next?"

"Ugh. How do I get myself into these things? This evening is the wedding. *And* I don't have a dress. I have to look good for this, especially after last night."

"So, we'll go shopping."

"I can't. I'm getting ready to go work out, even though I keep praying Nick won't be there."

"Chicken."

Jenn eyed her closet, hating everything she saw inside. "A chicken without a dress. Are you busy later today? Maybe we can shop then?"

"Absolutely. But first, tell me about this kiss."

"He's a *fifteen*, Suzanne."

"Are we back to the number thing again? I'm telling you, you're much higher than a five. Anything with boobs is a five. Ask any guy."

"But no way am I in double digits, which means Nick still outnumbers me. I might as well hold up the white flag right now. Why would I get involved with a man I don't have a prayer of keeping?"

"You are so weird. Nick's not some twentysomething stud out to score. He's got a kid and a head for business, and he isn't as wild and crazy as everyone else seems to believe. Speaking of children, how's the tutoring going?"

Jenn closed her eyes and winced. "It's been rough. Matt is

struggling and I'm not sure how to reach him. I've tried so many of the tricks we're taught in college, but nothing works. The problem seems to be more with reading than math."

"At least you're narrowing it down. That's good."

"Maybe. Nick's not any help, though. Matt needs supervised practice—you know how important it is for parents to be involved. That's partly why I was so insistent about him taking me to the family dinner. I made it part of our deal because I was still angry over the way he blew me off when I asked him to pitch in with reading lessons."

Suzanne chuckled. "I'll bet he didn't see that one coming. But he does run two businesses. His time is in pretty short supply."

"Yeah, yeah, but are his businesses more important than his son?"

"Of course not. Nick's not like that at all, and you know it. I just meant that of all the parents we deal with who slack off where their kids are concerned, at least Nick has a legitimate excuse. And a lot of them don't, as you well know."

"I know. I get that, but how am I supposed to get Matt to read in his spare time, if Nick won't help out a little bit? Reading to himself and getting the words all wrong isn't going to help Matt. And I'm not asking for a huge commitment, just a short session every day."

"Well, I could think of a way or two you might be able to coerce Nick into doing what you want," Suzanne said, suggestively.

Jenn sat on the edge of the bed, and since she wasn't able to do anything else she lay back and began doing stretches. "Tell me more about him. What's the problem between Nick and his parents?"

A pause filtered over the line. "Why do you ask?"

"Because obviously there's some tension but I don't quite have the nerve to question Nick, given his responses last night."

"I thought you said you kissed and talked?"

"We did, but I'd like more information."

Once again Suzanne hesitated a long moment, then sighed dramatically. "It's no secret in town, so I guess it wouldn't hurt to fill you in on the details. To be honest, I thought Nick would've told you by now—or you would've heard."

"Heard what?"

"What do you know about the Tulanes?"

"Other than surface information, nothing. I take it you knew Nick has a twin?" Jenn held the phone with one hand and raised the other over her head, holding in her stomach and stretching as far as she could.

"Ahhh, Luke. Now there's another hunk, huh?"

"They're *all* gorgeous. It's yet another reason for a chubby girl like me to beware."

"Stop it or I'll come over there and kick your butt, even though I'm supposed to be resting. Don't you believe in inner beauty versus outer beauty?"

"Only when the outer beauties are on a par with each other." Jenn covered her face with her palm. "And where are my manners? I forgot to ask about the baby. How are you?"

"Just fine. So far, so good."

"But you said you were going to do laundry, and you're supposed to be resting. Does Tuck know?"

"Shut up, I'm fine. Do you know how awful I'll feel if I sit around for nine months and then try to give birth? Talk about out of shape. Anyway, back to Nick...You got that all his brothers and sister, and his parents, are highly successful, right?"

"The country-club thing kind of delivered that message, but what does that have to do with Nick? He's successful, too."

"Yes, he is, but not like them. Did you talk to them last night? Do you know what they do? Jenn, Nick feels inferior."

"Inferior—you're kidding, right?" Her laugh was met with silence. "You're not. But *why?*"

Another pause. "I really wish he'd told you this. I hope what I say won't change how you look at him, because Nick is wonderful."

"Suzanne, tell me!"

"Nick is a high-school dropout. In fact, he's the only one in his immediate family—his entire family from what I've heard—that didn't graduate high school, much less go on to college. He barely has a sophomore education."

She paused midstretch. "Seriously?" But... How was that possible? He was so smart, so intelligent. Why drop out?

"Yeah. As soon as he was legally able to quit, he did. His family went *nuts*. We're not talking a little nuts, but completely ballistic. You have to grow up in a small place to really understand how weird it is for *everyone* to be involved in your business. The whole town talked about it and the more everyone talked and stirred things up, the angrier and more distant Nick became. There were times when they passed each other on the street and didn't speak. It was horrible."

Jenn lowered her leg onto the bed. "I had no idea."

"Nick doesn't like to talk about it. Anyway, not long after this happened, Nick's grandfather died. They were all close to Rosetta's husband and the funeral helped bridge the distance. At least a little bit. You know how things like that bring people together. Then Nick's girlfriend got pregnant and the whole mess started up again, when he refused to go to his parents for help. The girlfriend thought Nick would go back to the fold and she'd sort of sit back and enjoy the benefits of being a Tulane, but at the time Nick was a mechanic and he had no interest in his family at all. When things didn't go her way, she took off for Nashville."

Poor Nick. Poor Matt.

"Trust me, it was a big deal. The Tulanes aren't snobs, but image is important to them. Uh-oh, Tuck's home. I've got to run. I'll see you later. We'll talk more then."

"Okay, but… 'Bye," Jen said after the phone clicked in her ear. She pressed the button and lowered it to the bed beside her. *A dropout?*

Rolling to her feet, she finished dressing, her thoughts consumed by the surprising revelation. A dropout. A sophomore education. Her head whirled. And eventually her thoughts led her to more questions. But did she have the courage to ask them?

## CHAPTER FOURTEEN

NICK NOTED THAT Jennifer seemed preoccupied as he put her through the paces of her workout. Sweat beaded her forehead and dampened the hair at her temples, and her T-shirt—this one reading Teachers Have Class—clung to her breasts and distracted him more than he wanted to admit. It wasn't a good idea to get involved. He already knew the outcome. So why couldn't he stop thinking about that kiss? About spending the summer with her as more than her trainer?

He walked back to where Jennifer sat on a padded bench and handed her a heavier set of hand weights. "Do the lifts exactly as I showed you."

She waited, but then wet her lips and stared up at him. "Do you, um, have to stand there?"

Nick frowned, then realized he was standing right between her parted legs. Clearing his throat, he moved behind Jenn, facing her in the wall of mirrors. The problem was, the mirrors showed her dark head and big eyes level with his groin and the sight brought all sorts of ideas to mind.

He shouldn't have kissed her, because now that he had he wanted even more.

Jenn began doing the lifts, each one of them lifting her breasts.

"Nick? I need to talk to you about something and…I don't know how to bring it up."

Her words snapped him out of his sensual reverie and brought his gaze to her face. She'd closed her eyes, and her cheeks were hot pink. Was she thinking the same thing he was? "What's wrong?"

"Nothing's wrong."

He waited for her to continue, but she didn't. "What did you want to ask?"

"Never mind. It's nothing. I need to finish my reps. How many did you say?"

"I'll double them if you don't tell me."

Her eyes snapped open. "That's mean."

"That's life. Spill it. It's important, or else you wouldn't be dodging right now. Something to do with Matt?"

She inhaled and sighed, a trickle of sweat slowly gliding down the *V* of her shirt. He fought back a groan of awareness. He'd have to be dead not to notice that *Ms. Rose* was stacked. Good thing she taught little kids instead of adolescents. The boys in her class would be goners.

"Well, um, it's about…you. Why didn't you tell me you dropped out of high school?"

Her question hit him like a bomb. Heat, impact and then a surge of fallout in the form of embarrassment and humiliation. In an instant, he was sixteen again. And Jenn was the straight-A girl he'd asked to the winter dance. Back then he'd been shot down because the girl thought he was a dumb loser. The same held true now.

He stood there, frozen in time, as memories slid over him. Jennifer had arrived at the gym ten minutes late, with the excuse that she'd taken Suzanne's call. Looked as if Suzanne had filled Jenn on the details of his life in between vacation stories. "It's…old news. And none of your business. None of anyone's business but my own."

Jenn flinched, her eyes avoiding his. "Forgive me if I'm overstepping boundaries here, but I'm trying to understand. It doesn't change how I view you as a person."

"Doesn't it?" He didn't buy that. Not at all.

"Of course not. Look at everything you've accomplished."

"Some people say it's been given to me."

"But it hasn't been. You've worked hard to succeed."

"And you're wasting time. Thought you were supposed to go shopping with Suzanne? Finish your workout and get going."

"I'm trying to talk to you." She blinked up at him, her lovely gray eyes wide. "Nick, please. You've achieved a great deal. Your family might have impressive degrees, but you are just as successful running your businesses."

"My father disagrees."

"Maybe he does, but surely you don't need a diploma to tell you who you are?"

"No, but…" He ran a hand over his hair, messing it. "Look, I don't want to discuss this with you."

"Why not?" Her eyes softened. "I told you about my sister and the things my father said to me." When he didn't answer, she looked down and blinked. "All I'm saying is that I think this news makes it even more important for you play an active role in Matt's education. So you dropped out. It doesn't mean you can't help me help your son."

"For the love of—"

"Does Matt know you didn't graduate?"

He kept his silence and Jenn knew.

"Nick…Oh, Nick."

"It's not a big deal."

She shook her head slowly back and forth. "Who was it that said if you're bringing it up now, you haven't let it go? Why haven't you told him?"

"You're the one bringing this up. *Drop it.*"

"No. No, I won't, because if it's pride that's stopping you, you're going to have to decide which is more important."

He glowered at her. "You think my son needs to know I dropped out? That his friends' parents laughed and talked about me back then, made fun? You think that'll *help* him? The longer it stays quiet, the better."

"I disagree. I think Matt needs to know you care enough to keep him from getting so frustrated he makes the same mistake in the future." She lowered the weights, her rapid pulse visible in her throat. "Matt needs to practice his reading, and if you won't practice it with him, then you should find someone who will. Your grandmother or another family member."

"*No.*"

"Because you don't want them to know he's having problems? Nick, I know you don't get along, but it's obvious how much they love him. They wouldn't hurt Matt for the world."

"Maybe not intentionally, but it would still happen. Believe me. It's my job to protect him, my job to look out for him and that includes this. Your father said some nasty things to you growing up, the same as mine did. But I won't be that way with Matt. I won't undermine his self-confidence by going around telling everyone he—" he lowered his voice even more "—has some trouble in school. What kid needs that? It's like printing a label and plastering it on his forehead for the world to judge him by."

This wasn't the place for their argument. Granted, the gym was nearly empty, but this was a private matter. One he didn't want dragged up again, especially today of all days. Maybe he could claim an emergency at the grill? Not go to the wedding? "Finish your reps."

She hesitated a long moment, but when Nick turned away

to go make a call and possibly come up with an excuse, he heard her inhale and knew she wasn't going to give up.

"He needs help, Nick. Would you rather finish our discussion at the wedding later?"

Her words stopped him in his tracks. His knuckles popped. The mousy Ms. Rose had a backbone after all. Too bad she hadn't found it where her ex was concerned. "You wouldn't do that." He turned to face her.

"You have to begin taking the time to read with Matt. And if it takes making it part of our deal, I'll make it part of our deal."

"I'll get another tutor."

"No, you won't. You don't want anyone to know, and doing that would require telling more people. You know I'm discreet, even if I'm giving you a hard time about this. Plus, we have a deal, and it's one I'm holding you to."

He could easily imagine her adding "So there" to her statement.

"I'm only looking out for Matt's best interests. And yours, for that matter."

He hadn't asked her to. Didn't want her to. Nick counted to twenty, glaring at Jennifer as she caught her breath once more, the move revealing cleavage that he wanted to lean over and taste in spite of his anger. The thought brought a smirk. If he did, that would shut her up. "I told you, I'm too busy to play teacher." Nick narrowed his gaze on her, remembering how she wouldn't say she was worth it. Problems like that didn't just go away. "Or maybe you're doing this to pick a fight, to try and get me to renege on the deal so you won't have to own up to wanting to quit?"

"I'm doing no such thing."

He took in her appearance, letting her see what had been on his mind of late. Jenn gasped, and he smirked again. He could tell she'd lost weight. Could see the muscle tone developing in her arms and legs. He thought she looked fine before, but he'd admit that healthy foods and exercise had her glowing. "Sure about that?"

"Y-yes."

He surveyed her, his expression suspicious. "You're several weeks into your diet and you've been good, but now it's really sinking in. The junk food is calling you and you're obviously cranky from withdrawal. You want to quit, but don't want to have to say it, so if you piss me off enough to do it for you—"

"I'm not trying to quit!"

He could tell by the slant of her eyebrows and the way her mouth flattened into a thin line that he'd hit a nerve. Inhaling through her nose the way he'd instructed, she shoved her chin in the air and lifted the weights, exhaling through her mouth.

"See?"

"Yeah, well, keep going and when you finish those, start your next round. I'm going to make some calls."

"It isn't true, you know. What you think. It's not true."

He fought his frustration. Did all women talk this much? Argue? A part of him would admit to liking sparring with her, but another found her interference—

"It doesn't change who you are, Nick. Knowledge is power. I admire you for getting help for your son. I *respect* you for going so far to protect him, but did you ever think that knowing he's not alone in having difficulty might *help* him? It's your decision whether or not you tell Matt, but I think he would rather hear it from you."

Just like that, his frustration deflated. Did she mean that? Believe it? Or would Matt be embarrassed because of him? Nick couldn't handle that. Given how Matt was growing up so fast, it would come soon enough, anyway.

"What decision? What's going on with Matt?"

Nick bit back a groan and turned to find his twin studying them both from ten feet away. "Nothing."

Luke closed the distance between them, his attention divided between Nick and Jenn. "Looking good, Jenn."

"Did you want something?"

Luke's eyebrows rose and a slow smile crossed his face. His brother's gaze lowered to Jenn, sweeping her with an appreciative glance. "Ah, so it's true."

"*Luke.*"

Luke's smile grew to the length of a football field. "What?" he asked innocently.

Remembering what he'd seen last night as he and Jenn left the rehearsal dinner, Nick widened his stance and crossed his arms over his chest. "You and Shelby Brooks seemed to be hitting it off last night. Does our little sister know you were flirting with her best friend?"

Luke shuffled his feet, a dull flush rising on his neck.

"I'll, uh, leave you two to talk," Jenn murmured, standing and carrying the dumbbells with her. She walked over to freestanding bench on the far side of the room, her expression curious as she began another set of lifts.

Nick waited, hating the tenuous position he found himself in. He'd wanted the subject of Matt to be dropped, but he'd much rather argue his position with Jenn than face off with his brother about whatever it was that had brought Luke here. "What's up?"

Luke rubbed his neck the way he always did when he was on the fence about something. "Actually, it's about Matt. I wanted to know if you'd let him come stay with me for a couple of weeks. I'll fly him out and bring him back personally."

"Why?"

"I'm working on a computer project that's right up his alley. When it comes to new games, the company brings in kids to test the products and get their responses. I thought it might be nice to get some input from Matt. You know, something fun. Ma says he hasn't flown anywhere and we haven't spent a lot of time together. He's older now and pretty self-sufficient so… It would also take him off your hands for a bit."

"Matt isn't a problem."

Luke planted his hands on his hips. "I didn't mean to imply that he was. I just meant with it being summer vacation, you wouldn't need a sitter while you worked. Besides—" he indicated Jenn with a smooth tilt of his head "—you look to be a little busy right now."

He glanced across the room at Jenn and frowned. No matter what happened between them, it wouldn't last long. It couldn't, under the circumstances—not once the novelty wore off. And not if she found out the whole truth. "Jenn is just a friend."

"Uh-huh. Then why you were staring down her shirt when I came in?"

"She's also a beautiful woman. But I don't think taking Matt to California is a good idea. He's busy with ball, and I don't want him quitting so he can take off with you when the season's just started."

Disappointment clouded Luke's expression. "I forgot about him playing ball. He any good?"

Nick smirked. "Unfortunately, he takes after me."

Luke smiled, and shook his head. "He'll get better with practice."

The way he had? Nick sighed.

Luke fingered the plastic-covered top of the weight rest that was attached to the bench in front of him. "Anyway, that's cool. Just thought I'd ask. Maybe I can spend some extra time with him while I'm here. Take him riding or something?"

Did he really have to? Guilt stirred, but Nick pushed it down. "That would be better."

"You could come, too, if you like. Been a while since we've hung out and had some fun."

Nick immediately shook his head. "Not with Cyrus gone. Too much to do—you know how it is." Luke didn't like the response, but Nick didn't care. Did Luke have any idea how hard it was to look at him and see himself, minus the smarts? "That's all you needed?"

"You got a computer I could borrow?"

"Why?"

"I need to look up something."

"If you want directions to Shelby's, just ask."

"You know where she lives?"

"Things got interesting last night, huh?" Nick wasn't surprised. When he'd spotted them, Luke's tongue was down her throat and his hands were up her shirt. "Ridge Road. Drive along until you reach the old sawmill. She bought that little house by the creek."

"Thanks."

Nick chuckled, glad it was his brother on the hot seat for a change. "Alex's scrawny little friend grew up nicely, didn't she?"

Luke grinned. "Yeah. So…Matt. Gram said he's spending the night with her after the wedding. Maybe I can take him riding after church tomorrow?"

Nick nodded reluctantly, not ready to face the fact that the older Matt got, the more out of control things were likely to become. Being a parent was scary, and being a single parent was worse. Jenn was right. He didn't want Matt hearing the news from anyone else.

THE WEDDING went off without a hitch. The bride was resplendent in her white lace and the groom was visibly emotional from start to finish. Jenn watched the ceremony with a damp tissue crumpled in her hand and Nick at her side, looking every bit as handsome as she'd known he would. He wore another dark suit, this one with a power tie in bold red.

It just wasn't fair. Shopping with Suzanne had been a success, but the form-hugging dress that Suzanne promised was flattering and slimming just didn't compare with the effect of Nick's long, hard form in that suit. Especially since it made her want to rip it off him. She sighed deeply. *Don't be such an idiot. You're fighting with him, remember?*

"What are you thinking about?"

Squirming on the chair, she jumped at the feel of his whisper blowing gently into her ear and tried not to notice the shivers running through her as a result. Or the way his calloused fingers brushed her left shoulder. Back and forth, absentminded strokes that kept her from concentrating on the exchange of vows. Every now and again his thumb would move. Ease beneath the strap of her dress to stroke her skin. No wonder she was distracted.

*And loving every minute of it.*

How stupid was it to become involved with a parent? With a man like Nick?

Nick was overwhelming on a good day, a combination of chocolate, salty potato chips and diet-blasting gourmet coffee. No woman with breath in her could walk away unscathed.

The minister pronounced the couple man and wife just as the sun sank midway behind the mountain across from the country club. The announcement couldn't have been more perfectly timed, the couple silhouetted by the sun's glorious backdrop. The crowd broke into applause as Garret and Darcy sealed their wedding vows with a kiss. Jenn inhaled sharply when Nick's right hand appeared in front of her face. He brushed her cheek with his knuckles and wiped away a tear.

"Sorry." She tried to laugh off her silliness. "I always cry at weddings."

He smiled his sexy bad-boy grin at the revelation, even though he was probably still mad at her from this morning.

The newly married couple walked down the aisle, Garret beaming proudly and carrying his soon-to-be-adopted stepdaughter with his wife on his arm. The crowd began to disperse one row at a time and on a far end from the aisle, Nick snagged her arm in a gentle grip. "Come on. This time you're dancing with me."

# CHAPTER FIFTEEN

NICK TOLD HIMSELF IT was part of the plan. He was supposed to be Jenn's *guy friend* and that meant he had to dance with her. He hadn't last night because he'd been too pissed off about being at the rehearsal dinner in the first place, but now… Now it was part of the plan.

So what if it was becoming easier to pretend? It didn't matter. Not in the end. Look how fast the past weeks had flown by. Summer would be over before he knew it and they'd go their separate ways. Why not enjoy the moment while it lasted? The friendship?

"Why are you looking at me like that?"

Nick drew her closer, shuffled them into a shadowy corner of the dance floor away from prying eyes and continued the slow, swaying movements. That's when he felt the trembling, *her* trembling. Subtle, elusive, but there. And like a train racing out of control, desire shot through him and it was everything he could do to keep his hands to himself. She *trembled* for him. What guy could ignore that?

He liked her softness. After so many fights in school and after being made fun of because he sucked at sports, he'd finally found his inner athlete in the gym. Lifting weights didn't require hand-eye coordination and it had opened up a whole new world. He'd worked hard and he'd made his body stronger, since his mind wasn't what it should be. Unable to stop himself, he turned Jenn so that he blocked the view of the wedding party and let his palm drift to the curve of her hip and gave it a squeeze. Jenn muffled a gasp, her breath quickening against his throat. When her back was to the crowd again, Nick's hand was at her waist in the proper position.

It became a sensual game. Each time he turned her, his hands drifted low over her rear, or up along the sides of her generous breasts, then back into place. The music blended together, song after song, until finally she raised her head and gave him a passion-darkened stare he couldn't ignore. Brushing his lips over her forehead to feel her smooth skin, he scanned the room, noted the fact that the other members of his family were busy chatting up the guests and curled an arm around her to lead her out the closest door. He'd said goodbye to Matt earlier, knowing his son would be running around all night and hard to find.

Outside, the door had barely shut behind them when he pulled Jenn into his arms and lowered his head, kissing her the way he wanted to. "Yes or no?" he asked her softly, the words rough with passion he couldn't hide.

She blinked several times, her chest rising and falling rapidly, her eyes bright. He liked her like that, liked knowing that he made Ms. Rose hot. When she couldn't seem to decide, he bent low and kissed her again, using his lips and tongue, nibbling at her mouth until she moaned and arched closer. He nuzzled her, his nose brushing against hers. "Sweetheart, yes or no?" There was no need to clarify what he was asking her. She knew.

After a deep breath that had her breasts rising above the scooping neckline of her dress and left him weak in the knees, she nodded. "Yes."

NICK KISSED her yet again outside the country club. Long and deep and with more passion than she'd ever experienced in all her years with Todd. He kissed her when they reached the truck. Once more, inside the cab, when he pulled her close and slid his hand down to cup her breast, caressing her until they both moaned with pleasure.

He kissed her at every stop sign and every red light. Once he stopped in the middle of a deserted street because he couldn't wait until the next light. By the time they made it back to Nick's, they were both shaking.

And every time troubling thoughts about the consequences of her actions tried to intrude, she shoved them away. She deserved this. Him. Especially after what she'd gone through with Todd. Nick was everything a gentleman should be. Sweet. Kind. So hot that a girl forgot herself.

They stumbled through the back door, Nick's hands holding her face as his mouth devoured hers, her fingers pulling at his beautiful silk tie. He tripped on the bottom step, laughing roughly at his clumsiness, and her heart tugged at the sound. Growling at her playfully, he pulled her in front of him to precede him, his hands resting on her hips as her trembling legs carried her up the stairs. She couldn't have said how they made it to the top without tumbling back down.

And the moment Nick's apartment door closed? *"Nick."* He pressed her against the wall, his body hard and hot and rigid with need, his hips grinding erotically into hers.

"You are so beautiful."

She ignored the compliment and somehow managed to keep herself from uttering a denial, choosing instead to help his fumbling hands work at removing his suit coat and unfasten the buttons on his crisply starched shirt. Once the clothes were off, she spread her hands wide across his chest, sliding them over corded muscle and the light dusting of springy hair that curled around her fingers, appreciating the sensuous contours of his six-pack abs. He was perfect, so perfect.

"I love how soft you are." Nick dropped a kiss on her shoulder. "The way you smell." His tongue swept over her skin. "Taste."

Nick's rapid breathing matched hers, a testament to his desire for her. He tugged at the zipper of her dress and cool air danced on her skin from the vent above her head. She held her breath, waiting, so glad she'd gone the extra mile during her shopping excursion and purchased a sexy black satin bustier that plumped her breasts and tucked in her waist, along with panties that weren't something her grandmother would've worn.

Nick pushed the gathered shoulder straps of her Grecian-style gown, letting them drop to her waist. His nostrils flared as he eyed her breasts in her deeply plunging demi-bra. "Beautiful. You're going to kill me, Jenn." His hands trembled at her waist, a tight, oh, so, slow smile pulling at his lips as he stared down at her. "And I can't wait. You," he murmured, pressing a kiss to her lips. "Are." His tongue found hers and rubbed. "*Unbelievably* hot."

She couldn't help it. Twenty-seven years of ingrained self-doubt reared its ugly head. "You don't have to… I haven't lost all the weight. I'm still f—"

His mouth covered hers, swallowing the word with forceful purpose. Nick bent his legs, his knees bumping hers as he gripped her behind. Then he lifted.

"Nick!" She wrapped her arms around his neck and held on as he carried her through the apartment to his bedroom. She'd seen it from the doorway, even peeked in once during a tutoring session with Matt. But as Nick carried her in, all she remembered was a brown-and-cream bedspread, functional furniture and a basic neatness she admired.

Nick stopped beside the bed, his gaze on hers. But he didn't put her down. No, he lifted her higher, as if she were a hundred pounds at most, and opened his mouth. Her breath caught in her chest as his teeth found the lace-edged top of the bustier and gently tugged. The ties were tight, so nothing came undone, but then he kissed the skin between her breasts with all the care and dedication of…of… She didn't know what.

"Don't ever let me hear you say that again," he whispered against her skin, his mouth sucking at her body, sending a spiral of heat shooting down her and making her want to wrap her legs around his waist.

Lost in the fantasy, she wasn't prepared to be dropped. "Nick!" A surprised shriek escaped as she landed on the bed, bounced, legs sprawled and breasts jiggling free of the sexy bustier. And Nick liked it. She could tell that he did because his eyes sparkled and he wore an expression that no woman could possibly misinterpret. In that moment she wasn't anything but *hot*. Beautiful and alluring. Ready and waiting for Nick.

He cupped her ankle with one broad palm hand and removed a high heel. Then the other came off. They dropped to the floor with small thuds. That done, he slid his hands up her legs, lingering on the softness of her thighs as if he adored the feel of them, dipping his thumbs beneath the elastic band of her panties and slowly easing them off.

She couldn't breathe. Nick was watching her. He'd turned the lights on as they'd stumbled through the door of the apartment, and the indirect glow filtering in from the hall was more than enough.

But in that moment all the doubts, her insecurities, her faltering self-image, disappeared as she remembered Nick's words about attitude. Which was why, when his hands lifted to the cups of the undergarment, when they pulled and released her breasts, slipped behind her to tug at the strings holding the ribbed bustier in place, she lifted her chin and let her eyes urge him to keep going. She wanted him. She needed this. Regardless of the pain she imagined she might feel later.

Nick groaned. He lowered his head, his hungry eyes holding hers as his lips fastened over the crest of her breast. A final tug loosened the silky ties, and somehow Nick managed to pull the undergarment away from her body, leaving her naked and straining to get closer to him.

His hands fumbled with the belt at his waist and before Jenn could think twice or allow a single doubt to enter her mind, she helped him, holding her breath as the last of his clothing was shed. The shirt dropped from his shoulders and was tugged over his wrists, a button popping in the process. His belt, his shoes and pants, everything came off as she watched, and with every second she grew more and more ready for him. He was beautiful. Physically perfect in every way. Hers. For the night, if not for longer.

Seconds later Nick was lying beside her, his head on one hand and his free hand caressing to her throat and roaming to her thigh and back again.

"You okay?"

She nodded shakily, once, before she could change her mind. And she prayed that her vision was a little better than his and that he couldn't see her as well as she could see him.

"Stop," he ordered roughly. "Stop worrying about things that haven't entered my mind even once. Just feel." Nick dropped his head and kissed her again. What began as slow and easy quickly became hard and fast, and she writhed with pleasure. His hand plumped and caressed her breast, his thumb sliding over her in a stroke of heat, before he continued on to take her hip and pull her closer, snuggling her against his rock-solid body.

It was magic. Desire. Hard meeting soft, and it was good—so good. Emotions and feelings she'd never experienced poured over her. There wasn't a spot on her body that Nick didn't kiss or tease, touch or explore. He rebuilt the heat that had been cooled by her worrisome thoughts and then his hand slipped between her thighs.

She moaned at the contact and clutched him to her, opening her body and her heart, which were one and the same, no matter how much she might like to pretend otherwise. "Please, Nick. Please." She wasn't sure what she was asking for, knew she could only ask for so much.

Nick buried his face against her neck, laving the skin there before scoring it with his teeth in a gentle-rough nip. "Don't think, and don't move."

He rolled away from her long enough to take care of protecting them and then rolled back again to position himself. Settling himself comfortably over her, Nick smiled a sexy grin. His arms were locked, muscles clenching and unclenching as he held himself above her, and she knew that he was holding back simply because of her.

"Please." With her hands at his waist, she tugged at him, urged him down and earned a jaw-clenching rumple of desire.

"Slow. I don't want to hurt you, sweetheart."

Because it had been so long. Because he *was* hurting her, but it was a wonderful hurt. The burn and stretch actually added to the pleasurable sensations, and she rolled her head back and forth on the pillow. "Now. Please, Nick. *Now.*"

When he sank only a little farther inside her, she took matters into her own hands. Holding on to him, she lifted her knees and locked her ankles around his hips, using the strength he'd helped her acquire to pull him deep inside.

A low moan escaped and before she had time to do more than gasp at the unbelievable feel of him, Nick began to rock back and forth. Her breath caught in her lungs. Her nails dug into Nick's sweat-dampened back—she had to hold on to something. Had to hold on to him because she felt too much. And then she was flying, so close, and as he continued to thrust inside her, harder and faster, rougher, she heard a broken cry and realized the sounds of rapture were her own.

Pleasure burst through her, every muscle straining with delight, and she was acutely aware of Nick's groans, as well, as he watched her and found his own release.

THE RINGING OF the telephone woke him. Nick's arm tightened around Jenn's waist as he remembered a night, and a morning, well spent. Last night they'd made love a second time in the shower, and they'd taken things slow and explored. He loved how easy it was to put a rosy color on Jenn's cheeks. The softness and curves that she was so ashamed of made him happily aware of the differences between them.

And maybe this morning should have been awkward but it wasn't. With the sweet fragrance of her hair in his nose, he'd taken particular pleasure in waking her slowly, kissing the stomach she tried so hard to suck in and hide during the light of day before moving lower. They'd fallen asleep afterward, all tangled limbs and musky sheets.

The phone rang again and he shifted over her to grab the portable off the base, aware that his body was more than ready for another round when he pressed against her hips from behind. They hadn't tried that yet, they hadn't tried a lot of things, but he could imagine the blush she'd wear when they did. The thought made him grin.

Jenn blinked drowsily, looking soft and warm and everything feminine, and he dropped a kiss on her bare shoulder before hitting the talk button with his thumb. "Hello?"

"Nick?" Luke's voice was tense and Nick could hear Matt sobbing in the background.

"What's going on?"

"Matt's been hurt, and we're on our way to the hospital. I'm driving him in."

*"What?"* He sat bolt upright and Jenn did the same, as Luke's voice carried loudly over the phone. Her hands touched his back and arm, held him gently in comforting support.

"Dusty got spooked and threw him. Look, just meet us there."

"I'm on my way." He pressed the End button and tossed the phone down with a curse.

"He'll be okay," Jenn told him. "You go. I'll get dressed and walk home."

She held the bedsheet to her chest and shifted her feet onto the floor. He couldn't let her go like that, however. Anyone who saw her would know she'd spent the night with him and he didn't want people speculating about what Nick had done to leave her walking home in her wedding finery. Nothing said *morning after* like that. More to the point, he wanted her with him. Period. And he didn't have time to think about that too much at the moment. "Will you come with me?"

Her eyes widened a split second before her expression went soft on him. Her eyes, her face... She was so sweet.

"Of course. But I need to change clothes and...I left some things downstairs in the locker room. Could you go down and get them?"

Not without drawing more attention to their situation,

because he'd have to send one of his female employees into the women's locker room after her clothing, but what choice did they have?

Nick stood and yanked clothes from his dresser, hopping from foot to foot as he pulled them on. "I'll be back in a sec."

"Nick? He'll be all right."

Hands shaking, he pulled his shirt over his stomach as he rushed for the door. "He has to be."

# CHAPTER SIXTEEN

FIFTEEN MINUTES LATER they were at the hospital. They spotted Luke's rental car with its doors open beneath the E.R. canopy. Nick jogged inside the entrance, Jenn's hand in his. The smell of disinfectant made his nose twitch.

The waiting room held only a few people. An older couple and two women, one of them holding her arm. A man rubbed the back of an upset-looking young girl who seemed close to being sick on her daddy's lap.

"Nick, over here."

He followed the sound of Ethan's voice and saw his brother heading toward them at a run.

"I was just paged. They're in there."

Nick followed Ethan, still holding tight to Jenn's hand. They entered a cubicle and Nick swore under his breath when he saw Matt's leg, which was twisted at an odd angle. Matt stared at them all, wide-eyed, tear tracks staining his cheeks.

Nick moved to his son's side and leaned over the bed to kiss his head. "You okay, bub?"

Matt's lower lip trembled. "It hurts. And I won't be able to play ball."

"He's been given something to take the edge off his pain," Ethan told Nick, looking over Matt's file. "They're waiting on final X rays before taking him to surgery."

Nick swore silently, then forced himself to smile reassuringly at Matt. "You'll be fine. Don't be scared. Matt? You'll be okay."

Ethan finished studying the chart, a frown on his face. He set it aside and gently examined Matt's leg.

Nick's dread grew.

"But I don't wanna have surgery. Can't they just put a cast on it?"

Ethan met Nick's gaze and held it for a long moment before shifting his attention to Matt. "No gettin' around it, kiddo. Surgery is a must for this break. But you just wait until the girls get a look at the cool cast you'll have afterward. They'll be falling all over you." He winked at Matt. "Girls like that sort of thing."

An orderly came into the room. "And how is everybody today? You Matt?" He waited for Matt to nod. "Nice to meet you. I'm Rick and I'm your driver for today. You ready to race?"

Ethan squeezed Matt's uninjured leg. "Rick wins all the gurney qualifiers around here."

"I don't want surgery."

Ethan nodded. "I know, Matt, but like your dad said, it'll be okay. I'll be there the whole time. I promise."

"You'll do the surgery?" Matt asked, his eyes bright with tears.

"No, it would be a conflict because you're my nephew, but I'll be in the room supervising your doctor and flirting with the nurses."

"You always do that."

Even under so much strain they all chuckled.

A nurse stuck her head in the door. "Excuse me. Any of you parked in the E.R. entrance? A Dodge?"

"Me." Luke stood.

"We need it moved, please. I take it you're Mr. Tulane,

Matt's father?" The nurse smiled at Nick when he nodded and held out a clipboard full of forms. "We need you to fill these out immediately and report to registration so they can get everything cleared while your son's being prepped."

"I need to stay with my son."

"You can't go back, Nick. I'll stay with him." Ethan ruffled Matt's hair. "Are you ready to race?"

The orderly took that as his cue and began moving the gurney. Nick accepted the forms automatically, his mind too full to grasp all that was going on. His son was having surgery and was scared out of his mind, and the nurse wanted him to fill out paperwork?

"Wait." He leaned over and gave Matt a hug and a kiss. "I love you, buddy."

"I love you, too, Dad."

Nick heard the tears in Matt's voice and worked to swallow the lump in his own throat. "I'll be waiting for you when you wake up."

Matt sniffled, but stayed quiet.

"Better get to the starting gate." The orderly wheeled Matt out of the room.

Nick stood there like an idiot. What now? Where to begin? He had to get someone to cover for him at the garage and this evening at the Coyote. And he probably should call the insurance company or something before the papers started showing up, shouldn't he? And what about Matt's pediatrician?

"Take care of the forms and try not to worry. Registration will tell you where to wait for Matt." Ethan nodded at Jenn, and then paused by her side on his way out. "Thanks for coming with him."

Jenn was shaken by the sight of Matt so pale against the hospital sheets, his leg mangled. "Nick?"

He waved the clipboard in the air, looking as if he wanted to throw it across the room. "This is ridiculous. My son is having surgery and they want me to fill out forms?"

"It won't take long. Think of the paperwork you have at the gym for membership. The hospital has to do this upfront." She moved close. "Come on. Let's go fill everything out and get to registration so we know where to be when Matt is done in surgery."

Jenn led the way out of the E.R., figuring one of the nurses would tell Luke where to find them when he returned from parking his car. Nick stormed along beside her, glaring at the floor, and muttering under his breath about the papers in his hand.

"Nick? Nick, what happened? Where's Matt?"

Oh, not good. She felt Nick stiffen and saw his head jerk up. Nick's parents approached them.

"They took Matt to surgery," she explained.

"Did you get a second opinion?" his father demanded. "If the nerves are damaged, he'd be better off with a specialist."

Nick glowered at them. "Ethan checked Matt out. Someone else is doing the surgery, but Eth said he'd stay with him."

"Who? Which doctor? Ethan is a fine surgeon, but he isn't a pediatric specialist," Alan Tulane grumbled. "If it wasn't life or death, why didn't you tell them to wait for a specialist?"

"Dr. Tulane." Jenn glanced at Nick briefly before focusing her gaze on the irate man across from her. She wished she was dressed in something better than workout clothes, wished she had makeup to put on so she'd look halfway decent, but regardless of feeling like a bum, she wasn't going to let Nick's father berate him when Nick hadn't done anything wrong. "I know you're upset over the accident, but I'm sure if Ethan had felt there was a need for a second opinion *or* a specialist, he would have said something."

"She's right," Nick's mother, Marilyn, agreed. "Calm down, Alan. We're all worried about Matt, but it won't help anyone if we're arguing while he's in surgery."

Near the registration desk, Jenn spotted an empty area with four vacant seats. "Mrs. Tulane, why don't you head for the post-op waiting room while we fill out these forms? We'll be there as soon as things are done."

Separating the two men was key right now. Nick's body was tensed from head to toe, and his hands formed two rock-hard fists.

Marilyn flashed Jenn a grateful smile. "That's a good idea. Alan, let's go."

Jenn waited until the older couple had moved on, and then she gripped Nick's hand and tugged. "Let's go over and fill out the papers. It'll make things go faster at registration if they're already completed."

"Why didn't I call a specialist?" Nick growled.

"He's concerned, Nick. Just like you."

Nick dropped into a chair, swearing under his breath. Jenn dug into her purse for a pen and handed it to him. As if he were only now coming to awareness, Nick looked at the papers and blinked. He squeezed his eyes tight, then sat forward, the papers seeming fragile in his work-roughened hands. Seconds passed and still Nick didn't move.

Jenn frowned, pretending she wasn't watching him. She studied the various hospital employees as they went about their business. Finally Nick clicked the pen as if to write, held it over the paper and then hesitated before the tip touched the page. He rubbed his forehead.

"Nick?" She sat forward. "Is something wrong?"

"Why can't the people in registration do their damned jobs? They're going to make me repeat all this anyway."

"Stop," she whispered. "Blaming the people in registration isn't going to change the fact that Matt got hurt. Just calm down and fill the forms out."

A muscle vibrated in his jaw. He clicked the pen a second time. Stared at the papers and fumbled for his sunglasses.

"You don't have them. I think I remember seeing them in the apartment before we left. Sorry, I should've said something." She'd wondered about his habit of wearing sunglasses from sunrise to sunset. Other people probably thought he wore them to enhance an ultra-sexy image, but Jenn thought it had more to do with glare.

He rubbed his eyes again. Was something else wrong? Why didn't he fill out the forms?

Nick shifted on his chair, hunched over the clipboard. She heard the sounds of paper rustling and glanced down. Nick was moving the forms back and forth ever so slightly. Just like Matt.

Jenn noted his intense focus, the way he kept rubbing his head and the way his lips moved as he read. Almost as if he was trying to sound out the words?

An awful suspicion came into her brain. Surely not. Nick ran two businesses and was quite successful at them. There was absolutely no reason to think he couldn't...what? Couldn't *read?*

He rubbed his forehead harder and muttered another curse under his breath. And then Jenn thought of other things. The books on tape. The way Nick got upset when she'd asked him to read with Matt. Nick wasn't the type of father to blow off something like that. Not unless he couldn't do it. And if he couldn't do something, he—

*Hired help.* Suzanne's husband. His managers. Her.

Could it be true? Could he have built up such a solid wall of coping strategies over the years? Was it possible?

*You don't know that that's his problem.*

But what else could it be? Why wasn't he writing? Dyslexia was diagnosed now after a long series of tests and evaluations, but back in the eighties when Nick was in school, it wasn't. Especially in rural areas. Instead, kids were considered lazy and slow. Problematic.

"Give me the papers." Her voice was hoarse and shaky. She cleared her throat, hoping with all her heart she was wrong. She had to be wrong. It was just too painful a possibility to contemplate. But her head whirled with all the things she'd noticed while spending time with him, things she'd shrugged off as unimportant.

Nick lifted his head and stared at her, his eyes bleak. Beleaguered, as if he were waiting for an ax to drop. If there was a problem, he hadn't trusted her enough to tell her, and this wasn't the time or the place to confront Nick about her suspicions. Anyone upset, with a child in surgery, wasn't able to think straight or concentrate on filling out papers. And until she knew otherwise, she had to assume that was all his hesitation was about. Not about dropping out or not having a basic education.

But the look on his face. Nick seemed to be waiting for her to call him on it. Guilt, embarrassment. *Pride.* All the emotions were stamped on his features, and yet he appeared to be preparing himself to be blasted with censure. Meaning she was right?

He wiped a hand over his eyes, rough and angry. "You don't have to do them. Maybe you should go. You don't want to hang around here all day."

"I'm not going anywhere. Give me the papers."

"Seriously, you can leave if you want."

"I don't want to leave."

"Jenn…"

"Let me help you. I *want* to help you. Let me."

His face tightened even more but when he turned his head to look at her, his features were intentionally blank. Guarded. But so revealing. *Oh, Nick.*

She held out her hand and ignored the way it trembled. "Give me the papers. I'll take care of them." For now. Then she'd do everything she could to discover what level of reading he had and figure out how he'd slipped through the system. Some kids did. Smart, intelligent kids learned all the tricks there were in order to protect themselves from embarrassment and the teasing of their peers. And so had Nick.

*To protect himself from his family?*

No wonder they didn't get along. Nick's übersuccessful parents and siblings were a smack in the face to someone who couldn't— Her eyes misted with tears at the thought of what she'd made him do, the position she'd put him in at the dinner and then the wedding. Obviously Nick was functionally literate, but the thought of filling out papers with her watching him made him hugely uncomfortable.

She remembered the charts at the gym. How he'd slid them across the desk so that she would fill in the blanks. So many individual things that she hadn't picked up on.

Jenn cleared her throat and took the sheaf of papers and pen from him. "What is Matt's full name?"

Nick hesitated a long moment, rubbed his forehead and gave her a look she couldn't decipher.

"I'm not going anywhere, Nick. Please don't ask me again."

He released a resigned sigh. "Matthew Colton Tulane."

She filled in the blank, the moisture in her eyes blurring the words slightly. "Date of birth?"

SIX HOURS. Six damn hours of pacing the floor and enduring his father's frowning disapproval, his mother's worried

glances and Gram eyeing Jenn like fresh meat. And Jenn...
He was amazed she was still there. That she made eye contact
and smiled at him. Did she know? Guess? She had to. She was
too smart not to. Why had he thought he could actually spend
any length of time with her and have her not find out?

How much longer was this going to take?

"You should have called us," his father muttered for the
thousandth time. "If Luke hadn't called, we'd wouldn't have
even known to come."

*Thank you, brother.*

"I think it's understandable that Nick was more concerned
with getting to his son than making calls," Jenn said, her tone
gentle but firm. Almost as if she spoke to one of the children
she taught. "When you arrived, we'd only just gotten here ourselves, Dr. Tulane."

Gram smirked. Luke coughed. And Nick wondered how he
could get rid of them all.

Last night with Jenn had been...hot. A fantasy come true.
But after seeing the suspicion in Jenn's eyes when he
couldn't fill out those stupid papers, he knew whatever
they'd had was over. What had he been thinking? It should-
n't have gone so far. Kissing her was one thing, compliment-
ing Jenn to boost her self-image even though any man that
looked at her had to see how beautiful she was another given
in the scheme of things. But *sleeping* with her? Not a smooth
move. Jenn was probably kicking herself for hooking up
with someone like him, hanging around only until Matt
came out of surgery and she knew all was well. Women like
her did that.

"Garret called and Alex told him about Matt. He said to
keep him and Darcy posted." Luke stared at his hands. "Nick,
I'm sorry. I can't say it enough. Dusty has always been so mild

and easygoing. I've never seen her spook like that. The cat jumped out of the tree and the next thing I knew, Dusty reared."

"Accidents happen." It was hard to force the words out. He hadn't wanted Matt to go to California with Luke in case something happened and he was too far away to get to his son, but it just proved things like this could happen anywhere, at any moment.

The truth overwhelmed him. He'd felt like a failure before, but now… When was he going to face the truth? No matter what he did, no matter how successful he was in business, he didn't measure up. Because he wasn't Tulane material. Tulanes did better. They were well above average. This just proved his father had been right.

"Nick?"

He turned to see Ethan in the waiting room's doorway. Ignoring the rest of them, Nick raced forward. "How is he?"

# CHAPTER SEVENTEEN

"MATT'S IN RECOVERY. The break was a bad one, but with physical therapy Matt should be just fine," Ethan informed Nick.

His knees felt weak.

"Thank goodness." Jenn's arm slid around his waist and held him tight. Despite what they'd have to go through the next time they talked, Nick welcomed the comfort now, pulling her close and breathing in the sweet scent that was hers alone. Eyes shut, he sent up a prayer of thanks.

"When can we see him?" Marilyn asked.

"Tomorrow would be best. He won't really come to until then. The surgeon had to do some digging for bone fragments and Matt will be in less pain if we keep him under for a while. Nick, come with me and I'll let you see him before you go home."

"I'm staying."

"No, you're not. I'm on duty all night. I'll keep a close eye on him. There's no sense in you spending the night out here in the waiting room."

"Why can't I stay in the room with him?"

Ethan frowned. "Don't be alarmed by what I'm going to say. With any surgery there is a risk of blood clots, so since there was an open bed in ICU I asked that Matt be put there. He'll be monitored more closely that way. Hospital policy states no overnight visitors in ICU, however. Not even for children."

ICU? Was something going on that Ethan wasn't telling Nick? What if Matt woke up and he wasn't there?

"ICU is a good precaution," his father murmured. "He'll be fine."

His mother took his hand and squeezed. "Nick, you're going to have a lot to deal with when Matt wakes up and can't move around. Children aren't known to be patient patients."

"You've got that right," Ethan confirmed. "Come on. I'll take you back for a short visit, and then Jenn can take you home to get some rest."

"I'll wait here for you."

Jenn released him and took a step away as though she hadn't been aware he'd held her in his arms the entire time. "Thanks."

"Nick?" Tears brightened his mother's eyes, and as they overflowed she rushed forward and brought his face down to hers with her hands. "Will you give him a hug and kiss from me?" She kissed his cheek, gave him a quick hug and then stepped back, dashing away the tears with her fingertips.

"Uh…sure."

"Ethan, keep me apprised of the situation." His father waited for Ethan to nod before he looked at Nick, an intense expression on his face. "We'll be back tomorrow to visit with you both. Go get some rest, son."

It was as much a declaration of love as he'd gotten from his father since he was a kid. Nick nodded.

Ethan led the way to the ICU unit. Nick's throat grew tight when he saw Matt connected up to an IV, with an oxygen tube clipped to his nose. Matt's leg was wrapped from his toes to above his knee and suspended from a metal prop at the end of the bed.

"He's going to be fine. Dr. Potter did an excellent job,

and other than a scar I doubt Matt will have any long-term after-effects."

Thank God. Nick leaned over the bed and ran his hand through Matt's soft hair. Matt hated the cowlick that made him look as if he had a curl on his forehead. Nick smoothed his fingers over the swirl, pushing it to the side because he knew Matt would want him to. He was growing up so fast. He needed a mother's touch, someone to soften the edges and teach him manners so that Matt would learn that farting and burping weren't the best ways to win a girl's heart.

Leaning against the cold bed rail, Nick stared down at him and listened for every beep of his heart on the monitor overhead. Jenn was waiting outside, but Nick didn't know how to face her. Now that the day was over.

Now that they were over.

NICK WAS SO QUIET on the drive home that Jenn began to worry. He hadn't eaten all day—he'd been too worried about Matt to have an appetite. Her? She'd had to eat something to fend off her frustration so she'd munched on carrot sticks she'd found in the cafeteria. That just showed how much she wanted to change her unhealthy ways. What else could've turned her cravings for junk food into a veggie fest? Being with Nick made her want to be healthy, thinner, but more importantly it now made her realize that as perfect as Nick seemed, he wasn't.

*Is anyone perfect?*

Was she really only just figuring that out? Why not like herself, be herself? Love who she was as an individual. She wasn't a saint, but she wasn't a bad person, either. She had good qualities. Worthwhile qualities. Sighing deeply, she turned Nick's truck down the quiet street that led to her house.

"Come home with me."

Jenn slowed her driving at his words, the first he'd uttered since they'd left the hospital.

"Stop and get a bag. I don't…" He shook his head. "I can't go home by myself and know he's not there. I can't stay here, because it'll stir up too much gossip for you. Just stay one more night."

*One more night.* He was setting a limit to their relationship. Probably smart, since she was already in over her head. But he had a point about being discreet. If he left his truck outside her house the gossips would have a field day, and she had to consider what her students and their parents might think. Set an example.

Jenn pulled into her drive, her heart absolutely racing. *Just one more night.* Unable to deny her desire, she put the truck in Park. "Give me five minutes."

Ten minutes later she drove around the alley behind the gym and garage and parked. Nick just sat there and stared.

But as much as Jenn wanted to stay and be with him, they had to talk about what happened today at the hospital. "We have to talk, Nick."

His mouth tightened into a flat line. "I don't want to talk."

"I do. I insist, actually."

"Then maybe it would be best if you—"

"Let me rephrase that," she said, unwilling to let him off so easily and yet surprised by her boldness. "I'm coming up with you to talk about what happened today. As a friend— *your* friend. After we talk, we can decide if I stay."

No way was he going to give her the brush-off now. It might have been a split-second moment of weakness that had prompted him to ask her, but now she was there and she was staying until she had answers.

Without a word, Nick opened the passenger door. Jenn

climbed out the driver's side of the big Dodge, grabbed her tote bag, just in case, and followed him in. She led the way up the back stairs, wondering how things could have changed so much in twenty-four hours. Last night Nick had been trying to get her clothes off as they raced up the stairs. Now they were both dragging their feet and reluctant to face the conversation to come.

How could she bring it up? *I noticed you were having some trouble reading back there. Been doing that long?*

Yeah, that wasn't going to go over too well. Maybe he would raise the subject?

They entered the dark apartment and Jenn was glad when Nick ignored the lights. Sometimes it was easier to talk that way. Just like dancing. If you couldn't see it, maybe it wasn't so bad. This was bad, though. She knew it, sensed it in his behavior. And there was just enough moonlight streaming in at the edges of the curtains to show her that truth on his face.

"Nick, whatever you say stays between us."

He made eye contact, his jaw working as if he were grinding his teeth. He turned away and paced the floor like a caged animal. "It's my fault."

"What is?" She followed him into the living room, needing him to spell out whatever *it* was.

"The trouble Matt's having in school."

He stopped in front of the pictures on a wall near the hall leading to the bedrooms. School photos of Matt from kindergarten through third grade hung in black frames along with snapshots of Matt and Nick together. Fishing, at a football game. Guy stuff that dads did with their sons.

"Tell me why you think it's your fault. Is it about the papers today?"

Nick shot her a glare over his shoulder before turning

back to the wall, a child being punished for bad behavior. "Dixon would…"

"Todd has nothing to do with this. Neither does your family. I already told you, what you say stays between us."

Nick ran a hand through his hair, down his neck. "You know I dropped out of high school, but…you don't know why."

"I assumed it was because you had trouble."

A raw laugh burst from his chest. "Yeah, I definitely had some trouble. The same trouble as Matt. I can't…"

Her fears were confirmed. Nick's shoulders were lined, his back tense, and she searched for the right words to see her through without blowing everything. "Can't?"

Nick swore again, his head hanging low, nearly touching the frames in front of him. His hand fisted and hit the wall hard enough to make the frames clatter against the painted Sheetrock. "Don't make me say it."

"It sounds as though you need to."

"What I need…" He hit the wall two more times before dropping his forehead to his fist. "I don't *need* to be admitting this. Especially not to you."

Nick turned and pierced her with a glare. How many times had Matt worn the same expression? A combination of anger and pain and frustration. "I know what it's like, Nick."

"A brainiac like you? I don't think so."

"Oh, so that's how it is, huh? You think it was easy admitting to one of the most *gorgeous* men in Beauty that I have a problem overeating? That for way too long my best friend was a tub of Chunky Monkey? That in less than two years I've outgrown *two* sizes of clothes?"

"The weight isn't who you are—it's a product of what happened to you. You've gotten control of that now. This isn't as easy. It's not something I can get over. It's *me*."

"It's me, too. You're not getting it. And I'll never be completely *over it,* Nick, because with my body shape it will always be a battle. I doubt there will *ever* be a bad day when I don't hear the things my father and sister said to me. How many times have you told me that the key is to move on? That if I let them get the best of me, they win?"

"You can't compare the two."

"Why not?"

"That's not the same. *I can't read.*"

His voice was low, so pained, she barely heard him.

"This isn't about willpower or bad habits. You think I don't want to *help* my son? You don't think it kills me having to sit there and listen to him, when I want to help him, but I *can't* because I don't read much better? All it says to me is that I'm the loser my father and the rest of my family think I am."

"But you're not. No, you're *not.* Do you think Matt's a loser?"

"Don't try to psychobabble me."

She wanted to scream. "I'm trying to get you to see that if you have problems with reading, it's because you have a problem and not because you're a loser or lacking *intelligence.*" Jenn hesitated, then put her hands on his back, smoothing them over the taut muscles. She used brute force to turn him around and was surprised when he let her. "While we worked out and spent time together, I told you things. Now it's your turn. *Talk to me.*"

"What do you want me to say?"

Her eyes stung, but she forced herself to maintain contact. "I want to hear you say that you'll let me help you. Knowing this? What you just said? It doesn't change who you are, Nick. Not to me."

A rough laugh rumbled out of his chest.

"What?"

"You. You're actually going to stand there and tell me you don't look at me and see a big, dumb jock?"

"I *see* someone who knows what it's like to not be the person other people say they should be. I see a loving, caring father, an astute businessman who's attuned to his employees' needs and limitations. And I see a man I want to help, not change."

Nick stared at her a long moment, searching her eyes, her expression, for any sign of hypocrisy. "I've liked spending time with you." He lifted a hand and stroked her hair away from her cheek. "But for a brainy teacher you're not very smart. Dixon would say you should run."

"Todd has *nothing* to do with this—or me."

"It doesn't bother you that I'm this way?"

Jenn turned her face into his hand and pressed a kiss to his palm. Bother her? Yes. But not the way he meant. "Does it bother me that you went out of your way to get Matt the help he needed? That you're a great trainer and an honorable man? No, it doesn't. Nick, you're not an *ogre*. If it bothers me at all, it's because now that I know, I understand the struggle you've had to accomplish everything. I can only imagine what you've been through to get where you are today." He looked away as if it weren't true—or maybe the praise was hard to accept? Were they both products of their upbringing? "You've had to work ten times harder than anyone else, but you've done it and I admire you more for it."

A muscle ticked in his jaw, a slow, thready pulse. "My father used to call me lazy. He said I wasn't trying hard enough, that I fit the stereotype to a T, even though I sucked at sports. I wasn't a big, dumb jock, I was just big and dumb."

Her heart broke. Nick's hands were clenched, his face lined with pain, and however strong he was, he was equally vulnerable. "He didn't know what you were dealing with." To look at Nick one would think he had everything, but inside he was as flawed and messed up as she was. "Do you really think a person lacking intelligence could have had the success that you have? Nick, most dropouts only *dream* of owning their own businesses, much less owning *two* and running them successfully. It's a testament to the quality of your mind. To your drive to succeed despite the odds."

"Be careful," he murmured. "You're laying it on a little thick."

"Every word is *true*."

Nick slid his hand to the nape of her neck and tugged her closer. There they stood in his shadowy living room, their pasts laid bare, finding solace in each other.

"If it's so obvious to you that I'm intelligent, why isn't it obvious that you're every bit the diva that you want to be?" he asked gruffly. "You think someone other than a diva would have confronted me like this?"

A pleased smile pulled at her lips. "Really?"

"Like I said, it's a state of mind." He stroked her cheek. "Right now I'm seeing *major* diva qualities. And I like it. I like it a lot, sweetheart."

Meaning he liked her. It was there in his eyes. She saw it, wished he could say more, be more specific. But she knew better than to push. It was too soon, especially after what they'd just shared.

Jenn stared up at him, knowing from the human development class she'd taken that men saw acceptance differently than women. Women were emotional and men were physical. And right now Nick equated her acceptance of his reading ability or lack thereof with her physical acceptance of him. Her presence there in his arms. She knew that, but it didn't stop her heart from wanting it to mean even more.

Images filled her head, created a flush of heat that warmed

her skin. Just thinking about the night before made it hard to breathe. Did she dare *show* him how much she'd come to care for him?

He leaned his head back against the wall and sighed. "I don't ever remember being this tired. All I've done is sit in hospital chairs, but I feel as if I've run a marathon."

He practically had, pacing back and forth for an entire day. Working two jobs of his own plus managing his uncle's business for the last few weeks. Poor guy. Here she was thinking of making love and Nick was exhausted. "Worry will do that to you. Come on." Resigned, she took his hand in hers and led him into the bedroom, where she began straightening the sheets. "Don't just stand there. Get ready for bed."

He didn't move. "What about you? Do you want to stay?"

Her heart pounded, the smell of Nick on the sheets she was holding, subtle but there. What was she doing? What had Suzanne gotten her into?

She felt way too much for her *guy friend.* "I'd love to," she whispered. Because it was the closest thing to *I love you* that she would allow herself to say.

## CHAPTER EIGHTEEN

NICK LISTENED TO THE shower running in the adjacent bath-room, imagining Jenn naked inside. If he walked in there right now she'd probably freak out, because he'd see the excess weight she carried. She'd think he wouldn't see the kindness in her beautiful eyes, the way she scrunched her nose when confronted with a vegetable, or know the way she'd made him feel by offering to help instead of treating him as if he were mentally deficient. She'd meant what she said.

It was right there on her sweet, heart-shaped face and in her smoky eyes. She *meant* it. And it changed everything. He felt free, able to speak to her without guarding every word. Something he couldn't do—hadn't done—with anyone else.

He stared up at the bedroom ceiling, beyond exhausted but unable to sleep. The shower was turned off, the curtain pushed aside, and he twisted his head to see Jenn the moment she stepped through the bathroom door. She came out wearing an oversized T-shirt, her hair wrapped in a towel. She took it off and dried the long strands briskly, but stopped when she saw him watching her.

"I thought you'd be asleep by now."

"Can't sleep. Come 'ere."

"I need to dry my hair. At least run a brush through it."

"In a second. Come here." He held out his hand.

Jenn bit her lip and gave him a shy look before padding over and sitting on the side of the bed, her hand warm and moist in his. Not happy with the distance between them, he tugged her sideways. She laid down and Nick rolled over to spoon her, burying his nose in her neck. She shivered at the brush of his chin against her skin and the response humbled him. Jenn was such a good person, a woman any man would be lucky to call his own. Sexy and smart, soft. His. The tension inside him eased.

"You called the hospital?"

"Yeah. No change. Eth said Matt's asleep and doing great. I told him we'd be there first thing in the morning." He wrapped a hand around her waist. Sure enough Jenn sucked in her stomach. He kissed her neck, felt her shiver again. "Stop that," he ordered, gruffly.

"What? Oh. Well, if I had a stomach like yours…"

"I wouldn't be nearly as attracted to you." He ran his hand up her side, rubbed her back and shoulder, slid back down again, the feel of her hot and womanly. "I like your curves, sweetheart. All of them."

"I like your… The way you're hard all over."

He grinned and snuggled her closer. Now that she was in bed beside him, he felt as if he could rest. "Then I guess we like each other, don't we?" Nick closed his eyes. A weight had been lifted from him and he felt exhausted from carrying the load. It wouldn't be easy, it might not even work, but they'd take it slow and figure things out as they went.

"I guess we do."

He squeezed her again. "Good."

"YOU'VE BEEN LAID."

Jenn froze, the turkey taco halfway to her mouth. Embarrassment flooded her face and she glanced quickly around the restaurant to see if anyone had overheard Suzanne's announcement. "What, um, makes you think that?"

"I don't, um, know. Maybe the way you can't get that syrupy expression off your face."

Jen set the taco on her plate. Syrupy? "What's got you in a mood?"

Suzanne waved a hand in front of her face.

"Oh, I see. Tuck Junior's giving you fits and you're taking it out on me, huh?"

Her friend leaned backward in their padded booth and groaned, her face as green as the guacamole she'd asked them to keep in the kitchen. "Morning sickness is only part of the game. Apparently the little bundle has decided it would be great to make me sick the entire time he's in there."

"Oh. Yikes."

"Exactly. Which is why I have to concentrate on someone else—and that someone else is you." Suzanne fixed her with a steady gaze. "And Nick. When and where?"

"Uh…What's to say?" she murmured, picking up her supper once more. *Except that Nick keeps his promises,* she thought, smug and happy and freakishly satisfied all at the same time.

Having fallen asleep in his arms the night after Matt's surgery, she'd woken up in the middle of a climax. Then there in the full light of the morning sun shining through the bedroom windows, Nick had made love to her again. Every inch of her had been exposed and while she'd been embarrassed by the weight she still had left to lose, she'd forced herself to let go of her inhibitions and enjoy the moment.

Nick made her feel beautiful, just the way she was. Did she really want to spend her life trying to be someone she wasn't?

Right then and there, staring up into Nick's silver-blue

eyes as he kissed and licked and made her shake and quiver and gasp, she'd made a decision. No more worrying about her body image or her flaws or anything else. It was time to grow up and be comfortable with who she was, whatever her size. She'd learn to love the body she'd been given, instead of taking her problems and frustrations out on herself. Some people cut themselves, some people took drugs or made themselves throw up. She ate too much.

No. Correction—she *used* to eat too much.

"Jenn? Yoohoo?"

Her face turned red. "Sorry. Nick and I are…friends. And I'd appreciate it if you wouldn't talk about this to anyone or make any other public-service announcements about my love life."

"Meaning, you now *have* a love life?"

She couldn't discuss it. She and Nick both needed time to figure out their feelings. They'd spent most every day at the hospital with Matt until his release this afternoon, three days after his accident. She'd helped Nick move Matt and his many bouquets of balloons, gifts and cards home, then left father and son to spend some quality time together. "Give me some room to sort things out for myself, okay? Then I'll fill you in. In the meantime, I could use some help with something else."

"What?"

"Matt." She glanced around and lowered her voice. "I think he might be dyslexic." Maybe Nick, too. That was a subject she had yet to broach with him. *One step at a time.*

"Oh, no."

She nodded. "Maybe a touch of hyperactivity, too. He can't sit still after the first few minutes of working on something. I know boys learn differently than girls when it comes to how they study and work, but Matt is constantly in motion. Didn't you have a student last year who was diagnosed with dyslexia?"

"Yeah, but technically it's still not confirmed. It takes a long time to get an 'official' diagnosis because there's no specific test for the problem. It's more like a trial-and-error method of testing to see what works and what doesn't until a consensus is formed."

She chewed, but the remainder of her turkey-taco had lost its appeal. "I'm going to have to do a lot of research to help Matt, but I'm thinking I'll incorporate it into my paper for my HD class. It's the only way I'll be able to do them both this summer."

"And be with Nick," Suzanne added. "Jenn, just reassure me here. Things are good? I love Nick because he's a great guy, but I don't want either of you to get hurt."

She felt her lips pull up in a genuine smile. "Things are way, way better than good."

"But you're not going to talk about it?" Suzanne sighed. "That's just cruel. It's always the quiet ones who are the teases."

"COME ON, Ms. Rose says we need to do this."

Matt looked up at him with a wary frown. "But my leg's broke."

Nick smirked. "Good try, bub. Your leg is broken, but not your brain. Let's go. She printed an extra paper for me to do, too. We'll take the test together and practice."

"Why do you have to take it?"

Good question. One he wasn't sure how to answer. Except maybe by finally telling Matt the truth?

"How come you don't have to read, but I do?"

Yeah, definitely time. "Matt, whenever you were with Grandma or Nana, did they ever say anything to you about me not doing very well in school?"

"You *didn't?*"

Matt's eyes resembled saucers. Apparently he hadn't given

his family enough credit for not discrediting him in front of Matt. The thought shamed him.

"But you're smart."

"So are you. But, yeah, I had a lot of trouble in school and I kept getting into trouble. Kids… Some of the kids made fun of me whenever I was called on to read, and I'd get mad and act up. Eventually they stopped calling on me, because I kept landing in the principal's office afterward."

"I only got sent there once. How many times did you have to go?"

He smiled grimly. "A lot. Which is why, when I still had trouble after I started high school, I dropped out."

Matt couldn't have looked any more surprised. "You *did*?"

Nick nodded slowly. "I did. But I've always wished I had stuck with it and graduated. That's why, when I found out you were having trouble, I wanted to do whatever it took to help you—so you won't make the same mistake I did. This is important, Matt. Not something to take lightly."

"What did Nana and Grandpa say when you told them? Were they mad?"

"Yeah. They were mad. I wound up moving out and getting a job. For a while it was like an adventure, but when my friends were going to the prom and football games and having fun, I had to work. I missed out on a lot because of what I did."

"Wouldn't Grandpa and Nana let you go home?"

Treading these waters would be tricky. His parents hadn't dissed him and he had to give them the same respect. "They would have if I'd agreed to go back to school, but I was stubborn and too hardheaded for my own good. We fought a lot."

"Like you do now."

"You picked up on that, huh?"

Matt shrugged. "I miss not being able to go see 'em. Nana bakes really good cookies."

"That she does. And I'm sorry you're missing out, Matt. I never meant for you to be in the middle. Your grandparents love you."

"That's what Ms. Rose said."

Nick sat down on the bed beside Matt, careful not to jar his son's injured leg, which was propped up by a mound of pillows. "Yeah?"

"She said that they love me, even if I don't see them much. That grandmas and grandpas are like that." Matt scooted closer and put his head on Nick's chest the way he used to when he was younger. "She said it would get better, too. One day."

Maybe it would. *Maybe one day soon.*

Nick snuggled Matt against his chest and thought about that for a moment. Yeah, he could see that happening. So long as Jenn was by his side. She'd stepped in at the hospital and taken care of the paperwork without making him feel any less a man or embarrassing him in front of his family.

And now she knew everything there was to know about him and she'd stayed with him anyway, made love to him and never once looked at him as if he were a loser.

And that light he saw shining in her eyes when she looked at him? Did she love him, too? A woman like Jenn didn't share her body without an emotional connection. He might not be book smart, but he was smart enough to realize that.

He didn't know what he'd done to deserve her, but when he thought of the summer and beyond, he saw more. He saw a future. Jenn was the perfect woman to help him deal with his family. In the three days Matt had spent in the hospital, Jenn had smoothed over problems, eased the tension and had them all smiling on numerous occasions. Thanks to her, Nick had actually managed a couple of long conversations with his family without anyone getting mad or walking out. With her at his side, he could actually see a more amiable future for them all.

But she needed more time. Jenn's marriage had taken a toll and she still considered herself to be missing some indefinable quality. She wasn't, but until she realized that, she would need space to grow within herself. And when she was ready…When she was ready, he'd be there.

"You like her, don't you?"

Matt's question pulled him out of his thoughts. "Ms. Rose? Yeah. Do you?"

"She's cool. She signed my cast."

"I saw that." He'd watched her do it. Smiled as she'd teased Matt while carefully scrawling her name in loopy, feminine strokes. "She is pretty cool, isn't she?"

"Yeah. Will you sign it?"

He didn't hesitate. "Absolutely."

Matt rolled toward the bedside table and grabbed a Sharpie from his stash. Nick knew exactly where he wanted to sign the cast and chose the spot over Jenn's name. Frowning, he blinked, and wondered if his eyes were playing tricks on him.

"Dad, do you *like her* like her?"

Nick signed his name carefully and capped the marker, tossing it aside. "Yeah. Now, work on that test and quit trying to distract me, or we'll both be in trouble with Ms. Rose."

A WEEK LATER Jenn turned one of the many tests she'd had Matt and Nick take around for Matt to see, hoping the solution to their problems could be straightforward in the end.

*Please work.* Nick's timing couldn't have been more perfect. He'd mentioned, in passing, that when he'd signed Matt's blue cast he'd been able to read the other signatures perfectly, and that very morning she'd spent hours online researching the different forms of dyslexia. On one of the Web sites, she ran across a mention of something referred to as Irlen Syndrome. Instantly, her hopes were raised.

"Okay. Remember this?" Matt nodded and Jenn noticed he'd automatically squinted upon looking down at the paper. Excitement soared. "Read the first couple sentences."

"Mr. Baker…ran to the—the…" Matt lifted his hand and rubbed his eye, then began shifting back and forth on the seat where he sat. "Ran to the. Gate?"

"Yes."

"Gate. That's why…"

"When," she corrected softly.

"When he…"

"Matt, sit still." Nick pulled out a chair and sat beside his son, placing his hand on Matt's shoulder.

"It's okay. Actually, that's the perfect place to stop so I can ask you some questions. Matt, when you look at the paper, what do you see?"

"Letters."

"Okay. What do they look like?"

"I don't know."

"Try to describe them, please."

"They look…messy."

She clasped her hands in front of her and inhaled deeply. "Nick? Your turn."

Nick shot her an uncomfortable look. He glanced at Matt next.

"It's okay, Dad. I won't make fun."

Jenn gulped when Nick hesitated, his jaw clenching as he ruffled Matt's hair.

"Thanks, son. I appreciate that."

He squinted at the paper, but she noticed he focused more on the text in the middle of the page.

"Mr. Baker ran to the gate. That's when he...noticed a sack." Nick began shifting the paper back and forth in his hands, his eyes squinted. "Squ—squirming. By the side. Of the road."

Nick read for about five minutes. A passage that would've taken the average adult less than a minute or two at most. He strained to focus on the paper, and continually shifted it between his fingertips, his forehead pulled into a series of creases.

"Stop." She wet her lips and prayed she was right. "Stop right there."

## *CHAPTER NINETEEN*

BOTH TULANES looked at her with varying looks of wariness. Jenn smiled. "First, I want to tell you what I've been doing with all of these tests I've been giving you. I thought you both might be dyslexic. There is still a possibility, but we'll get into that later."

"Is that bad?" Matt asked, looking pale.

Jenn rushed to reassure him. "It's when you have trouble reading because your brain can't process the letters correctly."

"Oh."

She looked toward Nick, who just sat there wordless and tense. "Then in my research I ran across something else. It's called Irlen Syndrome and it has to do with light. Both of you, look at the page right now and tell me exactly what the letters look like."

"Fuzzy," Matt said. "And messy."

"Fuzzy and messy. Nick?"

He inhaled and squinted down at the paper. "They look fine at first, but after a minute or so it looks like the letters are…falling off the page. Distorted, like Matt said."

"So you move the paper back and forth because it helps hold the letters in place?" she guessed, based on what she'd read.

Both father and son nodded.

"Okay. First off, let me say that nothing has been scientifically proven. But people with lighter-colored eyes have a tendency to be more susceptible to headaches and light-triggered problems such as glare. Doesn't matter if it's sunlight or fluorescent light. Add eyestrain, and fatigue from trying to see correctly, and that causes a definite lack of attention, poor concentration, and poor reading ability." She smiled at them. "Which means your beautiful eyes might very well be the root of the problem."

Nick shook his head firmly. "My vision is twenty-twenty. I'll take Matt to have his checked, but he's never complained about not being able to see."

His expression begged her not to get Matt's hopes up.

"I understand. But it's not your vision—at least, not exactly. You obviously see fine without the aid of corrective lenses, *but* you're still seeing the letters as fuzzy, correct?"

Nick ran a hand over his neck and looked at her, getting impatient.

"It's not our eyes, Jenn. I'm sorry to disappoint you."

"I'm not disappointed, and it's not your fault. But I do want to try something. It might not work, and if it's dyslexia it won't help at all. But just try it?"

Nick nodded, albeit reluctantly.

Jenn dug out the clear-colored plastic sheets she'd special ordered. "One at a time, I want you both to take a sheet and put it over the page. If one of them helps you see the words even a little bit better, set it aside until you know which one works the best."

Nick shot her a questioning glance and sat forward, using the sheets only after Matt had put them on the page himself. There were nearly twenty sheets all together, and Jenn began to lose hope after most of the sheets had been rejected.

Twelve. Thirteen.

Matt kept going, a frown pulling his eyebrows together. *Oh, please work.*

Jenn glanced at Nick only to catch her breath. Nick had stopped and turned stone-still. He blinked. Blinked again. His mouth parting to release a rush of air.

*Oh, please.*

"Dad! Dad, this one works—the letters don't look messy!"

Nick swallowed, his Adam's apple moving slowly in his neck. "Yeah—" he raised his gaze to hers "—so does this one."

Jenn shot out of her chair and Nick met her at the end of the table. His arms surrounded her and lifted her high against his chest, his mouth finding hers in a kiss that made her wish Matt was elsewhere.

"Dad, you're kissing my *teacher!*"

Nick released her mouth, a chuckle rumbling up from his chest. They both turned to look at Matt and found him head down on the table, the back of his neck pink.

"Yeah, Matt, I am." His mouth near her ear, Nick whispered, "And that's only the beginning of what I'm going to do."

JUNE BLENDED into July with hot, humid days and long, humid nights. Nick loved watching Jenn work out, loved teasing a blush to her cheeks and pulling her into his office for a few hypnotic kisses that left them both panting and aching for more. But as they attended July Fourth fireworks, shared picnics, watched movies and did all the things that couples do, he was very aware that summer was passing quickly and August was right around the corner.

Jenn hadn't had much contact with her work friends, but what would happen when she went back to school and heard all the things that would no doubt be said?

"Whoohoo! Go, Tony! *Go!*"

The crowd around him burst into cheers as a kid on Matt's team rounded third and headed for home. Even though Matt wasn't playing, he'd wanted to be there with his team, and since Jenn had spent more time with him and Matt than she probably should have, she'd firmly set aside today to finish her paper for the human-development class. Her plan was to turn it in, spend tomorrow with Nick and Matt and pack, then leave for her trip.

Nick didn't want her to go, but he also couldn't ask her to cancel her plans. She hadn't invited him to go with her, either. Nor had she said a word about their relationship or what would happen to them once her tutoring sessions with Matt were over. His pride kept him from asking.

"Mind if I have a seat?"

The question jerked Nick out of his daze. His father stood with a hot dog in one hand and a drink in the other. Feeling the watchful eyes of those around him, Nick swallowed his dread and scooted over. Could they have a conversation without Jenn or Gram there to referee? "What are you doing here?"

"I come when I can." His father gave him a look. "You haven't been here much."

"The summer's been busy."

"I know. I always said the same thing."

Nick bit back the response that sprang to his lips.

"If you see your mother, I'd appreciate it if you don't tell her about the hot dog."

Nick hesitated, then smirked. "I'm not an idiot."

The comment hung there in the air between them. Looked as if his father wasn't the only one who didn't know how to keep up a conversation.

His dad inhaled and sighed, his gaze on the field. "No, you're not, but I sure treated you like one, didn't I?"

He didn't want to do this. Not now. Definitely not here. "It's over."

"No, son. It's not yet, but I'd like it to be. If I'd listened half as much as I yelled at you, we wouldn't be sittin' here like two lumps on a log."

But Nick understood the yelling now. His father had been frustrated, just as he'd been frustrated with Matt. He'd said enough to Matt about his grades that Matt had obviously felt the pressure to forge the notes sent home from school. Where was the difference?

"I'm sorry. I've never said that to you, but I am."

Nick leaned forward and put his elbows on his knees, glad that no one was sitting right next to them. As it was, many of the townspeople in the bleachers probably speculated on the two of them talking to one another, but no bystander could hear their words since they were keeping their voices low. To make up for years of yelling at each other? "Me, too."

His father cleared his throat. "Things look different, the older you get. I can see my impatience and hotheadedness now, the way I always blew up when you brought home a bad grade. I have excuses, Nick, but they don't matter. Not anymore. Work and marriage, pressures I reacted to when I was your age. That's why I mentioned the hours you keep the night of the rehearsal dinner, no other reason. I don't like the thought of you making my old mistakes with Matt. But I know it's none of my business and I'll do my best to keep my opinions to myself. Unless you ask for advice."

Nick bit back a rough laugh. Yeah, he'd have to be careful there, all right.

"If it's not too late, I'd like to ask your forgiveness."

From out of nowhere a lump formed in his throat and he

struggled to swallow. He knew what it must have taken for his father to ask that. "Why now?"

The bench *creaked* as his father leaned forward. "Matt's accident made me realize that I haven't done that well as a dad."

"A lot of people would argue that."

Dad turned his head, gave him a direct stare. "Would you?"

Nick thought about his life. Even though they hadn't gotten along, his father had always been there. He hadn't abandoned them, hadn't abused them. "Argue? No." He focused on the field once more. "But some things I needed to experience on my own."

His father didn't comment and Nick looked over, surprised to see his dad discreetly wiping away tears.

Nick clasped his hands together in front of him, his elbows digging into his knees. "I…had issues back then that you didn't know about," he heard himself say, his tone soft. "Things that made me feel as if I didn't belong in the family. Was too stupid to be a part of it."

"I made you feel that way."

His father's words hadn't helped, but they weren't the sole source of his inadequacies. "It was a lot of things, not just you."

"I hope one of these days you feel comfortable enough to talk to me about them."

"Yeah. Me, too." But not yet.

"This Jennifer Rose. She's a nice woman?"

"She's the best."

"I see. Things are serious between you?"

Jenn's image appeared in his head and he smiled. "Yeah."

His father chuckled. "I wore that look when I met your mother."

"Mom's pretty amazing." He glanced at his dad. "So is Jenn."

"You like her that much? If so, you'd better stake a claim soon, if you're going to."

The player at bat hit a home run and the fans around them roared. Nick clapped, but didn't stand up. He couldn't. Because he'd just realized that school began in a couple of weeks. A little over two. And she'd be gone most of the time in between.

Matt had made leaps and strides on the practice tests that Jenn had given him. She'd assured Matt and Nick both that Matt was ready for the fourth grade, and this time there would be no need to worry.

So what was he waiting for?

"Where are you going?"

He hadn't realized he'd gotten to his feet. "Can you keep an eye on Matt for a couple hours? He's in the dugout."

His father looked as if he'd just handed him the Nobel Prize for medicine. "I'd be happy to. But where are you going?"

Nick grinned. "I'm taking your advice for once. I'm going to stake my claim."

IT HAD TAKEN ALL afternoon to make up his mind and form a plan. He'd cursed a blue streak when he learned that it took weeks to get a passport. If Jenn waited that long, she'd be back to teaching school and unable to take time off to go on her trip. He couldn't ask her to wait, even if it would make the perfect honeymoon.

His parents had agreed to keep Matt overnight. His father was so excited by the idea, when Nick had called to check on Matt and ask, that Nick felt guilty. Years of distance wouldn't disappear right away, but things would improve. Thanks to Jenn.

After making his very special purchase, he'd put in a food order from the Old Coyote. Picked up flowers and candles. Then he'd gone home to shower and change. Now he parked in front of Jenn's house and couldn't believe his eyes. Of all the things to forget. Why hadn't he called to make sure *she* wasn't going anywhere?

He let himself into the house using the spare key. Finding a favorite radio station, Nick cleared off the dining-room table and arranged the flowers and candles, then put the food in the oven to stay warm. Turning toward the kitchen sink he paused, his gaze locking on a set of water guns lying outside. From there his gaze moved to the basketball beneath the old stringless hoop that was attached to Jenn's garage.

There was evidence of Nick and Matt throughout Jenn's house. Their old game system was hooked up to her TV and one of Matt's laundered baseball jerseys was folded neatly on the coffee table. Beside it was a T-shirt of his that Jenn had taken to wearing during their nights apart. He liked the thought of her sleeping in his shirts, but he liked her better wearing nothing at all.

*Bleep.*

Nick looked down at his cell phone with a frown. A missed call? Reminding himself that cell phones had a hard time with signals in the mountains, he hit the button to retrieve messages.

"Nick!" Jenn's voice brought a broad smile to his lips. "You won't believe it but *I finished my pa-per*," she sang, sounding more than a little giddy with excitement. "I typed the last of it this morning. Finally! I have some last-minute shopping to do for my trip and Suzanne called and asked me to go to her doctor's appointment with her, so we're going to make an afternoon of it. Anyway, I just wanted to let you know where I am and that I'll be home very soon. Probably around six or so." Her voice lowered. "I'm, uh, in the mood to celebrate, and I hope you will be, too. Bye!"

Still grinning like a loon, he clipped the phone to his belt. Tonight was definitely a night to celebrate. Jenn should be home anytime. He'd wait. Make a few calls. Get some work done. Think of all the things he was going to do to her after he asked her to marry him.

*But first you need to make sure that no one interrupts you.*

Jenn's desk was neatly organized, with a sheaf of papers stacked by the phone. Her paper? After all the research she'd done on dyslexia and Irlen Syndrome, he couldn't wait to…

It was printed on white paper like most everything else in the world, and so he narrowed his gaze to concentrate on the letters before pulling out his wallet and then frowning because he'd left his piece of blue plastic behind somewhere.

He groaned, remembering he'd last used it in the office of the gym.

Shaking his head at himself, he squinted, turned his back to the summer sun and struggled to read the words. He couldn't wait to get a pair of specialized tinted glasses.

*"Family dynamics…in Education: A Fa—Father's Struggle to Stop Gener-a-tional Illit-Illiteracy."*

His breath left his lungs and blood surged into his face. *What the…*

JENN LET HERSELF into the house, excited to know that Nick was already there. Suzanne's appointment had been amazing, the images of the baby so detailed that they'd seen the pout of its mouth and watched the heartbeat, loud and strong. She'd have to get started planning a baby shower after she returned from her trip. Oh, if only Nick would come with her. But how did you ask a guy to take a trip like that when things weren't…long-term? She'd like them to be, but Nick was the strong, silent type, and she'd pushed their relationship enough as it was. What if her notion of it and his were totally different? They needed to talk—that much was obvious. But how to raise the subject?

Then there was the small-town aspect of it. People in cities might not care if she went on a trip with Nick, but in Beauty it would be a constant topic of conversation. Not exactly how she wanted to start a new school year. She had to think about the big picture, and not just about her feelings for Nick.

"Nick? Nick, I'm home! Did you get my message? I—" She rushed to find Nick but broke off the moment she saw him. "What's wrong?"

His gaze narrowed even more and his expression was cold and hard.

Fear rolled over her. "Nick? Is Matt all right? Where is he?"

"Matt's fine." Nick stood from her desk chair, the papers in his hand rattling slightly. "But this isn't. *You had no right!*"

Jenn watched him anxiously. She wasn't afraid of him physically, and she knew Nick would never hurt her, but she'd never seen him this angry before—not even when she'd confronted him about not reading to Matt or after his fight with his father. "My report? The professor is tough, but I think I might get an A."

"An A. That's what my life is worth to you—an *A*?" He crumpled the papers in his hands.

"Nick! What are you doing? What's wrong?"

"What's wrong?"

"Stop repeating everything I say and just tell me."

"You're so smart, do I really have to explain it to you? You think telling the entire town I dropped out because I couldn't *read* is no big deal? That the news won't have an impact on Matt? On my family and my business?"

"Nick, I-I didn't use your names. Did you read it?"

He pointed a finger at her. "You didn't say *anything* about using me or my son as *guinea pigs!*" Nick turned and paced away from her, crossing her small living room in a couple of strides. "I should've known. Dear God, I'm a fool. I'm going to be the town idiot all over again!"

"No, Nick, *no*. That's not what I—"

"And to think I worked my butt off trying to help you while you wrote the thing... I brought you food, so you wouldn't have to stop to cook. I pitched in with Matt, so you'd have more time to complete your research. I mowed your damn lawn because you didn't have time. And in exchange this is what I get? Dammit!"

## *CHAPTER TWENTY*

"YOU DIDN'T READ IT! Nick, sit down and let me explain. Please, it's not like that."

His eyes. Nick's beautiful silver-blue eyes were dark and turbulent, bitterly angry. "I read enough. I read enough to know that even though you said you'd keep my problem between us, you were about to tell the whole damn world I was so stupid I couldn't figure out why the words didn't make sense."

"It wasn't just you. It was the teachers, the administrators—your family! Nick, don't you see how much this might help other people?"

"You said you wouldn't tell anyone and I trusted you."

Jenn felt ill and the fear inside her was growing, expanding. Doubling in size. "You can... You *can* trust me. Nick, please, read the whole thing. Maybe if you read it all, you wouldn't be so upset." Her heart pounded and tears stung her eyes. The look on his face. Oh, Lord, what had she done? "I didn't use your *names*. Yes, I cited you and Matt in my research, but it's an online class. The university is two hours away."

"Like half the people in town didn't go to the same school or have kids there now? You think they aren't going to put two and two together? Do you know what people are going to say when they find out? It's bad enough that so many people know I dropped out, but do you know how they're going to respond when they realize they've been doing business with a man who's barely literate? I'll be laughed out of town."

"No, you won't. Nick, please—"

He swore, the curse more graphic than any she'd ever heard him use. "I've spent the summer, nearly ever damn day, with you. You, with your name on every sheet of this paper. Do you really *think* they aren't going to see a big red flag when you talk about the subject and the subject's son? Everyone will know it's me. And Matt… *How could you do this to a kid?*"

"I'm sorry. I'm so sorry." She was trembling so badly that she had to hold on to the back of a chair. She knew better than to use real names, but she hadn't thought it would be a problem to include Nick as an example. Since she'd figured out the problem, Nick had begun to read voraciously. His speed and skill improved every day, and his reading comprehension was rapidly growing to match the verbal and audio skills he'd perfected over the years. She'd noted all that in the report. Described how the father who couldn't read comfortably now read nightly to his son—with such success that they were already on book two of *Harry Potter.*

It was progress. It was a huge success and her paper was outstanding. Definitely worth an A. But she hadn't once thought about Nick being upset. She hadn't thought about anything but helping them both and passing her class. "Nick, please. Calm down. I know you're angry, but I think…I think you're overreacting."

"Overre—" He raked his fingers through his hair. "You don't get it, do you? You don't have a clue what you almost did to me by turning this in, and you don't care."

She blanched, but Nick didn't notice. He was too busy pacing and cursing, to see her flinch. "Nick, please, calm down and think about this. *If* anyone realizes it's you, they'll see how far you've come. It's a story of success, not failure. It's about the way a dad should be." She twisted her hands into knots. "I'm sorry. I had to use the research I was doing to help you and Matt in my class. It was the only way I could spend time with you before the summer was over and…"

"And use me as a case study." He shook his head at her, and the man she'd come to know, the one she loved, was nowhere to be seen. "Glad you had fun, sweetheart, but it's over. We're done."

"Don't say that."

"Matt's up to speed and ready for school, and you're going on your trip." He shook his head. "The summer's finished. I'll pay for you to take the class again. You can write a new paper, but you are to leave me and my son out of it. Do you understand me?"

Jenn sucked in a deep breath. "Nick…" Her heart broke. "If I'd known you'd be so upset… If I'd had any clue, I wouldn't have done it."

His gaze narrowed on her, frozen and sharp. "Wouldn't have done *what?*"

She struggled to form the words. "It's gone. I—I already sent it. E-mailed it. I knew I'd be busy tomorrow and…I'm sorry. I'm so— *Nick, wait!*"

"Pack up our stuff and leave it at the gym."

"Don't *do* this!"

He stomped across the room toward her, but only because she stood between him and the door.

"I didn't do anything. *You did.* I knew from the beginning you were a mistake. I should've listened to my instincts."

She didn't know what to say to that. So she said the only thing she could say. "I'm sorry." The words were whispered,

thick and revealing. "I didn't mean to hurt you. Nick, please…
I love you, I didn't mean to hurt you."

A raw curse blistered the air. "Well, you've got a helluva
way of showing it."

SHE WASN'T GOING to cry. After Nick had stormed out and the
shock of his words had worn off, Jen had kept herself in motion to keep from thinking. She'd known from the beginning
it wasn't going to last forever. It would have ended soon regardless. But she hated what had happened. Why hadn't she
told Nick she was using him and Matt in detail? Maybe because she knew he'd react that way?

*Self-preservation. You knew he'd be upset, and you knew
it would matter, but you did it anyway. You still look at him as
a fifteen, and you see yourself as a five. Grow up!*

Jenn opened her gritty eyes and blinked wearily. After
tossing and turning all night, she'd stayed in bed for far too
long this morning, staring at the ceiling and remembering the
time she and Nick had spent there. Was she that self-destructive? That afraid of liking herself, of loving him?

She had to finish packing and make sure the house was
secure. She'd have to call Suzanne to see if she could run by
and water her plants, get her mail. Do all the things Nick had
offered to do for her while she was in Paradise.

Jenn went through the motions of getting dressed for a
workout. She couldn't stop now, no matter what. Maybe Nick
would be there and have calmed down. Maybe they could
talk—and she could apologize.

Dressed, she left showering and packing her toiletries for
later. She wanted to pick up the phone and cancel her trip, but
she was not about to do that. It had taken her all summer to
gain the courage to go by herself, and while Nick had never

said he'd go with her—and she'd never asked—it had been a secret fantasy of hers that he might come along. The two of them on the Caribbean island, playing in the surf. Making love and getting away from everything.

She was going. She had to go, period. If she could work up the courage to take that trip, then maybe she could find the courage to admit to Nick that she was afraid of what she felt for him and that… Had she really sabotaged herself?

She went downstairs and found herself rummaging through the refrigerator for sweets. That's when she knew she was in trouble.

The walls threatened to close in on her and she couldn't stand it a moment longer. She *wasn't* the woman she used to be. The Summer of Jenn had changed that.

Twenty minutes later she burst into the gym with all the attitude of a woman on a mission. Nick would calm down eventually. And he'd listen to her because he was such a nice guy. But why on earth *would* Nick listen to her after acting the way she had?

Jenn ignored the curious looks of the other patrons and kept walking toward the back. Maybe she was self-destructive to some extent, but screwing up with Nick was not going to ruin her new attitude toward life. Maybe she hadn't lost all the weight she'd wanted to lose, and maybe her fantasy dress still didn't fit, but that was okay. Her goal was to become satisfied with herself, and who cared if the dress fit? It was several years old and out of style, anyway. All it represented was her past with Todd, the person she *used* to be and not the woman she was now.

*And the part about where you destroyed Nick's confidence and trust in you?*

Guilt washed over her. Last night she hadn't been able to make Nick see her point of view, but today… Maybe today would be different? Nick had to come to terms with what had happened in the past. He couldn't read then. But he could read now. He was a smart, extremely intelligent man, and eventually he'd see that using a father-son example in a case study for a university two hours away, well, it would be okay. She'd stand by him. Help him. *Love him.*

But regardless of what the future brought, she had to deal with this situation in a healthy, mature way. It wasn't by striking out at Nick. Or herself. The only person hurt if she were to give in to temptation and drown her sorrows in chocolate would be herself. No more emotional eating for her. She'd made her decision.

Jenn didn't stop until she reached the heavy bag that was hanging from the ceiling at the back of the gym. The bag was surrounded by machines that faced the other direction. She wasn't adept at boxing, at any sport really, but at least she wouldn't have an audience.

"I'm here," Suzanne said, as she hurried up after Jenn. "What happened? You and Nick broke up? Is that what you said on the phone?"

"Last night."

"Last night? Why didn't you *call* me?"

Jenn tried to smile and failed miserably. "I wasn't in any shape to call anyone. Help me put this glove on."

"Wait a minute. You're *boxing?*"

"It's better than drinking. I need to hit something. And I need to cover my fingers so they can't shove food into my mouth."

"Uh-oh." Suzanne took the heavy glove and held it for her. "Talk to me."

"It's…" She would *not* cry. "According to Nick, we're over. And it's my fault. I did something stupid. Something really, really awful."

"What did you do?"

Gloves on, she whacked the bag once. Twice. Over and over again. Faster, harder. Until her arms ached and trembled with fatigue.

"That you or him?" Suzanne murmured.

"Both." Jenn was striking out at both their pasts, at all the people who'd hurt them. She kept up a good pace, hitting, kicking, kneeing the bag as many times as she could. Finally she ran out of steam. Her eyes were dry because she'd sweated the pain away.

"Feel better?"

Jenn shook her head slowly back and forth. "No," she whispered, the sound raw. "*No*, I don't, because I don't *want* it to be over. I'm so sorry."

"Tell him that."

"I can't. Nick doesn't believe me. I was just so happy that it made me afraid and…" She lifted her head. "Suzanne, I love him. See? I said it, but it *sucks* because Nick hates me now."

"Oh, hon. What did you do?"

She hesitated, but then knowing that Suzanne would keep it a secret, Jenn told her what had happened.

"I can't believe it. After all these years. Do you know how amazing it is that you were able to help them?"

The sound that emerged from her chest wasn't a laugh so much as a moan. "Nick disagrees."

"His pride is hurting. Badly. You can't blame him for that."

"No, of course not but…Suzanne, I can't take it back. A part of me knew he'd be upset, and I did it anyway."

"You didn't use his name. And before you tell me what a malicious person you are, let me say that I know better. You wanted to help other people like Nick. If someone, anyone, out there reads your paper and some good comes from it, isn't that worthwhile?"

"Of course it is. But it doesn't change the way I made him feel." Her shoulders slumped. "What am I going to do? And my trip—what about that?"

"Maybe you're not approaching this from the right angle. Maybe it's good that you're leaving town for a bit. It'll give you both some space and while you're gone maybe Nick can come to terms with the situation."

"It's way more than that."

"Then fight for what you want. You hurt him, yes, but people hurt the ones they love every day. We have to forgive and forget. And maybe… Maybe Nick is running scared, too. He loves you. Guys don't come over to mow their girl-friend's grass in ninety degree heat if they aren't in love. Maybe he's finally figured it out, and the news hit him like a ton of bricks. Nick probably needs some time to adjust and process things."

*And maybe Jenn shouldn't have ruined everything.*

Suzanne's words struck a chord, however. Nick certainly hadn't read the whole paper. Comprised of research, charts, graphs, and visual examples regarding the whole concept of generational education, dyslexia and generational reading problems, the case study was fifty-two pages long. He couldn't have read it that quickly, even with his tinted sheet.

*It doesn't matter now.*

Or did it? She glanced at her watch and noted the time. "I have to go."

"Are you packed? Ready?"

Jenn nodded.

"Are you *sure* you don't want me to drive you to the airport this evening? We could talk some more."

Jenn shook her head. This trip—the entire trip—was something she had to do on her own. Start to finish. But before she left, there was one more thing she had to do. "No, thanks. But thanks for being such a good friend."

"Yeah, yeah. Bring me back a cabana boy, then we'll talk true friendship."

IN A LOUSY MOOD and fast losing what was left of his patience, Nick hustled the waitress off with a loaded tray. Uncle C.'s bartender had called in sick again. Cyrus had tried to handle the crowd himself, but then he'd slipped on a spill and had to go see his doctor. That left Nick to cover the big game night after a full day's work and no sleep.

Nick filled another round of orders, cashed out a waitress who'd worked a double shift despite having a sick child at home and sent a message to the kitchen to hurry up the appetizer orders.

"Nick? Do you, um, have a minute?"

He froze at the sound of Jenn's voice. No way could she have the nerve to show her face after what she'd done.

Nick turned and, sure enough, there she was. One glance told him she'd had a rough night, too. Her eyes were bright and red-rimmed, and the muscles of her face were strained. "Aren't you supposed to be leaving?"

Jenn nodded and looked away. "I'm on my way to the airport now. But before I go, I wanted to drop this off."

"I asked that you leave Matt's things at the gym."

"I did. I took them this morning when I… When I went to work out."

Good for her. He'd figured she'd skip her workout today, all things considered. "Whatever it is, I don't want it." He smiled at the waitress who was heading his way. The last thing he was interested in was another woman, but Jenn didn't need to know that. "Hey, Cheryl. How's it going tonight?"

"Busy, busy." She sat her tray on the bar and rattled off five drink orders before sliding Jenn a glance.

Blond and stacked, Cheryl obviously didn't see Jenn as a threat. But Nick and Jenn had been in and out of the restaurant together enough that people knew something was going on between them. The waitress raised her eyebrows at the obvious tension.

"Let me know when you're ready to take your break."

Cheryl discreetly slid Jenn another glance. "I'll do that. But if I don't get a chance, are we on for later? Same as always?"

Jenn stiffened. Nick saw her with his peripheral vision and turned to find her looking ashen and on the verge of tears. He hardened his heart at the sight. Cheryl's "same as always" meant that instead of calling her bruiser of a husband, she would wait on Nick to close up and walk her safely to her car. "You know it. Here you go." He put the drinks on the tray and handed her a bill.

Cheryl shot one last look at Jenn and then gave him a wink of support before she took off.

Jenn stood. "I'd hoped we could talk before I left but... You've obviously moved on already."

If she couldn't tell the difference between a setup like the one he and Cheryl had just performed and the real thing he'd shared with her, he wasn't going to point it out.

"Here." Jenn dropped something on the polished surface. "I know you're mad at me, and you have every right to be. I screwed up and... I was afraid of getting hurt, so I think a part of me thought it might be better to hurt you first. I'm sorry for that. You have no idea how much.

"In my defense, I did it because I had a hard time believing someone like you could like someone like m-me. I guess I'm still fighting with the whole *I'm worth it* thing," she murmured. "Anyway, I hope instead of judging me by the title of my paper, you'll listen to this." She didn't look at him. "And know that if I could I… I care for you, Nick. And I was scared because…I love you." She shoved the case across the bar. "Goodbye, Nick."

## CHAPTER TWENTY-ONE

AFTER THE LAST CUSTOMER of the night headed out, Nick sat on one of the bar stools with an untouched bottle of Grey Goose on his right and a water bottle directly in front of him—along with the iPod Jenn had left. Wiped clean of everything but one selection, it held a recording of Jenn. Reading her paper.

She'd begun by explaining the complex process of diagnosing dyslexia and described how studies have shown it to be common in families. How she'd begun working with her "case study" only to find that while there were some similarities between symptoms of dyslexia and Irlen Syndrome, her case had no problems with directional instructions such as left, right, up or down as dyslexics often do. They didn't transpose their words when they were tired or stressed, but they often got severe headaches when they read. The list of comparisons and contrasts went on and on.

In her smooth, sweet voice Jenn quoted statistics, her research, how her case could have been another example of failure instead of a generational success had it not been for the father's determination that his son would not be doomed to the stigma associated with poor learning ability based on poor reading skills.

With every word she spoke, Nick heard love, support and her pride in all they'd accomplished over the summer. And his heart broke because despite the title and her reasons for using him in her paper, she'd made him out to be a hero. The paper was factual and statistic-heavy, but it gave genuine hope to the listener that despite the odds and his age, Jenn's case was able to receive help and could now read fluently after an amazingly short period of time. According to Jenn, he was a hero through and through.

"I thought I might find you here. She's gone, huh?"

Garret settled himself on the stool beside Nick. Someone bumped into him from the other side and he turned to find Ethan smirking. "What are you two doing here? How'd you get in?"

"You're not the only night owl around here," his uncle said from behind.

Nick turned and found his father walking up slowly beside his brother. "Hey, Uncle C., how's the hip?"

"Just a bruise. Enough to make me feel old, though."

His father and uncle made themselves comfortable at the closest table. Nick leaned his back against the bar, waiting for the wave of awkwardness to hit as it always did whenever he had to face his family. Seconds passed but it didn't happen. Not all of it, anyway. "What's going on?"

"The women are all still over at Garret's fussing over the perfect placement of wedding presents, hanging curtains and the like. Poor Matt's stuck right in the middle of it, but he still wanted to stay. We thought we'd come keep you company while you closed up."

Nick made note of his father's anxious expression, as if he was afraid Nick would take off—as he normally did when the family gathered together. He wasn't in the mood for this, but where would he go? As with the nights Matt had spent in the hospital, Nick didn't want to go home alone.

"Wanna play some Texas Hold 'Em?" Uncle C. asked with an optimistic grin. "Come on, boys, let's have some fun."

His brothers got up and joined the older men at the table.

"Nick?" His father watched him closely. "You're not playing?"

"Not tonight."

"That girl's got you pinin' for her, huh?" Uncle Cyrus scratched his balding head. "You should've gone with her." A frown formed on his face. "I keep tellin' you that you need to take one of those trips. Why don't you ever go anywhere? You'd like it. Me and Dorothy love going on those all-inclusive trips."

"I haven't gone because…I couldn't read." He blurted it out all at once, as surprised to hear the words come out of his mouth as the men in his family were to hear them. He cleared his throat, looked away, and then focused on his father, noticing he was the color of a dirty gray mop. "That's why I dropped out. I couldn't read."

A quick, sweeping glance of the others showed him Garret's mouth gaping open.

Realizing it, Garret quickly shut his trap and shook his head. "Why didn't you say something?"

"I didn't know why I couldn't do what I was supposed to do. I tried. Studied. I didn't want to admit I felt too stupid to learn."

"You're not stupid," his father growled angrily.

"One of the smartest men I know," Uncle Cyrus added. "Boy, you've got a business mind like no one I've ever known."

Ethan frowned. "So are you saying you're dyslexic?"

His father's fist hit the table and he looked sick to his stomach. "How did you find out?"

"Jennifer Rose," Ethan murmured. "She's got something to do with this, doesn't she?"

Nick nodded.

"That's what she's been doing this summer? I thought there was something serious going on between the two of you?"

"There is," his father told them all. "Nick told me it was serious."

"When was this?"

"At the ball game."

"Matt's playing ball with a broken leg?"

"Just hanging out with his team. And we were serious," Nick corrected. "But last night I told Jenn it was…over."

A roar of outrage blasted through the restaurant.

"Darcy's not going to believe this."

"I thought you loved Jenn?"

"You told me to stay away from her." Ethan glared at him for that one.

"That girl would be a mighty fine catch." Uncle Cyrus wiped a hand over his nose. "You sure you wanna call things off?"

He focused on his uncle's first comment and ignored the rest. "Jenn is a good woman."

"Then why break up?" Garret asked.

Nick turned away, grabbed his bottle of water and walked over to the jukebox. "Jenn wrote a paper for her human-development class at the university. It was about learning and relationships and how they tie together."

"And she used you in it," Garret deduced. "You didn't know?"

He shrugged. "I knew she was going to write about the research she'd done, trying to figure out what was wrong with me and Matt, but…"

"Something's wrong with Matt?" His father shoved himself to his feet. "Nick, why didn't you tell us?"

"He's *fine*. He had some trouble in school, but Jenn's got him up to speed."

"But you two have the same problem," Ethan pressed. "Is that what you're getting at?"

Nick dug deep for patience. "Yeah. Something called Irlen Syndrome." He explained what he knew about it and told them how the colored plastic sheets helped.

"So now you can read? The words make sense because of a piece of plastic?" Ethan shook his head, the doctor in him clearly skeptical.

"Yeah. Jenn…" Just saying her name made him miss her even more. "She said that since I listened to so many books on tape and worked in a business setting, my reading skills had developed anyway, compared to someone who dropped out and just stopped trying to cope."

"'Course they did," Uncle Cyrus said.

Nick's father moved over to where he stood and clapped a hand on his shoulder. "I'm sorry, Nick. I was so busy yelling at you to do better, I didn't think to stop and ask why you weren't."

"You were frustrated. Just like I was with Matt."

He squeezed Nick's shoulder. "I'm proud of you, son." Hesitating a brief moment, he pulled Nick into his arms and pounded him on the back, tears choking his words. "I'm *proud* of you. You didn't…You didn't behave like I did."

When his father let him go, Nick turned to face the rest of the group. "The reason I'm telling you this is because everybody is going to know once the paper makes the rounds. It probably won't take long for people to figure out that Matt and I were her guinea pigs."

"That's why you broke up with her?" Uncle Cyrus asked. "You need a thicker skin, son."

"Did she use your names?"

It figured that as an attorney Garret would be concerned with something like that. "No. She refers to us as the 'case subject' and the 'subject's son,' but everyone will know since they've seen us together all summer. She had no right to make a private matter public. Matt's going to be embarrassed."

"Matt—or you?" His uncle studied him, his gaze shrewd.

"No father wants his son to think less of him," his father murmured. "I understand that."

The weight on Nick's shoulders grew heavy. "It'll be like before. Which is why I…thought I should warn you before you heard it from someone else."

With an arm around Nick's shoulders, Alan Tulane turned to face the others. "But this time isn't the same, is it, boys?"

His uncle and brothers shook their heads in unison and Nick felt that he might just lose it.

"We've got your back, Nick—don't worry about it. I'm glad you finally told us." Garret sat forward in his chair. "But what happens now? When are you going to call and make up with Jenn? I have to know, because that'll be the first question Darcy will ask me when I tell her the news."

"Your mother, too. Do you love her, son?"

Nick didn't have to think about that question for long. Despite his anger, he missed her and he wanted her. "I couldn't see straight last night."

"And today?"

He wiped a hand over his face. "Yeah, I love her. She has a boatload of baggage left over from her marriage to Dixon and from her family. She doesn't feel…worthy. But I know deep down she wanted to help other people like me. Jenn's like that."

"But what if she does something like this again?" Ethan asked him. "What then? You were mad at us for years. Are you saying you can forgive her just like that?"

Garret silenced Ethan with a glare. "You'd know something

about relationships, if you ever kept a woman around long enough to have one."

"Boys."

Nick smiled grimly. "I don't think Jenn would ever do something like this again. Not after my reaction yesterday."

"So you have forgiven her?"

Had he? Looking at the male members of his family, Nick knew it was true. He had, because he couldn't imagine life without them—or her. Forgiveness was a process, a decision. One he'd made the moment the recording had ended. "Yeah, but I can't say what I need to say over the phone, and she's in the Caribbean for the next two weeks."

"So go to her," Uncle Cyrus ordered. "What're you waitin' for?"

"We'll take care of Matt. No worries there, son."

"It hasn't been that long since I supervised the garage," his uncle added. "Might be fun to be in the old stomping grounds."

"And Garret and I can keep an eye on the gym and help Uncle C. out here."

He was humbled by their immediate acceptance of him after so many years of distance. But wasn't that what they'd been trying to do all along? Get him to come back into the fold? "It won't work. I don't have a passport, and it takes at least three weeks to get an emergency one issued."

That stumped the lot of them.

Then Uncle Cyrus snorted. "Maybe you don't, but you do have a twin who gallivants all over the world. Why not borrow his?"

Garret shook his head with a groan. "As an officer of the court, I'm going to pretend I didn't hear that. I don't think breaking the law for love is an admissible defense."

"What time is it in California?" Ethan asked, taking out his cell phone. He pressed a couple of buttons and held the phone to his ear.

They wanted him to use Luke's passport?

Nick and his father walked over to where the others were sitting.

"This isn't a good idea," Garret muttered. "Just call her. She'll come home."

"I don't want her to come home. She needs this trip."

"He said he needs to talk to her in person, and using Luke's passport is the quickest way of getting him where he needs to be," Uncle Cyrus argued.

Nick tugged at his ear. "I'm not sure it'll work anyway. I don't know how to maneuver the airports. I can't go around holding up a piece of blue plastic everywhere. People will think I'm nuts."

Garret shot Ethan a baleful glare and stood up. "I have nothing to do with that," he said, jerking his head toward Ethan. "But I can help with the other problem. You got one of those plastic things on you?"

"Luke?" Ethan grinned. "You busy? No? Good. Have you ever been to the Caribbean?"

# CHAPTER TWENTY-TWO

JENN LET HERSELF INTO her hotel room and waved goodbye to the two sisters she'd met on the beach. Originally from West Virginia, the sisters had married and started careers, but they got together once a year for a sisters-only vacation.

Padding over to the balcony, she unlocked the patio doors and slid them open, letting the salt-laden breeze drift in. The view of the ocean was indescribable, a blue so clear and perfect it…

*Reminded her of Nick's eyes?* Fresh tears stung her lids and she blinked rapidly. She was not going to cry. She'd done enough of that lying in bed last night, listening to the surf crash against the shore.

What was Nick doing? Was he still furious with her? She missed him with every breath she took, and she'd picked up the phone a half dozen times to call him, only to set it down again. If he wanted to call her, he would.

This morning she'd walked the beach in her bathing suit without wearing a coverup. She'd sat by the pool and ordered one of those fruity drinks with an umbrella in it. Yeah, she was slowly finding her diva side. If only Nick were here to—

*Stop it! It's bad enough that you're here with a broken heart. Don't make it worse by calling Nick only to hear him hang up on you. Pining is useless.*

Sighing deeply, she entered her room and walked over to her closet. She was supposed to meet the sisters in the lobby in an hour. She had to shower and get ready, not to mention work up the nerve to dance. That was the plan for the evening. Meet the sisters downstairs and dance.

*Like nobody's watching.*

Forty-seven minutes later, she stared in the mirror and put the finishing touches on her makeup. Just in time. She grabbed a small purse from the table, checked for lipstick, keycard and some cash and made her way into the hall.

Downstairs she flashed the two women a smile, appreciating the way they let her tag along on their night of fun and considering them safe enough since both were married and only inclined to dance and enjoy themselves. She wasn't in the mood to pick up a man. Perhaps not ever again.

Music throbbed and vibrated, and inside the club Jenn smiled and nodded as they headed toward an available table near the dance floor. A waiter flirted with them, but Jenn didn't flirt back. It hurt too much.

"Ooh, I love this song. Come on, Jenn!"

Laughing at the others, she automatically shook her head. "We just ordered drinks." That was her wallflower excuse for the next five songs. Finally the sisters glanced at each other, downed their drinks and grabbed Jenn's hands, pulling her out and into a throng of dancers. Jenn took a deep breath, her body all arms and legs and no coordination—until she remembered why she was there.

She wasn't Jennifer Rose, the overweight, boring teacher. She was Jenn, the fun-loving, gotta-dance diva who'd planned this trip for *years,* paid good money for it and was bound and determined to enjoy herself. Somehow.

Another breath left Jenn laughing, her feet moving in time

to the beat. Body swaying, arms lifted, she raised her face to the sparkling lights overhead and *danced*. It was fast and fun and furious. And while she was a far cry from being good at it, she wasn't the worst one on the dance floor. Why had she waited all this time? This wasn't so hard. Never again would she hesitate to open herself up to new experiences. If she wanted to do something, try something, she was going to do it. Why worry about what people would say? There was only one power she'd ever answer to.

"That guy is sooo checking you *out!*" The blond sister yelled in Jenn's ear, dragging her back to reality. "And he's gorgeous. Go talk to him."

She shook her head automatically. "I'm not interested."

"Are you nuts? Look at him!"

Still moving in time with the music, she turned her head toward where her new friend waved and froze. Impossible. It wasn't Nick. Her eyes were playing tricks on her, because it couldn't be him. He was angry at her. He wasn't there. *Could it be Luke?*

No. No, she felt the sizzle of excitement, the butterflies in her stomach. Things she only experienced with Nick.

Blaming her imagination and wishful thoughts, she continued dancing until the song ended and another began. This one was slower, sexier, more in tune with couples than...

"You might not be interested, but he is. He's coming over here."

What? Jenn turned her head to see and there he was, moving toward her with an intense expression. "Nick?"

"You know him?"

She nodded, unable to take her eyes off him.

"Dance with me?" He held out his hand.

The sisters turned as one. "See ya!"

Jenn found herself flush against Nick's body, his eyes blazing as he studied her. The tempo was sensual and sexual and with his silver-blue gaze holding hers, she began moving against him, loving the feel of his arms around her. *If this is a dream, please don't ever let me wake up.* But the song ended too soon and a hard new dance beat gave her an instant headache.

"Want to take a walk?" Nick yelled.

She nodded, completely and totally dazed by his presence.

Outside, Nick led her toward the path to the beach. She stopped long enough to slip her heels from her feet and welcomed the feel of the sand between her toes. "It's really you, right?"

He flashed her a slow, tired grin. "Actually, no."

"Huh?"

Pulling her to him, Nick lowered his head and kissed her, deep and hard and thorough. When he lifted his mouth from hers, he sighed. "I'm not me. According to the passport I'm traveling with, I'm Luke. It was the only way I could get here to you."

Her heart stopped beating, then quickened. He'd done that for her? "Why did you come?"

"Because I love you. Jenn…I'm sorry I lost it. I overreacted."

"No. No, you didn't. I should've talked to you about using you and Matt in my paper."

"I would've said no. Like it or not, you made me realize it was time to face facts. My grandpa always said we reap what we sow, and all the lies I'd told, all the secrets I'd kept, they were suddenly coming back to haunt me. I couldn't escape the truth."

He stared into her eyes. The full moon and waves crashing against the shore made a perfect backdrop.

"It was time I told my family what was going on, but I wouldn't ever have done it if you hadn't written the paper and forced me to."

She blinked at him. "You told your family?"

Nick nodded. "And they were supportive—and angry that I hadn't spoken up sooner. All these years, I was too full of myself and my pride to know they'd love me regardless."

"Oh, Nick."

"Just as I love you exactly as you are."

She was not going to cry. Not now when she had so many things to be happy about. "You know I'm never going to be a size six."

He lowered his head and took her mouth again, kissing her deeply, wildly, not breaking the contact until her legs felt weak and she leaned against him. "I don't care. You'll always be a perfect ten to me."

She blinked rapidly, but the tears came anyway.

"Have I told you how much I like your dress?"

Jenn sniffled and dropped the shoes dangling from her fingers, wrapping her arms around Nick's neck and holding tight. "My Paradise dress didn't fit."

"It didn't do justice to the new you. Are you upset?"

Nose buried in his neck, she breathed deep, inhaling the fresh salt air and Nick's cologne. "Not anymore. Because you're right. It didn't go with the new me. I don't have to be a size six to be happy. Or loved. You love me?"

"I love you. And I'll buy you another dress. I promised I would."

She wet her lips, watching as his gaze lowered. *Think diva*, her mind whispered. The thought made her grin. "I've got a better idea."

"Yeah?"

"I'd rather you took this one off me."

# *EPILOGUE*

NICK LAUGHED as Suzanne shoved him through the doorway.

"Don't forget what I said. Do *not* forget."

"Okay, okay. Turn on the lights, right?"

Suzanne swatted him on the arm and he heard Tucker's chuckle from behind.

"He's teasing you, darlin'. He won't forget. Not if he wants to live."

The door shut behind him and Nick did as he'd been instructed. Door locked. Security system set. He did *not* turn on the lights. By the billiard tables, he hit SJ14 on the jukebox and stayed where he was. Stevie Ray Vaughan's "Pride and Joy" started with a pulsing beat, drawing his head up. Then he saw her. Standing on the only bare table among a restaurant full of candlelit tables, Jenn wore a knockout dress that showed her body off to perfection and ended midthigh. She wore four-inch heels, her hair had been curled and teased and she had a look in her eyes that screamed *vamp*.

Nick's chest seized up and his body caught fire. She was so damn beautiful. In better shape now than she had ever been, her breasts and thighs were still full and round and perfect, exactly as they were meant to be. She swayed to the seductive beat, her gaze holding his. Absolutely *everything* he wanted in a woman. In his wife, he thought, watching her diamond ring trail up her body and hold him entranced.

As Jenn rocked her hips, he moved toward her, helplessly drawn. And when he stood near, he held up his arms and caught her against him. "Come here, sweetheart."

Jennifer Rose Tulane gave him a flirtatious glance from beneath her long lashes and followed instructions, wrapping her arms around his neck and her legs around his waist.

"Happy anniversary."

He thought of the charm bracelet he'd purchased for her and smiled. He'd seen a spiky high-heel charm that would be perfect to mark this turn in Jenn's new life. "Will you do this for me every month?"

"Only on special occasions," she murmured, breathing against his mouth. "I wouldn't want you to grow bored."

"Never." He lowered himself into a chair with her draped across his lap. She kissed him, rubbed against him, and her fingers plucked at his shirt. "Other congratulations are in order, too."

"For what?"

Leaning over, she lifted the envelope from a nearby chair and handed it to him before going back to unbuttoning his shirt.

"What's this?"

"Open it. You'll like it." She spread his shirt wide and smoothed her hands over his chest.

He couldn't wait to do the same to her.

"I hope you don't mind, but I absolutely couldn't wait. I'll make it up to you though," she promised huskily, her fingers shifting to his belt.

How had he ever lived without her?

His body hardened still more. His brain was struggling to

function, since it lacked sufficient blood. Still, he recognized the address. "My GED results?" Jenn nodded. "I passed?"

Jenn slid one finger along his mouth, parted his lips and lowered her head to kiss him, her tongue slipping between his teeth to tease while her fingers stroked over him. "You *aced* it."

He locked his arms around her and hugged her close, thrilled with her breathless laughter in his ears. "You're amazing. I couldn't have done this without you. You know that, right?"

Nick let his hands roam, grasped her hips and ground her against him. He reveled with her gasp, the way her breath hitched in her throat when he discovered thigh-high hose and little else.

"I think you could have, but you know what they say…"

"What's that?" Her thighs tightened around him, a definite diva move if he'd ever felt one.

Nuzzling her nose against his, she smiled. "Sometimes it pays to sleep with the teacher."

\* \* \* \* \*

*Don't miss the next*
**THE TULANES OF TENNESSEE** *story*
*by Kay Stockham!*
*Coming in Spring 2009*
*from Harlequin Superromance.*

*Ladies, start your engines with a sneak preview*
*of Harlequin's officially licensed*
*NASCAR® romance series.*

## Life in a famous racing family comes at a price

All his life Larry Grosso has lived in the shadow of his
well-known racing family—but it's now time for him to
take what he wants. And on top of that list is Crystal
Hayes—breathtaking, sweet…and twenty-two years
younger. But their age difference is creating animosity
within their families, and suddenly their romance is the
talk of the entire NASCAR circuit!

*Turn the page for a sneak preview of*
*OVERHEATED*
*by Barbara Dunlop*
*On sale July 29 wherever books are sold.*

Rufus, as Crystal Hayes had decided to call the black Lab, slept soundly on the soft seat even as she maneuvered the Softco truck in front of the Dean Grosso garage. Engines fired through the open bay doors, compressors clacked and impact tools whined as the teams tweaked their race cars in preparation for qualifying at the third race in Charlotte.

As always when she visited the garage area, Crystal experienced a vicarious thrill, watching the technicians' meticulous, last-minute preparations. As the daughter of a machinist, she understood the difference a fraction of a degree or a thousandth of an inch could make in the performance of a race car.

She muscled the driver's door shut behind her and waved hello to a couple of familiar crew members in their white-and-pale-blue jump suits. Then she rounded the back of the truck and rolled up the door. Inside, five boxes were marked Cargill Motors.

One of them was big and heavy, and it had slid forward a few feet, probably when she'd braked to make the narrow parking-lot entrance. So she pushed up the sleeves of her canary-yellow T-shirt, then stretched forward to reach the box. A couple of catcalls came her way as her faded blue jeans tightened across her rear end. But she knew they were good-natured, and she simply ignored them.

She dragged the box toward her over the gritty metal floor.

"Let me give you a hand with that," a deep, melodious voice rumbled in her ear.

"I can manage," she responded crisply, not wanting to engage with any of the catcallers.

Here in the garage, the last thing she needed was one of the guys treating her as if she was something other than, well, one of the guys.

She'd learned long ago there was something about her that made men toss out pickup lines like parade candy. And she'd been around race crews long enough to know she needed to behave like a buddy, not a potential date.

She piled the smaller boxes on top of the large one.

"It looks heavy," said the voice.

"I'm tough," she assured him as she scooped the pile into her arms.

He didn't move away, so she turned her head to subject him to a *back off* stare. But she found herself staring into a compelling pair of green…no, brown…no, hazel eyes. She did a double take as they seemed to twinkle, multicolored, under the garage lights.

The man insistently held out his hands for the boxes. There was a dignity in his tone and little crinkles around his eyes that hinted at wisdom. There wasn't a single sign of flirtation in his expression, but Crystal was still cautious.

"You know I'm being paid to move this, right?" she asked him.

"That doesn't mean I can't be a gentleman."

Somebody whistled from a workbench. "Go, Professor Larry."

The man named Larry tossed a "Back off" over his shoulder. Then he turned to Crystal. "Sorry about that."

"Are you for real?" she asked, growing uncomfortable with the attention they were drawing. The last thing she needed was some latter-day Sir Galahad defending her honor at the track.

He quirked a dark eyebrow in a question.

"I mean," she elaborated, "you don't need to worry. I've been fending off the wolves since I was seventeen."

"Doesn't make it right," he countered, attempting to lift the boxes from her hands.

She jerked back. "You're not making it any easier."

He frowned.

"You carry this box, and they start thinking of me as a girl."

Professor Larry dipped his gaze to take in the curves of her figure. "Hate to tell you this," he said, a little twinkle coming into those multifaceted eyes.

Something about his look made her shiver inside. It was a ridiculous reaction. Guys had given her the once-over a million times. She'd learned long ago to ignore it.

"Odds are," Larry continued, a teasing drawl in his tone, "they already have."

She turned pointedly away, boxes in hand as she marched across the floor. She could feel him watching her from behind.

\* \* \* \* \*

*Crystal Hayes could do without her looks,*
*men obsessed with her looks, and guys who think*
*they're God's gift to the ladies.*
*Would Larry be the one guy who could blow all*
*of Crystal's preconceptions away?*
*Look for OVERHEATED*
*by Barbara Dunlop.*
*On sale July 29, 2008.*

# REQUEST YOUR FREE BOOKS!

## 2 FREE NOVELS PLUS 2 FREE GIFTS!

HARLEQUIN®

*Super Romance®*

### Exciting, emotional, unexpected!

**YES!** Please send me 2 FREE Harlequin Superromance® novels and my 2 FREE gifts (gifts are worth about $10). After receiving them, if I don't wish to receive any more books, I can return the shipping statement marked "cancel." If I don't cancel, I will receive 6 brand-new novels every month and be billed just $4.69 per book in the U.S. or $5.24 per book in Canada, plus 25¢ shipping and handling per book and applicable taxes, if any*. That's a savings of close to 15% off the cover price! I understand that accepting the 2 free books and gifts places me under no obligation to buy anything. I can always return a shipment and cancel at any time. Even if I never buy another book from Harlequin, the two free books and gifts are mine to keep forever.

135 HDN EEX7  336 HDN EEYK

| Name | (PLEASE PRINT) | |
|------|----------------|---|
| Address | | Apt. # |
| City | State/Prov. | Zip/Postal Code |

Signature (if under 18, a parent or guardian must sign)

Mail to the **Harlequin Reader Service:**
**IN U.S.A.:** P.O. Box 1867, Buffalo, NY 14240-1867
**IN CANADA:** P.O. Box 609, Fort Erie, Ontario L2A 5X3

Not valid to current subscribers of Harlequin Superromance books.

### Want to try two free books from another line?
### Call 1-800-873-8635 or visit www.morefreebooks.com.

* Terms and prices subject to change without notice. N.Y. residents add applicable sales tax. Canadian residents will be charged applicable provincial taxes and GST. Offer not valid in Quebec. This offer is limited to one order per household. All orders subject to approval. Credit or debit balances in a customer's account(s) may be offset by any other outstanding balance owed by or to the customer. Please allow 4 to 6 weeks for delivery. Offer available while quantities last.

**Your Privacy:** Harlequin is committed to protecting your privacy. Our Privacy Policy is available online at www.eHarlequin.com or upon request from the Reader Service. From time to time we make our lists of customers available to reputable third parties who may have a product or service of interest to you. If you would prefer we not share your name and address, please check here. ☐

HSR08R

# HARLEQUIN

*Super Romance*

# COMING NEXT MONTH

**#1506 MATTHEW'S CHILDREN • C.J. Carmichael**
*Three Good Men*

Rumor at their law firm cites Jane Prentice as the reason for Matthew Gray's divorce. The truth is, however, Jane avoids him—and not because he's a single dad. But when they're assigned to the same case, will they be able to ignore the sparks between them?

**#1507 NOT ON HER OWN • Cynthia Reese**
*Count on a Cop*

His uncle lost his best farmland to a crook, and now Brandon Wilkes is losing his heart and his pride to the crook's granddaughter...who refuses to leave the land her grandfather stole from them! How can he possibly be friends with Penelope Langston?

**#1508 A PLACE CALLED HOME • Margaret Watson**
*The McInnes Triplets*

It was murder in self-defense, and Zoe McInnes thinks she's put her past behind her. Until the brother of her late husband shows up, and Gideon Tate's own issues make him determined to seek revenge. Not even her sisters can help Zoe out of this mess. Besides, she thinks maybe Gideon is worth all the trouble he's putting her through...and more.

**#1509 MORE THAN A MEMORY • Roz Denny Fox**
*Going Back*

Seven years ago Garret Logan was devastated when his fiancée, Colleen, died in a car accident. He's tried to distract himself with work, but he hasn't been able to break free of her memory. Until the day she walks back into his pub with a new name, claiming not to remember him...

**#1510 WORTH FIGHTING FOR • Molly O'Keefe**
*The Mitchells of Riverview Inn*

Jonah Closky will do anything for his mom. That's the only reason he's at this inn to meet his estranged father and brothers. Still, there is an upside to being here: Daphne Larson. With the attraction between them, he can't think of a better way to pass the time.

**#1511 SAME TIME NEXT SUMMER• Holly Jacobs**
*Everlasting Love*

When tragedy strikes Carolyn Kendal's daughter, it's Carolyn's first love, Stephan Foster, who races to her side. A lifetime of summers spent together has taught them to follow their hearts. But after so much time apart—and the reappearance of her daughter's father—will their hearts lead them to each other?

HSRCNM0708